The Angels' Share

I was burning up with desire and, as the warmth of his tongue collided with the pressure in my sex, I thought I would explode immediately.

To calm myself, I rode Dominic's face in long, light strokes, barely allowing his outstretched tongue to dip between my lips. How he moaned each time my wetness left his face, like he couldn't bear being without the taste of me. Then I allowed him to beat against my clitoris and he brought me to within a breath of orgasm with the skill and speed of a humming bird's wing.

'Stop.' I was breathless. 'Did I ask you to make me come yet?' I reached behind my back and grabbed the thick girth of his cock, administering a sizeable squeeze to let him know I meant it. Dominic let out his loudest moan yet although I wasn't sure if it was from pleasure or pain.

The Angels' Share
Maya Hess

BLACK LACE

Black Lace books contain sexual fantasies.
In real life, always practise safe sex.

First published in 2006 by
Black Lace
Thames Wharf Studios
Rainville Road
London W6 9HA

Copyright © Maya Hess 2006

The right of Maya Hess to be identified as the Author of
the Work has been asserted by her in accordance with the Copyright,
Designs and Patents Act 1988.

Typeset by SetSystems Ltd, Saffron Walden, Essex
Printed and bound by Mackays of Chatham PLC

ISBN 0 352 34043 6
ISBN 9 780352 340436

*All characters in this publication are fictitious and any resemblance
to real persons, living or dead, is purely coincidental.*

This book is sold subject to the condition that it shall not, by way
of trade or otherwise, be lent, resold, hired out or otherwise
circulated without the publisher's prior written consent in any form
of binding or cover other than that in which it is published and
without a similar condition including this condition being imposed
on the subsequent purchaser.

1

Two hours into the journey and the swell caused passengers to stagger from their seats in search of a place to lie down or thrust their faces somewhere obscure. They clutched onto tables, railings, each other, as the ferry lolled through the Irish Sea and the endless darkness of a night crossing. Grown men, tinged with jaundice, paled while their wives comforted wailing children and tried to be stoic during the four hours it took to reach Douglas Harbour.

I sat cross-legged, wedged on a plastic-covered banquette with a can of Coke nestled in the crook of my knee and my diary cradled in my left arm. I nibbled the end of my pen, watching the passengers' sickness transform from mild discomfort at the start of the journey into outright illness by the middle. I wrote about the unusual last week of my life, my thoughts punctuated by extra-loud shrieks as a rack of glasses crashed from behind the deserted bar. Silence followed and then the boom and thunderous vibrations as a twenty-foot wave hit the bows side on.

'Excuse me, is anyone sitting here?' A young woman teetered up to me, thrown off balance as if she'd drunk a bottle of rum. She grabbed the chrome rail to the side of my seat, her backpack causing her to stoop and hunch. I was keen for her to take the empty space because, like me, she didn't look in the least bit sick. There was no chance I'd have to scoop my belongings or heave my legs away from anything projectile. She grinned and then giggled before releasing her grip on the rail. 'Look, no hands.' Her steep Scottish accent made her sound even cheekier than she looked.

'I think we're the only two with our sea legs on,' I replied. 'Feel free.' I patted the orange plastic, at which she took off her pack as deftly as a winter coat, dumped it on the floor and sat beside me.

'Steph,' she said. Pointlessly, I thought, as I doubted I would ever see her again.

'Ailey,' I replied to be courteous, realising it was the last sociable gesture I would make for a long time.

'Going home?'

I considered her casual question very carefully. Having left my home nearly a week earlier, I would be lying if I said yes. I was six bus rides, eight hitched lifts, a train journey, much walking and two ferry crossings away from home. The dust, the heat, the dogs, the guitars at night seemed an eternity away. I was steeped in my mission.

'Yes. I'm going home,' I answered, looking at her directly. 'You?'

'Nah. I've been travelling Europe for months but before I go home to Scotland, I'm going to visit someone on the island.'

'The Isle of Man isn't much of a place to end such a glamorous trip.' I took a swig of Coke.

Steph was thinking now, her dark eyes pulling together to make a narrow groove above her straight nose. I didn't mean to shatter her dream.

'But it has a beauty all of its own,' I added.

'You're right.' Another cascade of crockery followed the biggest dip starboard we had encountered so far. Several predictable screams ensued and then the inevitable silence during which the four hundred passengers held their breath to see whether we were still afloat. 'I'm completely tired of cathedrals and big cities and expensive tourist attractions. My visit to the island is a treat before I have to go back to work.'

I could have asked her where she'd been, how long she'd been away, what her work was, where she lived, did she have any brothers or sisters? Our conversation could have easily filled the remaining two hours. The fact was, I didn't care. I turned my mouth into one of those polite smiles that carefully punctuates the end of a meaningless chat; a kind of facial semaphore signalling that I didn't want to talk any more. So she really took the hint, I hoisted up my tatty pocket-book to create an A5 barrier between us and continued writing.

'I've just come from France. Paris, to be precise.'

'Nice,' I said without looking up. *She's been to Paris*, I wrote.

'I had great sex there.'

Slowly, I lowered the pocket-book barrier, being careful to lay it face down so she couldn't read that I'd been writing about her, and reinserted the pen between my lips. I put on a patient, interested look so that she might divulge a little about the great sex she'd had in France but the little witch unbuckled a side pocket of her backpack, plucked out a copy of *To Kill a Mockingbird*, put up her own literary barrier and began to read.

I left her alone for fifteen minutes, frantically scribbling notes in my book about the young woman I'd met on the Isle of Man Steam Packet. And I also made note that we were about the only two passengers who weren't being sick or lolling about with droopy eyes and our hands clapped to our mouths. I glanced at her a couple of times, just so I could get an accurate description for the record, and wrote everything that I knew about her so far: she'd been travelling; she'd got a temporary job on the Isle of Man; she was reading Harper Lee; she didn't get seasick and she'd had good sex in Paris.

'That should be *great* sex,' she suddenly said, causing me to hug my pocket-book as if it was a newborn baby. 'Good sex implies it was pretty average and what I had in Paris was way above that. I wouldn't mind if you put fantastic or out-of-this-world or mind-blowing. Any of those will do but not *good*, please.' Then she went back to reading her book and I blushed and scribbled out 'good', inserting 'great' instead.

I pretended to jot down a few more thoughts although I was really doodling in the margin while squirming with embarrassment and I bosomed my book as if I was playing poker for my virginity. It may have been my imagination but I suspected that the waves were pounding the vessel less frequently and no longer washed over the salt-encrusted cabin windows. I stood up and stretched.

'Would you like a coffee or something to eat perhaps?'

Steph slowly looked up from her book, clinging on to the words as if she was pulling gum off her fingers. 'No thanks,' she replied with a tight smile. She also stretched and looked around the boat. It was a sorry sight with exhausted passengers draped over each other or the floor as they searched for oblivion from their misery.

'Me neither.' I sat down again. I'd only asked so I could perhaps glean more about her sexy story and add it to my book. What are the chances, really, that you meet a stranger on a boat who offers you a glimmer of a good, no *great*, sex tale and then clams up and reels the whole thing back in as if she'd never mentioned it?

I snapped the elastic bands around my well-worn pocket-book and slid it deep into my backpack. Then I fastened all the catches and pulled the straps tight. I couldn't risk it falling out. The thought of a stranger, or worse still someone I knew, reading my thoughts and desires and wild ramblings that more often than not ended up describing my wildest fantasies was more than I could bear. The book was private and that was that. Even my oldest friend Nina had never peeked at one word and I'd been writing a journal for many years. I had volumes of diaries, not just this book, all padlocked away in a metal casket and hidden at the back of our grain store, where I knew they were safe. It was always my current, exposed volume that caused most concern. They really were very private thoughts.

'Maybe I will have a coffee then,' Steph said. I grinned and staggered down the boat to the drinks machine. Minutes later, we were chatting like best friends, trying not to slosh coffee from our polystyrene cups, while she provided plenty of detail about Paris. I planned to write it up in my diary later and knew that the luxurious thought would keep me fired up until I found where I was going and got settled in.

Briefly, my stomach lurched like the Irish Sea surrounding us. What if, after fourteen years, the cottage wasn't there anymore? I hadn't considered that it could have been washed away during years of storms worse than this one. And I hadn't thought either that it might be occupied now and not the sporadically used clandestine retreat of any estate workers who wanted to get their leg over when the boss wasn't looking.

'We did it for thirty hours solid. Oh, except when he cooked for me and we ate on the balcony overlooking Notre Dame.' Steph clasped her hands at her chin, eager for my response. But I was overcome with apprehension and while I had been listening to Steph's sexual escapades around Europe, I was a bit concerned that I would be spending the night in a ditch.

'And everyone in the street below could see up my little skirt. I didn't have any knickers on but I didn't care. I just gorged on the wonderful food and then went back inside, whistles and cheers below, to start all over again with what's-his-name.'

'Wow,' I said flatly. I could virtually feel the wind stinging my face and the sheep nuzzling my ears as I nestled beneath a hedge in desperate need of a good night's sleep. Having been on the road for what seemed like a lifetime, crashing in cheap hostels and hitching lifts, riding buses and living on crisps and sausage rolls, well, it was all wearing a bit thin. My big adventure was testing me and I just needed to get where I was going. I looked out of the cabin window.

'Hey, look! The lights of Douglas.'

Steph peered out into the blackness and ceased regaling me with her Paris story. We both remained silent as the string of Christmas fairy lights that was Douglas Promenade grew larger and larger. I felt my heart skip and jump with both fear and nostalgia. It had been fourteen years. Tears filled my eyes as I remembered the same scene but in reverse. My mother and I sat in a darkened corner of the boat, hardly speaking as we watched our life disappear on the horizon. We had quite literally been kicked out.

'It's so pretty,' Steph said and I had to agree. The once busy Victorian seaside resort boasted a lengthy crescent-shaped Promenade complete with horse-drawn trams during the summer months. It was a folly of a town, these days given over to a small helping of tourists and a thriving financial community. The Isle of Man has always attracted the rich. Now the forgotten heiress had returned to claim what was rightfully hers.

Moments later, as we approached the harbour walls, the vessel's rolling transformed into a gentle rocking and then a virtually motionless passage to the docks. The engines quietened apart from a few purposeful groans as the captain guided his craft into place. As if awakened from a hundred years' sleep, the passengers came back to life and gathered their belongings. An announcement guided all foot passengers to the disembarkation point and Steph and I helped each other with our packs. Mine was stuffed so full and heavy that it took her several attempts and much fiddling about with the straps and clasps to make it go on my back. Eventually, she had it in place and we said our good-byes.

'I hope you have as much luck here as you did in Paris.' I winked at her and she grinned back, her slight body bowing once more under the weight of her belongings.

'Oh, I will,' she called and headed for the bus stop. She obviously knew where she was going and I didn't want to be delayed with anymore idle chit-chat. I pulled my purse from my pocket and fondled the few notes that remained. Soon I would be running on empty and forced to find work but there was one luxury that I couldn't afford to do without, especially at this time of night. As I walked to the taxi ranks, it felt as if the ground was swelling and crashing beneath me, as if I was still aboard the ferry. The offshore breeze nipped my cheeks, causing me to pull the knitted hat I had bought in London further down over my ears.

'Can you take me to Niarbyl?' I peered in through the driver's window and he slowly nodded, undoubtedly wondering what a single young woman would be wanting with such a remote place at ten thirty on a Sunday evening. 'You can just drop me at the cottages on the main coast road. I'm visiting nearby.'

I had previously planned what to say. I needed to slip seamlessly back into island life and crawl silently into my chosen hiding place while I investigated where I once belonged. I remembered that the local people had a strict sense of their environment, especially on the west coast. Newcomers might as well wear a flashing beacon on their heads announcing their arrival or place an advert in the local paper. Mine would read: *Long-lost heiress returns.*

I heaved my backpack onto the rear seat and climbed in beside it. We left Douglas via the harbour road, taking the TT motorcycle track as far as Ballacraine before heading for Glen Maye, Dalby and finally down the rugged coastline towards Niarbyl. It felt as if we were travelling through blue-black ink, so dense was the darkness. Perhaps it was tiredness or fear and apprehension at what I might find at the supposedly deserted cottage, but I fought to stay awake during that taxi ride, despite my unknown fate. The beach hideaway was on the western tip of the Creg-ny-Varn estate and I wouldn't get a proper glimpse of my surroundings until first light.

'You sure you just want dropping here, in the middle of nowhere?'

I was standing beside the cab as it puffed hot, white exhaust into the salty sea air. It would most likely be the last bit of warmth I felt for ages. 'I'm sure,' I replied confidently. No point in arousing his suspicions. He'd only blab to old Bill down the pub that this girl was on her own at night, who'd tell his missus, who'd tell her cousin, who'd tell his mate and poof! My cover and mission would be blown when the impostor who had taken over my late father's property discovered I had returned.

'How much?' My fingers rifled through my remaining notes. I'd have to risk a trip to the shop at some point.

'Twenty-five,' he said, virtually removing the money from my frosted fingers before I had the chance to count. I watched the red tail lights disappear into the distance and all I was left with was the faint glow from the windows of a cottage perched on the hill above the craggy cliffs. The little house screamed warmth at me, something I was in great need of. The last fourteen years of my life had been spent in Southern Spain, running barefoot around our community with nothing more than a square of hand-painted cotton tied at my waist and, as I got older, my breasts too. Now, standing quite alone in the darkness with distant, haunting memories of my childhood, I juddered against the northerly wind even though I was wrapped up in many layers of clothing. A noise at the cottage door forced me to duck, as quickly as my pack would allow, into the shadow of a hedge.

'Who's there?'

The cottage appeared as a patchwork of grey stone punctuated by small amber squares of delicious light and warmth. In the middle, I could see a larger rectangle of light – the open front door – and a tense silhouetted figure virtually filling the gap.

'Who's out there? Show yourself.' It was a man.

I held my breath and watched him stare out into

the bleak night. I prayed that no cars would pass and what he saw would be nothing more than a black fog, dotted perhaps with the odd star or lone, screeching owl. I was so cold that I thought he would hear my shivering. For a moment, that was an appealing thought. I could stride out of the hedge, hands up as if I was surrendering, and beg for a hot bath and some food. I pinched my arm as I imagined myself offering a read of my diary in return for his hospitality and a bed.

The man shook his head and finally turned, closing the door with a bang. I sighed heavily, realising that I hadn't breathed for the last minute. I hauled myself out of the wet bushes and squinted through the darkness ahead. In the two cones of taxi headlights, I'd noticed a small sign indicating the narrow lane to Niarbyl. If I remembered correctly, there would be a bumpy private track a few yards further on leading down to the rocky beach – the very last leg of my journey home. I hoisted my pack further up my back, gripped the straps in my gloved hands and set off towards the rocky beach, praying that the cottage was derelict.

The pebbles ground together like oversized gravel announcing my arrival. For the last few hundred yards of my walk, I had been searching for lights reflecting on the shore – a certain indication that someone was living in my planned hideout. So far, there was only darkness but I dug my fingers into my woolly palms and gritted my teeth anyway, plodding on with the weight of my life on my back.

I had brought with me the most useful items I could muster in Spain. A torch, which I had turned off as I descended the difficult path to where the tide licked the black, mussel-encrusted rocks; three boxes of matches and a dozen candles wrapped in a plastic bag; half a litre of Miguel Torres brandy, drinkable only in the most dire and desperate of circumstances (none of my hardships so far had come close to warranting consumption); some warm clothing, which had been difficult to procure from a wardrobe that consisted mostly of cotton and silk; and an assortment of gadgets and useful implements such as a tin opener and a penknife. And of course my journal.

The ground rose and fell invisibly beneath my walking boots. I balanced as best I could, occasionally lurching forward to grab at a sharp rock for support. Thankfully, there was no light at all on the tiny half-moon beach coming from where I remembered the cottage was located. All I could see was the frilly edge of the now much calmer sea as it dragged up over the natural defence of the rocks jutting out into the water. The moon, half obscured by cloud, provided an annoying dimness by which I picked my way closer to the cottage. I could hear my heart pounding – or was it the rhythm of the waves? – as I placed my hand on the low stone wall that marked the front boundary of the tiny property. If that was still standing after all these years, then surely the house was too. I traced the line of the wall around to where I recalled the opening that led to the low front door, but stumbled and fell, catching my knee on a rock.

'Ouch!' I tried to stand up but, with my pack weighing me down, I couldn't get my balance. I unhitched the straps and wriggled free, nursing my aching knee. 'I don't care if there's anyone in there,' I spat in a terse whisper. I clicked my torch back on and muzzled it with my gloved hand, allowing just enough light to pick my way to the front of the cottage. I stepped to the side of the door and furtively angled my face so that just my eyes were peeping over the window sill. There was nothing to be seen except blackness and the sugar-frosting of years of salt and cobwebs. I did the same with the other front window and then tentatively walked to the side of the cottage to peer into the tiny bedroom. There were no back windows or rear garden. The cottage was built jutting out from the cliff with its behind sunk firmly into the gritty slate and a well-eroded thatch perched on bowed rafters as if the whole structure was wearing a yellowed toupee with a raggedy fringe.

'I think you're empty, aren't you?' I reached up and brushed my hand fondly through the low straw roof. I was talking to a house. If anyone was inside, then I had my excuses planned. I was a lost walker searching for a non-existent bed and breakfast, a foreign tourist with an out-of-date guidebook. Applying a heavy accent, I would barely speak a word of English.

I reached for the latch on the door and pressed down. It wouldn't budge. I pulled off my glove and ran my hand over the weathered wood, searching for a padlock or bolt or any reason why it wouldn't open. When I was a child it was never locked, my father insisting that the local fishermen use the place freely. It was an island tradition. The Manx rarely bothered with security, partly from their desire for warm hospitality and partly because of a low crime rate. I tried the latch again, harder this time, and felt a little movement. Taking a deep breath, I lunged at the door with my shoulder and boot and on the third attempt it gave, causing me to crash inside with the stealth of an elephant.

I stood perfectly still, waiting to see if I had disturbed anyone. Nothing. Sighing and finally realising that the cottage was mine, at least for the night, I fetched my pack and balanced my torch on the small table in the centre of the room, allowing me to find the candles. I smiled, both with a big grin and internally. I had done it. I had got to the Creg-ny-Varn estate and secured my initial domain. It was the first victory in my personal battle to grasp what was rightfully mine.

With three candles lit and positioned strategically so that each area of the small room was illuminated, however dimly, I dropped into a dusty armchair – I remembered the faded floral coverings so well – and took a moment to survey the abandoned remains of the cottage. The internal walls were still whitewashed although smeared with grime and a trim of lacy cobwebs. The flagstone floor was covered with several threadbare rugs and the only furniture remaining (I'm sure there was more when I played there as a child) was a bleached pine table with a couple of ladder-back chairs pushed underneath and two armchairs surrounding a low table. Everything was arranged around the heart of the cottage, the black cast-iron cooking range, which looked as if it hadn't been lit for years. Balls of soot and twigs and straw from birds' nests littered the fire basket and I wondered whether trying it out would set the whole place ablaze.

To one side of the fireplace was a tall cupboard. I vaguely recall my father secreting various objects in there when we came to the cottage for his beloved weekend fishing trips. I opened the creaking door and was faced with an array of belongings that I would take time to sift through over the next few days. It amazed me that all this stuff had remained undisturbed for so many years. I felt a single tear prickle my eye but quickly swiped it away. I hadn't come to the island to cry over what was lost.

Then I noticed a pair of binoculars.

'Heavens above,' I said out loud. I brushed off the dusty case and pulled out the glasses. 'I adored staring out to sea with these.' Pointlessly, in the dark, I aimed the binoculars out of the window. Aside from a runway of mottled moonlight dancing atop the breakers, there was nothing visible. I couldn't wait until morning to gaze at passing ships. But just as I was turning away from the window, just as I was about to pack the binoculars away and unfurl my sleeping bag, I caught sight of a pinprick of light passing in front of my eyes. I swung the lenses back towards the cliff top, where I was sure I had seen a flash of amber light sweep past my view. Sure enough, once I had focused and adjusted my eyes to this close-up way of viewing the world, I had in my field of vision the most surprising, delightful scene anyone could ever hope to stumble across.

Reluctantly, I pulled the binoculars away from my eyes, simply to catch my breath and take stock of what I had seen. It appeared that I had aimed the binoculars at the cottage high up on the cliff top where the taxi had dropped me earlier. I hadn't realised that it would be visible from the beach but the angle of the beach cottage and the curve of the coastline afforded an excellent opportunity for getting advance intelligence on my nearest neighbours, who could possibly be a future threat to my mission. At this point in time though, the only threat the cottage inhabitants posed was to remind me that it had been simply ages since I had indulged in sex. Even the quick flash of their two bodies had created a knot of desire in my knickers that

I knew wouldn't budge until something was done about it. I glanced around the empty cottage.

'You're looking hot tonight,' I joked to myself in the dusty, cracked mirror that hung lopsidedly above the fireplace. Then, 'Fancy a tumble?' I swallowed hard before tentatively bringing the binoculars back to my eyes. My vision adjusted more easily this time, allowing an immediate close-up of a creamy pair of full breasts with angry turned-up nipples being alternately chewed upon by, judging by his body size and shape, the man who had called out from the cottage doorway earlier.

'This is a bonus', I crowed. I had resigned myself to virtual celibacy while I claimed my father's estate. I wasn't sure whether to rejoice, because now I would have more to add to my fantasy-filled journal, or to become insanely jealous that, yet again, I was missing out on heated passion and the joy of being with someone special.

Erratic glimpses of the couple finally caused my exhaustion and tension to wane as I relaxed into the unexpected role of voyeur. I shifted a dusty armchair to the window and settled down to watch the unsuspecting pair. It was a moment I couldn't sacrifice to unpacking my bag and fetching firewood. To give a clearer view, I removed my hat and rubbed it over the grimy window, polishing the couple's performance. I could see that the man was still dressed. The woman was naked from the waist up. It appeared that they had only just begun their antics.

'Do they know I'm watching?' I pondered out loud. 'Did they suppose that someone was on their way to this cottage and they hoped they might get spotted?' The thought that they were putting on a private show gave me a tingle in my nipples. I pushed one hand inside my many layers of clothing and located my breast, albeit through my sweatshirt. 'Lucky pair,' I whimpered as I realised just how in need of comfort I was. There I was, alone in a freezing, derelict cottage that could be washed away by a freak wave at any moment, with no warming fire, no bottle of red wine to share with a lover, no clean sheets to slip between when the flirting and innuendos had reached a critical level. I was tired, hungry, cold, dirty, scared and the loneliest I think I'd ever been.

'I'll feel better in the morning,' I mumbled as I reached inside my pack for the emergency bottle of Spanish brandy. Briefly, I was reminded of home – my simple *cortijo* in the beautiful mountains, the ever-present sun, my friends, the tranquil existence of life in remote Spain. But I didn't regret my mission, especially now as my first night's company was assured, although it was passion by proxy.

I sipped from the flask and was instantly warmed from the inside. I would curl up by a roaring blaze later and write up my diary with the comfort of the brandy. Things were already looking up. I had Steph's sexy tale to add to my journal and now this. I removed my weatherproof coat and three other layers of clothing until I was sitting in my silk camisole and unbuttoned jeans. I tried not to shiver.

'On with the show,' I said with a giggle. I focused the binoculars and was immediately filled with disappointment. The pair were nowhere to be seen. 'Perhaps they thought I'd lost interest in them or maybe they've gone to finish things in another room.' I slowly scanned each window of the cottage and, aside from the warm glow and open curtains, there was nothing to be seen. I wondered if signalling would encourage them to continue. Risky, I knew, revealing that someone was inside the usually deserted beach cottage, but I was so keen for something more than just my own fingers that I even considered running up to their front door and begging them to continue.

I blew out all the candles and held the torch up at my window. Flicking the switch on and off, slowly at first then gaining speed, I hoped to catch their attention. Living on the coast, I assumed the couple would take notice of flashing beacons, even if they did appear to come from land. I stared at the cottage while signalling frantically with the torch.

'Yes!' I cried out as the man reappeared. 'Don't disappoint me now,' I implored. An expanse of naked flesh filled my view. They had undressed. The detail of the man's almost still body was stunning. It was as if he was standing three feet in front of me, showing off his athletic physique before he lunged at me. Only in this case there would be no lunging. Not at me, anyway.

'What are you doing?' I whispered, taking another rationed sip of brandy without lowering the binoculars. The man's head, with his sheet of back muscle facing the window, appeared to be dipping and bobbing although not in any particular rhythm. I ran my tongue over my finger and traced a circle around my left nipple. 'Your tongue is like velvet,' I said to him, imagining me lying beneath his naked body and his mouth toying with my breasts. 'Take it all in your mouth.' I cupped the small mound of my neat breast in my palm and squeezed it lovingly, as my man in the window would surely do if he could see me now. How I wished for a reciprocal viewing!

Suddenly, the woman came into view. The pair were standing sideways to the window and indulging in the most passionate, consuming kiss I had ever seen. I pressed my finger to my lips, imagining a mouth bearing down upon mine, lapping the taste of brandy from my tongue. So soft was the effect, so vivid the response of the woman's body rippling in the window, that I imagined it was her mouth searching mine – all for the benefit of her lover, of course. I grinned at my wicked fantasy. It would go in my diary along with a lifetime of erotic encounters, fantasies and beautiful people. What anyone did with them when I was dead and buried, well, that was another of my erotic imaginings.

The man's mouth dragged down his lover's neck to her bosom. He heaved her weighty breasts together, lavishing each chocolate disc with his tongue and coating it with a skim of saliva that I could actually see glistening in the lamplight. My own nipples burned for attention. I consoled myself that, other than organising the cottage and buying supplies, my first mission would be to find an expendable, anonymous man for a few hours of no-strings passion. I wouldn't even tell him my name. In reality, I knew this was unlikely however much I desired such a scenario, but the thought went nicely with the visual feast on the cliff top.

The binoculars were becoming too heavy to hold with one hand so I had to make do with sporadic bursts of touching myself. My show couple had moved on. The man was gripping the woman's girth while he pulled and pushed her pelvis. I saw by the delight on her face that her clitoris was bumping on and off his tongue, giving her tantalising shots of hot, moist pleasure. I could feel it myself as I allowed my finger to creep beneath my jeans and inside my knickers. His tongue, my stiff little bud. He could do that for as long as he liked in his warm, cosy cottage with his voluptuous wife watching in jealous annoyance. How I longed to be in there with them. But, considering my situation, it was about as likely as the impostor in my family home giving up the Creg-ny-Varn estate willingly.

Then, as if the couple were playing entirely for my benefit, the woman came up to the window to show me her aroused body. She pressed her nipples onto the glass then leaned forward so her breasts squashed into what looked like an almost edible marshmallow. With her face tipped sideways, she took the outer lips of her lightly shaved sex and pulled upwards so that the shell-pink folds were completely visible. Everything about this woman reminded me of consumable treats. Served on a plate, she would have made the most delicious dessert and I envied her lover having the chance to taste all her flavours. But I made do with what I had and dipped my own finger into the flow of white juice around the edge of my pussy. As if sucking on a lollipop, I pretended that he had allowed me a sample of his wife's sweetness. And it was true. She tasted of warm honey and gooey, pink candy.

Something else was happening to her, apart from the thrill of exposing herself to the night. Gradually, the pulsing became more noticeable and her face and breasts began to slide up the glass panes before quickly dropping down again. There was no doubt that her lover was shunting her from behind, unable to wait for any more foreplay. Part of me was disappointed. I didn't want him to come yet, snap the curtains closed and curl up in bed with a cup of tea. I wanted to watch them drive each other to a place where they could think of nothing but orgasm; where their bodies were catapulted into oblivion at the last possible moment, where nothing else in the world mattered, not even the delight of discovering they had been watched, as their minds crumpled beneath waves of pleasure that not even the sea beneath them could mimic.

I needn't have worried. My untouchable man had swung his woman around and had her on her knees with his cock forced down her throat and an expression on his face that told me she was kneading his head with the skill of a well-trained lover. He leaned against the wall as she worked on him and I was thankful for her short hair, which allowed me an uninterrupted view of the veined erection delving a disconcertingly long way down her throat.

'Do you give lessons?' I wondered, in awe of her skill. 'I sure would love to learn from you.' I inserted a finger inside myself and hooked out an ample amount of moisture, smearing it around my lips and clitoris in readiness for the finger-frenzy I would soon be embarking on. Just these initial touches mailed signals of a long overdue yearning for a body-cramping climax to tired and distant parts. My fingers glided between my smooth lips, encouraging them to swell and pout.

My athletic couple were wrangling against gravity. Having prepped myself and teased my body to an on-hold status with occasional flicks of my clitoris and a moistened stirring of my nipples, I watched eagerly as they ravished each other in a sweaty, hungry display of abandoned lust. The woman had her man's bursting balls pressing on her chin as she licked the space behind his sac. Then suddenly she was manoeuvred upright and her legs were hoisted around his waist as he prepared to enter her again. They staggered a little and she tossed her head back, laughing at their struggle, but soon he was in and she rode him like a jungle animal, clutching him around his waist. He had his hands under her buttocks for support. I panned up to their faces where their mouths were gaping and their tongues pressed together. The woman's fingers dug into her lover's shoulders and her legs gripped him tightly, forcing their genitals together. It took almost all my concentration to keep the binoculars steady while I fumbled in my knickers.

As the pair bucked in the backlit window of the cottage, I squirmed and moaned and brought myself to near maximum arousal without crashing over the edge. I'd see when they came and I wanted to do it with them. Timing things correctly while holding the binoculars steady and keeping my clitoris on fire was not an easy feat. I sharpened the focus as the pair slowed for a moment and the man wetted his finger. I watched him, magnified so it appeared that I was in the room with them, as he inserted a finger in the woman's exposed bottom. Her body tensed as she took the first joint, then another, and then she whispered something to him. He grinned and slipped a second finger inside her, right up to the knuckles. I imagined the cramped feeling this must have provided around his deeply seated cock. I had often desired such a sensation myself, perhaps with two men frantic for my body, each vying for space. In reality, I would never dare suggest such an act.

I saw that they were set for the finale. Their masks of concentration, the woman's determined stare as she pulled her sex up and down the shaft of her man, not only for his pleasure but to ignite her own climax, indicated that just seconds of the display remained. If only I could have yelled out to them to continue; that I hadn't seen nearly enough of their lovemaking, that it had been over a week since Marco had visited my *cortijo* in the middle of the night as the cicadas sang out and my white mosquito net billowed in the breeze. So long since his leather-coloured erection had sought me out.

I flicked the tip of my clitoris and imagined that it was one of the exhibitionist couple eating me up. I didn't care which. My fantasies were often filled with other women, usually present to help my masculine character get the most from me. The pretty women I concocted were expendable fancies, usually frighteningly attractive and perfect, and while they were seemingly innocent and naïve on the outside, when it came to pleasuring my body they were naughty vixens. Another secret fantasy: making love to a woman. It was all in my journal, with which I would cuddle up later.

When I saw the pounding slow, when I saw the woman lay her head on her man's shoulder and gradually slide off his spent body, I put down the binoculars and probed myself while rubbing my clitoris until my sex tightened around my fingers. The shivers of an extended, overdue orgasm worked up my spine, across my shoulders, into my neck and mind and back down again into my toes. I flopped in the chair and laughed as I remembered that I was still wearing my walking boots, having simply unfastened my jeans.

I put the binoculars to my eyes again and located the cottage window. A dim glow emanated from behind closed curtains. Funny, I thought, to shut out the world *after* the act. It made me wonder: did they know I was watching? I could only hope that they would perform again soon.

I layered myself in sweaters and jackets, having been kept warm previously by my steamy observations. My body hummed from near-perfectly satisfied thrills, my lucky discovery of the cliff top couple having sated my need for a man. My fingers alone would have never sufficed.

I relit the candles and began to arrange the cottage to suit my needs. I peeked into the back room and recoiled, fastening the door behind me. Birds and other wildlife had been in residence, entering through the broken window, and the room would need a massive clearout before it was vaguely habitable. For now, I would have to sleep on the two armchairs pushed together. At least, if I got it going, I would be near the fire.

I searched at the side of the cottage by torchlight, where I recalled my father storing driftwood and logs he had dragged from the cliff top. Sure enough, as if no one had cranked up the stove since my childhood adventures, I found a pile of dry wood in a ramshackle shed attached to the cottage. Back inside, I cleared out the fireplace as best I could in the half-light. I sneezed a couple of times as ancient dust and soot wafted into the air. To test the draw, I balled a piece of old newspaper lying on the table and lit it in the grate. After an initial surge of grey-white backdraught into the cottage, the chimney sucked up the smoke beautifully. With the skill of a Girl Guide I arranged knots of newspaper, kindling and some of the driftwood before setting light to the lot. Within minutes, I was sipping again from my emergency brandy flask and warming my toes by a blazing fire.

'Nothing quite like it,' I said, referring to the open fire although wondering if perhaps I was conjuring an imaginary friend. Had the loneliness of my predicament got to me already? Having become a voyeur, was I now inventing company? I laughed and shook my head in despair.

A month ago, running away from my home without telling a soul where I was headed would have seemed a fleeting insanity. Setting out on the trail of my fortune was as likely as setting foot on Mars. But it was true. I was hiding out in a little beach cottage, preparing to launch an intelligence operation and attack on the man who had stolen my family home. I admit, it was upside-down fun: being secreted in a far corner of Creg-ny-Varn, concealed by a veil of sea mist and a heavy determination to regain what was rightfully mine, stirred something primal within me. I may have been leading a simple life for the last fourteen years, some of my closest friends having dropped out of the rat-race and become passionate about all things home-grown, but I wasn't a fool. I knew about business from my father and my four university years in Granada had given me a cosmopolitan outlook. Whoever had stolen my inheritance was in for a shock.

I pulled my tightly stuffed sleeping bag out of its sack and puffed it up for maximum warmth. Despite the crackling fire, I could still see my breath condensing as I exhaled. It would be another few hours before the cottage finally warmed up after years of abandonment. Strangely, as the fire pumped out heat, I felt the walls reach out and hug me, as if the house was pleased I had come to its rescue. Depending on how long my mission took, I planned to make the place more homely. Not only would it be practical, making my transition into such a contrasting climate more bearable, but I wanted to do it in my father's memory. I truly believed he would be shocked if he saw the sorry state of the beach house.

I pulled my backpack close to the armchairs and climbed into my sleeping bag. Once snuggled inside, I dared to remove my jeans and outer coat but refused to cast aside my sweaters and socks. I rummaged around inside my pack and drew out a rather crumpled bag of tortilla chips, a squashed packet of sandwiches and a bottle of water. I began to stuff my face when it occurred to me that I should write down the luscious sex I had just had with myself thanks to my cliff top neighbours. Had it not been so perilously cold in the cottage, I would have clambered off my makeshift bed for another peek, just to see if they were offering another performance.

I searched the main compartment of my pack but couldn't locate my pocket-book. Puzzled, I concluded that I must have stashed it in one of the outer pouches but no, it wasn't there either. Sitting upright, I emptied the entire contents of my luggage onto my legs and rifled through it desperately.

'I know it's here. I put it away on the ferry!' Memory flashes of stuffing the book deep in my pack and securing the straps were followed by a cold sweat and prickles of fear as I realised that my most private possession – probably the most private possession of anyone in the entire world – was either lost or, worse still, stolen.

'What am I going to do?' I wailed. I dragged my fingers down my face. Aside from the year of work that had gone into this particular volume, I'd been looking forward to writing up my temporary ferry-mate's antics in Paris. The thought of the ferry company's staff finding my innermost thoughts and reading them to each other at fag break sent me into a panic. I leapt out of the armchair bed and hopped about the cottage searching for my journal. 'Think, woman, think. You came down the beach, left your bag outside, humped it inside, put it over there...' I briefly fumbled about outside in the dark, near the wall where I had initially dumped my bag. Nothing. I trawled the inside again, even the bird-infested bedroom, but nothing. I could only hope that daylight would render my diary visible, where candlelight had been insufficient.

I was about to climb back into bed, my search terminated by freezing limbs, when I stopped in my tracks and began to shake my head. Only little ripples of realisation at first but soon my dark hair was tossing wildly from side to side as I began to groan and wail as the truth hit me.

'No, no, it can't be. The evil witch!' I threw back my head.

I remember thinking a few hours earlier: *I know my backpack is heavy and awkward but how can it take anyone so long to adjust my straps?*

'The little thief! Steph hadn't been helping me at all. She was raiding my pack!' I groaned again. With the deftness of a magician, she must have palmed that book as quickly as any four of hearts. 'Damn her!' I yelled, pacing about and pulling my hair. My only consolation was that I knew she was still on the island. I would just have to find her before she learnt too much about me.

Back in bed, lulled into a fitful sleep by waves that sounded so close I thought they would appear under the front door, I gradually began to warm up as the fire crackled and spat. My eyes kept dropping shut but then I'd jump awake as a particularly loud wave pounded the rocks on the beach. I'd blown out the candles so the only light was from the stove. Crazy images patchworked together behind my eyelids – the colourful life I had left behind, my epic journey from Spain and arrival on the island, the ferry, the crashing waves, seasick passengers, my pocket-book, Steph, panic, the rocks, the subterfuge, my inheritance, binoculars, the couple on the cliff, the figure that passed across the window just as my eyes dropped shut...

When sleep finally came, only two things were certain: I had to find Steph and I needed to know who had taken ownership of Creg-ny-Varn.

2

I woke to the same sound that lulled me into sleep. A shaft of sunlight passed across my face, warming my skin but making my eyes screw up into slits. The first thing I did was reach between my legs and feel a moist residue from the night before. I grinned, rolled onto my side and drew a finger up and down the slippery line between my lips. The images of the previous night's display were still fresh in my mind and it occurred to me how lucky I was to have such considerate neighbours. I giggled at the thought and caught sight of the binoculars still on the window sill. The white early-morning sun proved just how much of a mess the place was. But I didn't care, not yet anyway. Housework could wait and at least there was still a fire in the stove.

I grinned and struggled within the sleeping bag to remove my knickers. I needed a couple of quick orgasms to set me up for everything I had to do that day. It felt as if my pussy had been swollen all night, judging by...

I froze.

Someone was outside the cottage, crunching the pebbles in my barnacle-covered front garden. A dog, too – I heard yapping and the creature being called to heel. I unzipped the sleeping bag and, in a panic, searched for my knickers that were buried somewhere at the bottom of the feather-filled sack.

'Christ, where are they?' I gave up and cowered on

the armchairs, trying to quickly assess my situation, the reality of which had ebbed and flowed several times a day since leaving Spain, like the salt-tide washing the rocks outside the cottage. Since my departure, I had felt free and trapped, frightened and fearless, cowardly and brave. My emotions were a confused surge, leaving me unable to discern the difference between what I wanted and how to get it.

In spite of my turmoil, I realised that if I was discovered so soon in my mission, I would be truly washed up. Word would travel around the island within hours that the Callister girl had returned, alerting the enemy. I had to get rid of whoever was outside my hideaway or lie low until they went.

I crawled to the window on all fours and slowly raised my eyes above sill level. Through the grime, I saw a man in a long jacket standing on the tallest rock in my front garden, staring out to sea with apparently no purpose other than to stare at the pale blue-grey horizon of another Manx morning. His dog, a scrawny terrier, jumped from rock to rock, sometimes slipping but quickly regaining its foothold. I never expected to see anyone down on this small, inhospitable beach, especially at this time of year.

The man turned to face the cottage and I ducked, but too slowly. He must have seen me, even through the muck and salt on the window. I waited, hardly daring to breathe. Apart from the regular small crash of waves dumping seaweed and driftwood onto the shore, there was nothing to hear. I trembled beneath the window, hugging my sweatshirt around my knees.

Then there came a sudden and urgent series of knocks on the door.

'Hello?' He called through the salt-bleached timber. I visualised his lips pressed close.

'Damn you, go away,' I hissed.

I glanced at the stove. Flames still licked at the giant log I put in during the night so that I'd have warmth in the morning.

'The smoke,' I whispered pitifully, realising that he would notice the grey-black curls from where he stood on the creaky front deck. I cradled my head in my hands.

'Anyone home?' He knew there was.

I had no choice. Which looked more suspicious – a disused cottage where a figure was seen lunging out of sight and a fire is lit but no one answers the door, or a disused cottage being given a new lease of life by ... I thought frantically ... by someone plausible?

I stood up, feathered my fingers through my straggly, sleep-mashed hair, breathed in deeply and opened the door. I forced a grin that told him I'd lived there all my life.

'Morning!' I said, as if I was expecting him for breakfast. Then I stopped abruptly, my mouth hanging open stupidly and my feet glued to the floor. He was the man from the cliff top cottage and was just as sexy, just as alluring at close range with his clothes on as he had been last night.

'Hi,' he replied in a drawn-out, already suspicious voice. His eyes were everywhere at once, flicking up and down my semi-dressed body and then into the dark cottage behind me. 'So there is someone here.' He called the terrier to heel. 'Welcome to Niarbyl,' he said, evidently very curious.

'Well,' thanks,' I said, desperately trying to reanimate myself. If I acted defensively he was far more likely to suspect something was up than if I behaved like someone with a right to be there. 'Would you like to come in?' Instantly kicking myself for the invitation,

I stepped aside and beckoned him in. I glanced longingly out to sea as if it was a possible escape route.

The man, as rugged as the rocks on the beach, attached a lead to the dog's collar and stepped inside, ducking his head under the perilously low lintel. 'What brings you here?' he asked.

Suddenly remembering my state of undress, I turned around helplessly a couple of times, as his dog might do before it lay down to sleep, and rummaged around the armchairs in search of clothing.

'Are these what you're looking for?' He bent down and picked up a pair of my knickers from underneath an armchair.

My head thumped with a sudden rush of embarrassment before I iced over and turned into a glacier. I wanted to hurl myself at his hand, make a grab for what he had plucked off the floor, yank the flimsy lace from his grasp, but all I could do was stand and stare at him while he offered me my panties.

'My knickers,' I finally said in a voice as brittle as meringue. Before I could say anything else, he was sitting down on the makeshift bed and once again staring around the cottage. I reached out and took my underwear and also retrieved my jeans before silently retreating to the animal-infested back room. 'Won't be a minute,' I called out as if trying on a new outfit in a boutique. I hopped and staggered in the dimly lit room while forcing my legs into the denim. I returned still wearing a pink flush on my cheekbones but also a smile that assured him this was nothing out of the ordinary.

'I hadn't expected visitors at this hour of the day,' I said.

The man patted the dog's tan and white rump as it skittered around his ankles. He leaned forward, his eyes wandering around the cottage as if he was on a reconnaissance mission. 'I'm sorry if I disturbed you,' he said. 'It's just that there hasn't been anyone here for such a long time and I wanted to make sure things were ... you know...' – he trailed off and stared directly at me – '...OK.'

'I understand.' I stood primly before him, trying to suppress a laugh as the dog spun in circles.

'Lewis,' he replied and stood up briefly, extending a hand.

I took it and said, surprisingly easily, 'Ailey.' There was no way I was revealing my surname.

'Nog.' He gestured to the silly creature and grinned, his teeth too white for a man with stubble, a dirty parka and worn-out boots. 'The dog.'

'Nog the dog,' I repeated because there wasn't much else to say.

'Are you on holiday?' I could tell that his question was laced with hidden meaning. *What are you doing here?* was what he meant to say.

'Kind of.'

'Not the best time of year to be exploring the island.' Nog finally became still and sat between Lewis's legs.

'The scenery's dramatic,' I said. 'How I like it.'

'Been here long?'

'Just got here actually. It's my uncle's cottage.' No response. 'Great-uncle?' I added for no particular reason, except perhaps to confuse him.

Lewis stared at me, his experienced eyes scanning my body, trying to assess if what he saw concurred with what I was saying. They were pale-grey eyes soaked in something dangerous, marinated in years of salty island living that had given him a weathered look and made him appear older than he probably was. My best guess was forty-two. It was at that point that I realised his undeniable attractiveness, despite our age gap.

'So you're a relation of Ethan Kinrade's.' It was a statement rather than a question although his intonation did slow considerably on 'Kinrade'.

I closed my eyes and tried to swim because I was fast sinking below the surface. I needed to be vague. Getting Lewis and his silly dog out of my cottage was a priority but I found myself engaging him – or was it him engaging me? – in an exchange of information about my great-uncle Ethan. Whoever he was.

'He seems very young to have a great-niece.'

'Oh yes, he is, isn't he?' It was agonising. 'But here I am!' I held out my hands in a kind of personal fanfare and twisted my legs awkwardly. My shuffling feet did something to Nog, however, and the dog leapt at the over-sized socks that had dropped to my ankles. Although painful, the distraction was welcome.

'Nog, leave!' Lewis finally persuaded the terrier that my socks weren't black rabbits. 'I'm sorry,' he said with a clean, unsuitable grin, his eyes lingering on my breasts. 'You were saying, about Ethan.'

'I was?'

Think, woman, think. Lewis waited patiently for my response. His black jeans stretched across his thighs and his parka falling open to reveal a grey, oil-stained sweatshirt. A large, veined hand with surprisingly neat nails rubbed at the stubble on his chin while he sized me up, waiting for my reply.

'There's nothing to say really. I haven't seen him in years. We have this' – I thought frantically – '... arrangement. I'm allowed to use the cottage when I visit.'

'So, you stay here,' Lewis asked, gesturing around the dilapidated room, 'and not in Creg-ny-Varn Manor?'

'I like the tranquillity,' I said, surprising myself. I was beginning to believe my own story. 'Being so close to the sea, nature, the elements – I love it.' I held my breath, waiting for him to accept my lies.

'I'm going fishing later,' he said unexpectedly. We both stared out of the window at the blue-green chop of a December morning.

'Really,' I said croakily, thankful for the digression.

'I can guess what you're thinking,' he said.

No you can't.

'That I've come to sell you fish.'

'The thought hadn't crossed my mind.' If only he knew how grateful I was to be discussing fish.

'Do you cook on that?' He nodded his head to the stove.

'I intend to but I think it's best suited for making tea and I reckon even that will take ages.'

'I can wait,' he said, grinning.

'You'll have to wait a long time then, because I don't have any tea, milk or fresh water.' Surely this was signal enough for him to leave although, strangely, I didn't completely want him to go. I was intrigued by the way his appearance contradicted his manner. He was obviously a highly educated and worldly man and yet evidently lived a simple life on the island.

Lewis ignored me, stood up and walked over to the window. My heart pounded as he picked up the binoculars that I had left lying on the sill. It was now imperative that he leave.

'Where do you live?' I asked, desperate to drive him homeward.

'Old Bridge Cottage.' He put the binoculars to his eyes and gazed out to sea. 'It's the grey slate cottage on the cliff.' He panned around the vista for a moment and then something must have caught his eye because he jerked the binoculars to the left again. 'Good heavens,' he said, lowering the glasses for a beat. 'You can see it from here. Who would have guessed that my place was visible from down here on the beach?'

'Heavens, indeed,' I echoed. 'But I wouldn't know,' I added. 'I've not used the binoculars yet. I found them lying on the sill when I arrived yesterday.' I felt my face turning scarlet.

At this, Lewis turned around and stared directly at me. His pale-grey eyes, set in a face that was too experienced to be conned by the likes of me, twinkled within the confines of his weathered face.

'So you haven't been tempted to spy on your surroundings? Or your neighbours?' He stood motionless with the binoculars poised at his chest. The only movement about him was the wry smile he was failing to suppress.

'Of course not,' I replied, adding such a large measure of shock to my voice that I sounded like a guilty child caught red-handed. 'Besides, it was pitch-dark when I arrived so I wouldn't have been able to see you or your wife.'

It felt as if the ground had dropped away and I was speeding towards the earth's centre at the speed of light, my entire body burning with shame, embarrassment and humility. One word, *one word*, had confirmed to Lewis that indeed, I had been spying. How else would I have known he had a wife?

Lewis placed the binoculars back on the window sill, walked to the door and clicked his fingers. Nog obeyed and trotted to his side. He turned abruptly and narrowed his eyes as if to say, 'I hope you enjoyed the show'.

'I expect to catch dogfish or cod later. I would very

much like to share whatever I land with you. I'm a superb cook. Dinner at my place, say eight o'clock?' The harsh features softened and he offered a charming smile. He pushed his fingers through his wind-tousled hair and took hold of the dog's lead. 'Elizabeth would love to meet you and you can tell us all about yourself and your great-uncle. The man's quite an enigma.'

If I say yes, will you go away and leave me alone? I thought. My mind raced and I fiddled with my fingernails. I glanced at the binoculars that might as well have been labelled 'I've been spying on you', but then I was lost in his eyes, which told me going to dinner at his house would prove to be a warm, hospitable and thoroughly enjoyable evening. My mind was made up, regardless of the risk to my predicament.

'I'd love to come!' I almost squealed. 'I've never had dogfish before.'

'Excellent,' he replied. 'I do hope you have a torch to find your way up the path.' And he winked, leaving me remembering how I had flashed my torch the night before.

I spent the next hour resurrecting the interior of the cottage as best I could. Without fresh water, cleanliness was nearly impossible but I found a broom and a bucket and after I had swept the floor, I drenched the table and windows with sea water. It would have to do. I beat the dusty armchair cushions against the jagged rocks, which gave me an idea for breakfast. When the cottage was as homely as I could make it and had lost most of its fusty smell, I returned to the rocks and used my penknife to loosen two dozen blue-black mussels from their bed of fuzzy seaweed. I stoked the fire and seared the shellfish on the now blazing flames. One by one, they hissed and popped open, revealing delicious salty pouches – the best breakfast I had ever tasted.

I licked my fingers clean and drank the last of my water. As well as my initial manoeuvres on Creg-ny-Varn Manor, I would have to make sourcing fresh water and food a priority. A trip to the local shop was risky as I was sure that the villagers would recognise me, or at least see the similarity between me and my mother. I was convinced that the scandal surrounding our shameful departure fourteen years ago would still be flowing in and out of their thoughts as regularly as the tide that washed the shore each day.

My appetite sated by my unusual breakfast and my body warmed thoroughly by the cast-iron stove, I wrapped up in layers of clothing topped off by my dark-green waterproof. If needed, it would at least provide some camouflage for my advance on my family estate. I even considered attaching twigs and leaves to my body so as not to be spotted when stalking the property's grounds. I giggled at the thought as I picked my way across the debris-littered beach.

Yesterday's storm, which had abated before I arrived at the cottage, had delivered an interesting array of gifts on the pebbles. I hauled several pieces of driftwood to the back of the beach to dry out under the shelter of the cliff and pocketed long lengths of orange twine. Tin cans and plastic bags were tangled with moss-green seaweed and I even spotted an unopened packet of crisps bobbing about in the froth.

I climbed the steep path that led to the cliff top track and, after fifteen minutes of tramping through the wet, springy grass, I was walking along the road towards the village. The sky pressed down like sodden blankets and I took some comfort in this, hoping that the promise of rain would keep other walkers at home or the mist that pooled in the valleys would shroud the road and render me invisible. As I walked under the occasional stark skeleton of a tree deformed by the insistent westerly wind, plops of water dropped onto my tightly-drawn hood, making me feel as if I was in a portable tent. The island's climate was so dissimilar to my whitewashed *cortijo*, which baked for three hundred days a year in a white hot sun, that I felt as if I was hydrating, somehow unfurling from over a decade of desiccation.

A car sped around a corner and swerved to avoid me. I sidestepped onto the verge, narrowly missing being clipped by the vehicle. A visit to the island's hospital would be a good way to wreck my mission. As tempting as it was to hitch a lift, risking the idle chit-chat that would inevitably ensue was tantamount to knocking on the front door of Creg-ny-Varn and greeting the impostor, Ethan Kinrade, himself. As I continued the thirty-minute walk on foot, I contemplated the man who had stolen my inheritance.

So far, I knew only two things about him – his name, thanks to Lewis revealing it, and that he was a thief. I guessed at other unattractive traits he was sure to possess and imagined him to be a big man, enormous in fact, with wobbling pale flesh fattened by his easy good fortune and generous living. He would have a servant to tend to his every need, while he sat in a quilted jacket smoking my father's pipe by the marble fireplace in the library, reading my family's books. He would rise at ten and have his clothes spread out by a maid. He would breakfast in the orangery, followed by a leisurely walk around the estate. After a lunch of quail's eggs and poached salmon, he would nap on the Queen Anne chaise-longue taking in the view to the coast before drifting into a deep, contented sleep. His evenings would be filled by recounting his good fortune to other scoundrels whom he had befriended, while they quenched their thirst with crystal glass after crystal glass of the estate's finest Glen Broath whisky.

My walk became a purposeful march and I puffed as the mist finally gave way to a regular spattering of rain. I balled my fists as I strode to the lane that would take me to the perimeter of the main estate.

'Who does he think he is?' My angry words went unheard and dropped to the road in bursts of hot breath. Lack of information frustrated me nearly as much as being forgotten in my father's will.

It was pure chance that I ever discovered my father's death, having acquired an out-of-date copy of *The Times* left behind by a pair of English tourists. I treasured that newspaper, even though it was several months old and had been used by the tourists to wrap pottery souvenirs in the boot of their hired car. They stayed in our *cortijo*, my mother providing bed and breakfast to supplement our income, and they let me have the newspaper when I spotted them rearranging the contents of their luggage. I read every page meticulously, catching a breath of the British life that I often missed. I even read the obituaries.

I believe in fate. How else would I have learned of my father's death? My mother appeared saddened for a while but then went about her business in her usual diligent manner. But the words 'Sole Heir Gains Manx Millions' swilling about in my mind finally drove me to leave my Spanish home and return to the Isle of Man where my estranged father had died. The heir's name had not been printed in the newspaper, fuelling my curiosity further. I was aware that my father had remarried after my mother and I were driven off the island but apart from that I knew nothing about the man I had once gambolled about the garden with as a playful child. My mother had never encouraged contact and I had grown up believing he didn't want anything to do with me.

I walked close to the leafless hedge as I turned up the lane and proceeded away from the coast. I soon caught sight of the white painted pillars that supported the ornamental wrought-iron gates and, as I tentatively approached the entrance to the long driveway, I saw the name 'Creg-ny-Varn Manor' etched in a large slab of slate. It was tempting to stride confidently up to the gates and press the intercom buzzer and demand access to my home but I had another method of entry planned. Glancing around to make sure there were no cars coming or walkers approaching, I pushed my way into the waist-high bramble hedge and scrambled over the wooden fence that separated the adjacent field from the Manor's formal gardens. The tangled hedge provided perfect cover as I scooted towards the house, bent low with my body skimming the thorns. I was beginning to feel the damp seeping through my clothes. I wiped the back of my gloved hand across my rain-glazed face and sniffed, unsure whether the cold air had made my nose run or if it was the sight of my childhood home.

I reached the end of the hedge, the point at which the topiary garden intersected with the field and the lower corner of the Glen Broath whisky distillery. The long slate barn, housing the mash tuns and copper stills, flanked the southern boundary while the tall slate-clad roof of the kiln house dominated the matching grey sky. Nothing had changed in fourteen years. I was suddenly startled as a low rumbling noise and what sounded like the hiss of brakes filled the air. As I peered through the thorny hedge, I saw a coach load of tourists disembarking, evidently set for a tour of the distillery. Thankful for the diversion, I pressed on. After easing myself through the scrub and gorse, I bypassed the bustling yard, wound my way through neatly clipped box sculptures and crept around to the kitchen garden of the Manor. I was thankful, at least, that Mr Kinrade had seen fit to keep the beautiful gardens immaculate.

'Can I help you?'

I froze. The voice was deep and assured, causing the skin on my back to prickle with fear. My peek through the kitchen window thwarted, I used those few precious seconds as I turned slowly to conjure an excuse. I straightened my back, but even standing tall I was only shoulder height to the man who had caught me red-handed. I swallowed and smiled through the drizzle, realising that I must have looked a terrible sight with my hood strung tightly around my rosy, wet face and my muddy walking boots and wet jeans. I wasn't sure he would even recognise me as female – a good thing perhaps, since remaining unidentifiable was paramount. I hadn't bargained on being caught, let alone so soon into my mission.

'I was just admiring the beautiful gardens,' I croaked. 'Even at this time of year, they are truly impressive.' I smiled, hoping to warm the hard, angular face that glared back at me.

'But that's the kitchen, not the garden.' With his green Wellington boots, his arms folded over a waxed jacket and his dark hair flattened against his forehead by the rain, he seemed likely to be the estate's gardener. A quick glance behind him to a wheelbarrow containing an assortment of tools confirmed my guess.

A few more compliments about his work would surely ensure my release.

'I wanted to see if there was anyone home.' I shifted uneasily. 'Just to say how I much admire the topiary.'

'It's a private estate,' he continued, holding his stance firmly. 'The coach tour's over there.' He finally moved, making a quick gesture towards the grey buildings of the Glen Broath distillery. He was assuming I had strayed from the party, offering me the perfect alibi.

'I'm sorry,' I said with a grin. Remaining casual was imperative. I loosened the tie of my hood, pushed it back and shook out my long hair. 'But I couldn't resist a glimpse. I'm passionate about –'

'You're trespassing.' The powerful voice, the unwelcoming stare and hard features remained but I noticed his eyes flick down my body as my hair settled in long, dry swathes.

'Are you the gardener?' I pushed my hands deep into my jacket pockets and dug my fingernails into my palms. He was right. I was trespassing. I was a stranger in my own home.

He nodded and couldn't seem to help the twitch of his jaw or the small swallow that fluttered in his throat. 'Passionate about what, exactly?' he asked.

'Gardening, of course!' I took a chance and walked past him to the formal shaped beds of the kitchen garden, thankful to escape the corner in which he had me trapped. I knew little about ornamental plants and shrubs, especially British ones, having grown up eking out an existence in the olive and orange groves in Spain. Our garden stretched to pots of geranium and creeping, scented jasmine roaming wildly over the veranda but my horticultural knowledge pretty much ended there. I did, however, recognise a few twiggy herbs in the kitchen garden. I plucked a sprig of lavender and crushed the spiky leaves between my fingers.

'I love lavender,' I said, inhaling the scent and taking a few more steps away from the gardener. In a moment, I would be retracing my path and thinking of a better way to gain entry to Creg-ny-Varn Manor.

'That's rosemary,' he said flatly and, before I could admit how silly I had been, his hand was fixed firmly around my wrist in a painful grip that caused me to drop the leaves at my feet. 'Who are you and what do you want?' He pulled me closer and our puffs of white breath mingled as I tried to concoct a believable story. He virtually shocked the truth out of me.

'I want to see ... Ethan Kinrade,' I stammered, refusing to surrender to the man's aggressive demeanour. He was only the gardener yet acted as if he owned the place. I pulled my arm but the grip tightened. 'You're hurting me.'

'Mr Kinrade's not home. He's gone away.' The gardener's voice dropped a little, almost saddened as he spoke. 'I don't know when he'll be back.'

The grip on my wrist slackened too and I took the opportunity to yank myself free. I could have run and hunkered down in the beach cottage for a couple of days to rethink my plan, but something prevented me from turning and fleeing back to the road. This man was a valuable source of information. He knew Ethan Kinrade.

'You're getting wet.' His tone changed, strangely softened, perhaps by my increasingly bedraggled condition. But his sudden concern threw me off guard and I was unprepared as he took hold of my arm again. Stupidly, I allowed him to drag me across the garden.

'Where are you taking me?' I stumbled through the wet grass beside him as we headed for a small building tacked onto the rear of the big house. The tool room, I recalled.

'Somewhere to dry off and talk.' He opened the wooden door of the ramshackle hut and virtually pushed me inside. Once my eyes grew accustomed to the dim light, I saw that it was not just a tool shed any more but a gardener's den with an old sofa bed, a rug and upturned onion crates positioned amongst the numerous gardening implements. 'Sit,' he ordered and fastened the door shut.

Vague childhood recollections filled my mind of gathering poppy seed heads that had been hung up to dry in this very room, of searching for worms in buckets full of mud, of happy days playing in the sun. How times had changed. The gardener lit an oil lamp, bathing the grey slate walls in an orange glow.

'Take off your wet jacket.' He tossed me a towel and draped my coat next to the wood burner in the corner. He took off his own weather-proof jacket and mussed up his damp hair so that it reclaimed its natural shape. His outdoor clothing had given nothing away of his undeniably lean and muscular body and, as I rubbed my face and neck with the towel, I tried to ignore the covering of dark hair on his arms as he pushed up the sleeves of his checked shirt.

'Thanks,' I said, passing back the towel. I stared down at my boots, feeling like a naughty child.

'You're not from the coach party at all, are you?' He poured two shots from a familiar bottle of Glen Broath single malt and handed one to me. 'Drink and get warm,' he ordered, 'and sit while you tell me your story.'

Despite there being room enough beside him on the

shabby sofa, I chose to kneel beside the wood burner. My legs ached from my long walk and the December drizzle and cold had finally ground into my bones but there was no way I was succumbing to the cosy exchange this rather arrogant man now appeared to be offering.

I shook my head in admission. 'No, I'm not from the coach tour.' Perhaps it was the way he had gripped my wrist and dragged me into his den but I found myself opening up and wanting to tell him my entire story. There was something surreal about the situation, something reckless. Of course, had I been caught by Ethan Kinrade himself, then that would have been different. He couldn't possibly be told of my intentions yet.

'I have to speak with the owner of Creg-ny-Varn.' I took a large mouthful of the whisky and coughed. I wanted to wipe the tear from my left eye.

'Like I said, he's not home.' The man leaned forward, his rigid arms braced against his knees, the shot glass circling between his fingers. Unexpectedly, he grinned, the temporary warmth of his expression equalling the glow of the lamp.

'What's so funny?' I was sure he was mocking me.

'You,' he exclaimed. 'You're not a very good liar and an even worse snoop.'

'It's true,' I protested. 'I came to see Mr Kinrade and —'

'Then why not use the front door like anyone else?'

He had a point but I could hardly admit to wanting to spy on the man. It seemed that he took my silence to signal defeat.

'Look,' he said in a much warmer voice. 'I can probably help you.' He patted the empty space on the sofa. 'But you really need to relax first.'

'You mean you can get me into the house?' My eagerness brought a small frown onto his forehead.

'If that's what you want, then yes. I doubt Mr Kinrade would mind.'

Things were looking up already and, to prevent him reneging, I tentatively took the place beside him. 'You have a key?'

He nodded. 'I am in sole charge of the house. The maid comes a couple of times a week and when the boss is away, as he often is, then the place is all mine. Now, tell me your name.' To my shock, he placed a hand on my rain-soaked thigh and squeezed gently. With those dark eyes to lead me astray, he could have told me anything and I would have believed him.

'Ailey Callister,' I replied, completely forgetting my covert mission. While I was mentally chastising myself for advertising my name, I failed to notice how pale the gardener became.

The mahogany four-poster was immaculately made up with an antique bedspread in duck-egg blue and an abundance of feather pillows in lace shams. The bed was the centrepiece of the impressive period room, which was filled with Georgian furniture and paintings.

'Mr Kinrade's room?'

The gardener, who had reluctantly revealed himself as Dominic before we left the hut, stood in the bedroom doorway, having tailed me as I nervously wandered throughout the deserted house. I was feeling quite strange inside.

'Technically, yes.' He ventured into the room, perhaps also feeling uneasy that we were prying on its absent owner. 'Although I don't think he sleeps in here much.'

'Oh?'

But Dominic fell silent and when he walked up behind me, so close that I could feel his breath on my neck, I dropped onto the plush bed to avoid another painful grip on my arm. Impulsively, I kicked off my boots and nestled in the mountain of pillows. However temporarily, I was finally home.

It didn't occur to me immediately that I had effectively advertised myself for sale. I had no idea how it looked to Dominic, who had already made his own discreet advance by allowing me to feel the brush of his desire on my neck. I simply lay, staring up at the rich curtains of the bed canopy, fantasising about how it would feel when I reclaimed my beautiful family home.

To my shock, I felt the bed dip as Dominic, whom I had met only forty minutes ago, positioned himself beside me. I risked a glance and saw that he was lying on his side, his head propped on his bent arm and his face unnervingly close. I looked away immediately.

'So, what is it that you want with Mr Kinrade that necessitates snooping around his house and lying on his bed?'

Should I answer truthfully? I bit my lip and sat upright, kicking myself for having climbed onto the bed. I pushed my hair back and swallowed, easing myself towards the edge of the satin bedspread. I had already let my real name slip so would being honest be such a disaster? Perhaps Dominic would be willing to help me. I took the half-lidded gaze he poured over me to mean that he would have done anything I suggested. I couldn't move. Instead, I offered a deep stare in return and let my mouth drop open in case a suitable reply should come out.

'Are you a stalker? Do you have a crush on Mr

Kinrade?' Dominic asked, shifting himself closer so that my next move away would be onto the floor.

'Good heavens, no! That thief is the last person I'd want to –'

And it was done. Dominic's mouth was on mine. I was being kissed by a virtual stranger in Ethan Kinrade's bedroom. I pushed away and stood up, grabbing onto the bedpost for support because my legs wouldn't work.

He followed the advance with information that skittled my mind almost as much as his lips. 'I know everything about the man. I could tell you his innermost thoughts, his desires, his intentions. I can tell you his favourite food, what car he drives, where he went to school and who his friends are. I could even tell you what aftershave he uses.'

Dominic wasn't at all affronted by my withdrawal. In fact, my reluctance to return his kiss seemed to fuel him more. For the third time in less than an hour, he gripped my wrist, pulling me back onto the bed.

'You know him that well?' I asked nervously, allowing Dominic to lay me down on the pillows again.

'Better than you can imagine.' The gardener's lips nipped at mine but didn't deliver the forceful kiss I had expected. My heart jammed against my ribs and a voice screamed in my head to run back to the beach cottage. A mild waft of whisky coupled with the tang of rain and bonfires drifted from his body, instantly annihilating my senses. Looming above me, Dominic coaxed me with his mouth, nuzzling, biting and nipping at my face and neck until he thought I was ready to hear his offer. I was too busy coping with his teasings to initially absorb what he said.

'If you take your clothes off, I'll tell you everything

you need to know about Ethan Kinrade.' His mouth stopped work and his eyes narrowed, assessing my reaction.

I was stunned. Dominic had verbally clouted me on the side of the head. Everything I had travelled so far to learn was being offered to me in a convenient package and all I had to do was strip and give Cregny-Varn's gardener a glimpse of what lay beneath my drenched layers. Momentarily, I was keen to shed my uncomfortable clothes but the idea of prostituting myself to gain the upper hand over Ethan Kinrade was not something I had anticipated in my mission. I was prepared to stoop pretty low: to rummage through waste bins, to intercept mail, to eavesdrop telephone conversations, to peer through windows. But to offer my body, to lay myself vulnerable in the heart of the enemy's domain for a virtual stranger – even if he was paying in a currency that would wipe out the need to delve further – was a tough deal to make.

'Well?' Dominic brushed a finger under my chin as if he had known me for years.

Absurdly, I thought of my lost diary and how I could fill many pages with the day's events. I mentally skimmed over the reams I had already written about ridiculous and unlikely fantasies, many touching on situations uncannily similar to the one I was currently in. Attractive strangers forced themselves upon me; faceless and nameless men whom I would never encounter again stole an hour of my life to cram me with a lifetime of sexual memories. And here it was. On a plate.

'Well?' I protested. 'Well, I think you're a shameful man without morals or a scrap of decency and if your employer knew what you were up to behind his back, he'd sack you for sure.' It helped my conscience to put up a little struggle, made it seem not quite as painful as I unfastened my jacket.

'I think Mr Kinrade would understand.' Dominic watched intently as I stood beside the bed and allowed my wet coat to fall to the floor. 'In my situation, I'm sure he'd do the same.' His undeniably attractive smile broadened his face and it was then that I noticed the intent in his eyes. Before, there had been duty stored in the deep suede of his pupils, possibly a matter-of-fact dullness when he escorted me to the brick shed. Now, in a place where he should feel uneasy, another man's domain, his eyes drooled and spread over me as if he was unwrapping a chocolate bar. Quite simply, the man was filled with lust.

I stood in my sweatshirt and jeans. 'Everything?' I asked. I didn't like it that it felt as easy as being at the doctor's for a medical check. A part of my mind had shut down temporarily, or was it that a new part, a yet unused section of my personality, was awakening? I felt wicked, almost forgetting the prize of information I would gain for my trouble. I was enjoying it and it didn't feel in the least bit troublesome.

'Everything.'

I pulled my sweatshirt over my head and stepped out of my jeans and thick socks. I unbuttoned my shirt and removed that along with the two T-shirts I had layered on for warmth. Dominic laughed at how much I was wearing but was quiet when he saw the very core of me standing in front of him in nothing but a shell-pink camisole and knickers.

'I'd never have guessed that such a pretty thing was tucked away under all those clothes.' It seemed that he didn't know what to do with his hands. They clamped together, kneaded a pillow – perhaps pretending it was my flesh – pushed through his still damp hair, toyed with his own clothing briefly before reaching out and sliding down my naked thighs.

'You never said anything about touching,' I said. The sensible part of me had finally found a voice although it was slammed by the new, adventurous me. His large hands hadn't only brushed against my skin. It was as if he had taken hold of a long-hidden emotion and squeezed it gently to release a deluge of need that quickly saturated every part of me.

'I couldn't resist.' Dominic's words were choked, as if he too were struggling with an inner demon that was intent on doing everything it shouldn't. 'Just undress. That will be fine.'

'And you promise to tell me everything I want to know about Ethan Kinrade?' I paused, hands on the hem of my camisole.

'Anything you ask,' he confirmed. I was reassured that he must know the wretched man very well indeed and so stripped my body of its remaining garments as quickly as possible. The sensible part of me screamed at me to get this over and done with.

There was suddenly a palpable stiffness in the air. The situation appeared, to both of us I think, ridiculous. My nakedness caused me to notice things I hadn't given a thought to when I first entered the room, such as a chill in the air comparable to that outside, and the slight musty smell as if the room hadn't been used for the entire winter. The dimness alerted me that the heavy damask drapes were closed and several pieces of furniture had been covered with sheets, forming bulky ghosts around the room's perimeter. And while I absorbed the minute details that my raw state rendered me notice, Dominic gorged not on my nakedness but more, I think, on my neediness.

Strangely, breathlessly, he viewed me as if studying an oil painting.

'Is this OK?' I was asking him for approval, a compliment even, and my body responded by gathering my tan circles of nipple and tightening them into points. Perhaps it was the chill, too.

'Very fine.' Dominic spoke slowly and cleared his throat, his voice sounding as if he had consumed a cocktail of sand and seawater. 'Beautiful, in fact.' He sat up and moved to the edge of the bed. 'Turn around. Let me see you from behind.'

I was for sale. I was delivering my body for knowledge and when my back was turned, I couldn't help the grin that cut across my face. I couldn't wait either to find my diary so that I could write it all up in a flurry of frantic scrawl that such a thing had happened. To me!

'I like this bit of you.' An express train of warmth and tingling drove up my spine as I felt the broadness of Dominic's hands settle on the small of my back, just where the flesh of my buttocks flared gently from my hips. 'You have a dimple.'

I turned around, preparing to defend myself. I didn't want him pulling me off balance and getting me back onto the bed. The deal was a look, nothing more. But as I faced him again, his hands remained in the same position and were now gently resting either side of my pubic mound. I should have moved but I didn't, and neither did he, making him appear to be warming his hands by a fire. And indeed he was. *My* fire.

'So where is Kinrade now?' I locked eyes with him. A deal was a deal, even if he did have his fingers a breath away from me neglecting to ask any useful questions at all. To my horror, Dominic shrugged.

'Not sure, to be honest.'

'Well, when's he back?' The quiver in my voice reflected the tiny waves that amplified between my legs. I pressed my knees together in an attempt to keep him out.

'Not sure of that either.' Dominic slid his hands together by an inch. Several of his fingers now nestled in the fine triangle of hair at the top of my legs, preventing me from delivering the indignant reply he deserved.

'Do you know *anything* about him?' I bored hard into his eyes, determined to get some kind of an answer for such risk.

I was kept waiting as he frowned and allowed his thumbs to drift into the furrow that led to my sex. His touch was preceded by an electrical force field that acted as an early warning to my body. Useless, however, in that it caused meltdown rather than retreat. I tried to concentrate in order to remember the details that Dominic would hopefully reveal but it took all my willpower to stop my hips rocking as his thumbs eased slowly to where they shouldn't.

'I think it's only fair that you give me details,' I said. 'I've more than lived up to my side of the deal.'

'He's a lonely man,' Dominic replied. His hands paused in a moment of thought. 'He lives here by himself and, well,' he looked to the fireplace, a bleak tinge to his eyes, 'I think he resents it.' Dominic withdrew his hands from my body as if I was in the way of a sudden rush of feelings and then he gestured around the room to indicate, I supposed, Creg-ny-Varn.

'He doesn't like the Manor?' My delight was hard to conceal.

'The emptiness of it, rather than the place itself.' Dominic sighed.

'You must know him very well.' I almost felt guilty

at digging up an obviously emotive subject. 'But he's lucky to have you as a friend. You obviously care about him.' But my guilt passed quickly. I was standing naked, allowing a virtual stranger to prise between my legs. My own emotions rose and I reached for my clothes.

'No, don't. Please.' There was seriousness in the gardener's voice. 'There's more I can tell you.'

I clutched my camisole to my breasts, not sure I could hear this naked. I wanted to learn everything about the man who had obviously conned his way into the estate but more than that, way more, I wanted to ease Dominic back onto the bed and allow him to become my living fantasy. The push-pull force was too great so I stood dumbly before him with my thoughts behaving as if I was drunk and my body teased to unbearable dizziness by Dominic's gaze and brief touch.

'Mr Kinrade understands his responsibility to the estate. He manages the place impeccably. The distillery exports whisky all over the world and Glen Broath has made quite a name for itself in the States.'

'But?' I didn't want this although knew I had to dig for information. What I really wanted was Dominic delving into me.

'But he never asked for the role. You have to know him to understand that.'

It was my own fault for accepting such a deal. Whoever said 'never mix business and pleasure' was right. The line between information and potential bliss was blurring fast and I had to decide on which side of it I was standing. I breathed in and closed my eyes briefly.

'That's my problem. I don't know him. I do know,

however, that he is an impostor.' Then I stepped forward and allowed the weight of my body to topple Dominic the gardener back onto the antique bedspread before silencing my own mouth by investigating the hard line of his jaw with my lips. He didn't slacken as I had expected but tensed as my words ricocheted between us. I could only deduce that he knew and cared for Ethan Kinrade very much. And it was the ignition between my legs, however tentatively it had been applied, and the crazy situation in which I found myself, that caused me to unravel Dominic and coax his surprisingly unwilling body to respond.

I curled my fingers inside the top of his checked shirt and prised the buttons open to reveal a grey T-shirt that clung to the blocks of muscle on his chest. He lay still and allowed me to precisely kiss his face and neck. My body was draped half over his, my legs entwined around the roughness of his jeans, and I had all but forgotten that I was naked and responding loudly to my new-found assertiveness. As my desire for the virtual stranger increased, my actions became more urgent, to the point where I wrestled him out of his clothing so that he was lying on the quilt in his shorts and wearing nothing but a blank expression with only the tiniest breeze of a smile.

'You don't seem so keen to learn about Mr Kinrade any more.'

Was he telling me or asking me? I didn't care. I was awash with an exceptional craving: the need for danger, frivolity and the compulsion to pleasure him senseless. I sanctioned my behaviour on the grounds that I need never see him again. It was all in my diary, which, for now, I tried to forget was lost.

'I want to learn about *you*.' It was half true although

I didn't want his life story. But I did want to know what lay beneath his cotton shorts. 'Are you going to let me find out?'

Dominic nodded in a way I hadn't expected. He was a gardener, a man used to heavy work and the outdoors, his body covered in skin that had seen many summers working without a shirt and muscle that was lean and honed, and I would have expected him to demonstrate his acceptance with more vigor. Instead, he simply gave a tentative bob of his head and quickly averted his heavy, doleful eyes, like a naughty eighteen-year-old boy caught with his pants down. My heart slammed against my ribs and my lungs vied for space as my breathing quickened.

'So, what should I do to you?' I didn't mean my voice to be quite so loud or to pull his face into line with mine so eagerly but somehow, strangely, provocatively, I felt he needed to be taught a lesson. 'You can't just go around ordering women to take their clothes off, you know.' Something delightful skipped through my body, a kind of sparkle on a string threaded through every vein. Shame might come later but, for now, I was enjoying this.

To my surprise, Dominic lifted up one of the many pillows and pulled out several long, silk scarves from underneath. He handed them to me, still wearing that modest look with eyes deeper than they had any right to be. I wasn't experienced in such things but instinctively knew that the offering was an encouragement to render him helpless. That sparkle again, fizzing through me.

'Spread your arms and legs,' I ordered in a voice that was developing a harshness I never thought possible. Dominic emitted a low rumble that I took to signal approval so, just to let him know who was now in charge, I told him I would have to bind his wrists and ankles extra tight to the bedposts. 'It's your own fault.' I kneeled over his body to fasten the knots. My breasts bobbed perilously close to his mouth as I leaned over and my pussy, lining itself with a skim of moisture, hovered near shorts that had risen with the erection they obviously contained. 'You shouldn't have been so rough with me earlier. My turn now.' I gave him a sweet smile as I checked each knot again with a sharp yank.

I sat beside his stretched body and took a long, hard look at what was on offer. Aside from the appealing yet mysterious face, framed by a mass of dark brown hair, and the sinewy neck, leading to a torso muscular not from meticulous and vain exercise but from years of toil caring for hundreds of trees and acres of parkland, aside from the long limbs covered in just the right amount of hair, there was the pale blue cotton of his shorts to consider. I hardly dared to look let alone think of touching the cloth and its contents. I did notice, however, a blot of damp on the fabric at the peak of his evidently eager cock.

Was it really me that reached out and stroked him from the hair between the mounds of his pecs, across his warm belly and over the rigid contents of his boxers, finishing up with my fingers gently kneading the soft cushion of his balls? I loved the feeling of cotton covering its needy filling. So much of me wanted to dive right in there, pull off his underwear...

'Oh no!' I felt stupid, inexperienced and instantly wished I hadn't said 'oh no'. Dominic didn't say anything because I think he already knew. He glanced over to the night-stand and winked at me and it wasn't until I looked there that I realised what he meant.

I reached out and picked up the stainless steel scissors that were muddled amongst a book, a comb and other similar bedroom items. Dominic had anticipated my predicament, which was now going to be wicked fun rather than the nuisance of having to untie him again.

'You'd better not move then,' I said, dragging the cold metal of the closed blades across skin that fell away beneath his shorts. He twitched briefly but then arched his back and moaned as I daringly pushed my face into the cotton package and took a draught of his scent before administering a playful nip to his shaft. 'You smell good,' I said, brandishing the blades. 'Hold still.'

I carefully cut into the cotton – how else was I going to get the things off? – and peeled away the cloth as I snipped. It was like my birthday as the beautiful gift inside was revealed. Dominic's erection sprung free of the shorts and looked up at me with a glint in its eye. I held still and breathless, sitting astride his legs so that I'm sure he could see the beads of moisture escaping from between my thighs. I trailed the scissors up the gossamer skin of his shaft before teasing the paler dome at the top. Dominic's head lunged from side to side and the tension on his wrists increased as he could barely stand the cold, light touch. I put the scissors back on the night-stand and leaned forward on my hands so that I was on all-fours above the poor, writhing gardener.

'Do you make a habit of this?' I asked sternly. 'How many other young women have you tricked into nakedness?'

'None, really. You don't understand –'

'Damn right I don't. You made a deal and it's quite obvious that you know nothing of use about Ethan Kinrade.'

To silence Dominic, who was evidently ready to protest, I surprised him – and indeed myself – by shifting forward and dropping my pussy onto his mouth. I reached out and gripped the bedposts for support, which allowed me to manoeuvre up or down and adjust the pressure and position of his tongue. I was burning up with desire and, as the warmth of his tongue collided with the pressure in my sex, I thought I would explode immediately.

To calm myself, I rode Dominic's face in long, light strokes, barely allowing his outstretched tongue to dip between my lips. How he moaned each time my wetness left his face, as if he couldn't bear being without the taste of me. Then I allowed him to beat against my clitoris and he brought me to within a breath of orgasm with the skill and speed of a hummingbird's wing.

'Stop.' I was breathless. 'Did I ask you to make me come yet?' I reached behind my back and grabbed the thick girth of his cock, administering a sizeable squeeze to let him know I meant it. Dominic let out his loudest moan yet although I wasn't sure if it was from pleasure or pain. With my face covered in a tangle of rain-wetted hair, I turned and immediately dropped my mouth to his groin. My breasts pressed against the soft covering of fuzz on his lower belly and I couldn't help it that my buttocks rose into the air like a freshly cut peach that was too juicy by far for Dominic, even in his restrained position, to ignore. Like a mirror to my own actions on his cock, I again felt the heat of his mouth between my legs except this time his tongue was delving high inside me. Every push he made somehow urged his cock deeper down my throat until I was massaging him with the softest, innermost part of my mouth. If I couldn't prise information about Kinrade from him, then I could at least use him to relieve my fantasy-fuelled condition.

But however hard I tried, first filling my mouth and then my sex as I turned and lowered my freshly primed pussy onto his near vertical erection, I didn't like it that I had been tricked by a mere employee of Ethan Kinrade, especially when the stakes were so high. I felt him pulse inside me as I spoke.

'You're a damn liar and fraud, Dominic whoever-you-are, and you deserve to be left tied to this bed until the maid finds you.' I leaned forward and dug my nails into his muscle-bound shoulders and in response he bucked as high as his pelvis would allow. Shockwaves as bright as lasers needled through me so I ground myself onto him to build up the waves that precede an orgasm. I didn't care if he was approaching a climax or not although, judging by the thickness of him inside me and the clenched expression stretched across his face, I took a guess that he wasn't far away.

'You could be the maid,' he said in jerky syllables. 'The current one is leaving so ... Mr Kinrade ...' – he paused and breathed heavily, thrusting beneath me – 'Mr Kinrade is going to need another one.'

I didn't care about maids and, at that moment, I didn't care about Ethan Kinrade either. I sat bolt upright, arched my back and closed my eyes as the signs of inescapable orgasm began. The tension in my sex increased until I was forced to hold perfectly still, as if trapped in the eye of a tornado, until the crashing tide plundered my mind and body and I was thrown into euphoria by Dominic's insistent cock. Even when

I had come, and I know he felt my contractions because he moaned in rhythm, he continued to pound inside me. Within thirty seconds, another string of waves washed through me and Dominic, still pumping hard, burst open inside me and I swear that I felt seven or eight hot jets fire into my core.

I dropped forward onto his panting body and then rolled off. I laughed. 'We could do with a maid to clear up this mess,' I joked, remembering his pre-come comment. I dipped my fingers in the mixture of juice and semen ladled over his groin. 'She could lap it all up for us,' I said naughtily.

'If you take the job then you can begin work right away,' he said and I knew he was serious by the deep tone of his voice, although he did wink playfully. I raised an eyebrow. It was a possibility. It would allow me to snoop around the house freely and get me into the very core of Kinrade's stolen domain. Plus, I would have a source of income until I claimed my rightful inheritance.

'OK, I accept,' I said with a grin. 'But won't Mr Kinrade need to interview me himself?'

'He trusts me completely,' Dominic replied. 'Besides, I think I've seen enough of you to know that he'd consider you perfect for the job. When can you start?'

'How about right now?' I teased, thoroughly pleased with myself for having turned around what could have been – aside from the quenching of my desire for sex with a stranger – a rather fruitless day.

Then, as I plunged my face onto his semi-hard cock, dutifully cleaning up the mess as any good maid would, I realised that I was on the brink of unleashing too many fantasies all at once. Perhaps it was the sea air, or the no-risk feeling of being away from my home in Spain. Whatever it was, I found myself aroused again by the thought of the evening ahead at the cliff top cottage with Lewis and Elizabeth. But for now I concentrated on my role of maid and did a superlative job of cleaning up Dominic the gardener.

It wasn't until much later, when I was tucking into Lewis's superb dinner, that I wondered how Dominic had known about the scarves and scissors in Ethan Kinrade's bedroom.

3

Elizabeth opened the door and her momentarily blank expression told me that either she wasn't keen on my presence for dinner or Lewis had forgotten to tell her about the invitation.

'Oh. Yes,' she said slowly. I didn't detect an outright lie in an attempt to cover lack of knowledge but I didn't notice much friendliness either. 'Come in out of the cold.'

Old Bridge Cottage exuded warmth and the tang of herbs and log fires, distinctly noticeable in the air even while I was walking through the drizzle from the beach hut. The lure of relaxing by a fire was almost as good as my torch in guiding me through the dark, and the thought of tucking into Lewis's catch kept me going on the tricky path up from the shore.

'I'm Ailey,' I said, hoping it might animate the woman because strangely she was standing quite still, staring at me intently. 'From the beach cottage.' I held out my hand, which she eventually took, returning a delicate, barely-there handshake.

'Elizabeth,' she said, exhaling at last and giving me a sweet smile. 'But you can call me Liz.'

On seeing the woman at close range, my mind was flooded with my voyeuristic antics of the previous night. My cheeks reddened and, rather than detecting embarrassment, I hoped she would blame the chill night air for my sudden flush.

'Ailey, you made it!' Thankfully, Lewis emerged

from the low kitchen doorway drying his hands on a tea towel. 'Liz, take Ailey's coat while I fetch her some mulled wine. She must be chilled to the bone.'

Indeed I was. Any remnants of heat from my earlier encounter with Dominic had sadly dissipated into the Manx winter. Following my unplanned encounter with Creg-ny-Varn's gardener, I had taken a shower and made myself a hot drink. Dominic didn't seem to mind and Ethan Kinrade wasn't there to care. Besides, after several hours in the place, the Manor had already begun to wrap its arms around my heart. As much as I loved my life in Spain, Creg-ny-Varn had always been my home.

'Sit by the fire and get this inside you.' Lewis planted me in a fireside chair and handed me a glass of warm wine that was scented with nutmeg, cloves and orange. 'I hope the walk from Niarbyl wasn't too difficult in the rain and dark.' He stood with Liz, the pair looking down at me, as if I was a stray pet that had returned home. 'It's a long walk. Dangerous, too,' Lewis continued.

'It's not far as the crow flies though, is it, Ailey?' Liz's earlier meagre smile blossomed into a full-blown grin, lighting up her small, pale face. It was unspoken but the understanding between us was palpable and I think they were still enjoying the feeling of having been watched during their lovemaking. Personally, I was squirming with embarrassment.

'I'll have to get used to the walk, I suppose.' I wanted to change the subject but Lewis insisted on talking about the cottage.

'It's a bit cut off, for a young girl living on her own.' He placed his arm around Liz's small waist and pulled her towards him. I looked away, not wanting them to think I was studying another of their displays of affection.

'I like being alone,' I said, which was mostly true although I had relished my earlier liaison with Dominic. I'd barely had a second to ponder my encounter at Creg-ny-Varn, having afterwards walked a further couple of miles to a shop in order to stock the cottage with provisions. Then I'd cleared out the back room and tried to make the whole place more homely. The result was pleasing and I'd even collected some shells from the beach to decorate the window sills and lit a fire for comfort for when I returned from dinner with Lewis and Elizabeth.

'Did you catch anything?' I asked. The warm wine drizzled pleasantly down my throat and my skin was beginning to tingle from the flames. Lewis looked at Elizabeth fondly and made a silly expression.

'Did I catch anything, she asks. Talking of which, I'd better check on the sauce.' Lewis left the room and Liz sat down on the opposite side of the inglenook.

'He's pleased with himself,' she said. 'He got a massive haul, most of which is in the freezer, and he's given away some of the cod. You could take some back with you, if you like.' That sweet smile again, lighting up her delicate features beneath a cap of trimmed blonde hair.

'Thanks,' I said, not really wanting any. The few provisions I bought earlier had to be tinned because I didn't have a refrigerator.

Our conversation drifted between life on the island versus a London existence and the benefits of living in a warm climate. I had got as far as telling her that I had travelled from southern Spain but was loath to reveal much more about myself in case it somehow filtered through to Ethan Kinrade upon his return. Then Lewis announced that dinner was ready and Liz guided me through to the dining room where we were greeted by a small, round oak table laden with a colourful feast. But my reprieve from awkward questions was short-lived and, as Lewis was tucking into the starter of crab cakes and chilli dressing, he asked eagerly about my arrival at Niarbyl. Clearly, my dinner invitation had been for no other reason than to find out about their new neighbour.

'I was telling Liz about your great-uncle Ethan up at Creg-ny-Varn. We've seen him around locally a few times. He hardly looks old enough to have a great niece.' Lewis poured three glasses of chilled Pinot Grigio and raised his glass. 'To new neighbours,' he said and Liz echoed his toast although in a slow, thoughtful voice. 'So tell us, what's the chap like? As I mentioned earlier, he's quite an enigma around here. None of the locals seem to know anything about him.'

'Well,' I began, slipping a piece of the delicious starter in my mouth so that whatever I said would have to be brief. 'He does like to keep himself to himself.' I chewed the crab slowly. 'Mmm, is there tarragon in this?'

Lewis nodded. 'We've not seen a Mrs Kinrade. Do you have a great-aunt?'

'Parsley, too? Perhaps a dash of mustard?' I took a long sip of wine in an attempt to buy extra seconds. 'No, he has no wife,' I slipped in before asking where Lewis learnt to cook.

'Self-taught, aren't you, darling? Purely an accident of living a bachelor's life in London and trying to impress the women with your domestic skills.' Liz laughed and leaned back in her chair. 'I was more impressed by your legal skills, however.' They exchanged winks and I made a grab for the subject change.

'You're a lawyer?'

'When it suits him,' Liz answered on Lewis's behalf. 'He prefers bobbing about on his boat to battling in court.'

'Can't say I blame you,' I added. 'Do you have offices in London? Do you commute?' My questions came thick and fast.

'When I have to, yes. I have a practice there and also on the island so I flit between the two. When I get off the twin-prop at Ballasalla airport, it's like something in me unplugs with the first breath of Manx air.' Lewis certainly seemed to relish his island life.

'And what about you, Liz? Are you from the island?'

'Originally, yes. I went to London to study photography, met Lewis and after spending a few hectic years together, we decided to live up here as much as we could. My work's flexible. I'm away quite a lot on shoots.'

'How interesting.' And that wasn't a lie just to keep the conversation off Ethan Kinrade. I'd always been fascinated by photography. 'What's your speciality?'

'Nude women,' she replied directly and began to clear the plates, knowing that she had set my mind spinning just as much as theirs were whizzing, frantic for my personal story and details of Ethan Kinrade.

Lewis had roasted the freshly caught dogfish with oregano, basil, thyme and garlic and then drizzled it with lemon and olive oil. He served it with sliced potatoes baked with pecorino cheese and a green salad and it was the tastiest fish I had ever eaten. Lewis was obviously passionate about food, although his lean, healthy physique didn't suggest this.

'How long will you stay on the island?' Lewis asked, pouring another carefully chosen wine. 'Are you here for Christmas?'

'No, I hope to have my business taken care of by then.' I realised my mistake only when the couple both looked up from their food. They paused from eating and waited silently to hear more. 'But it's nothing really. I've hardly any business at all.' I was making things worse.

'Business with your great-uncle Ethan?' Liz asked. She had indulged me with polite chit-chat about her life and interests and, since she had kindly invited me to dinner, it felt churlish not to allow them a glimpse of my mission. What harm could it do to reveal a few basic details? Lewis might even be able to offer me some legal advice regarding my stolen inheritance. I had to get one thing straight though.

'Ethan Kinrade is not my uncle.'

Two gasps preceded the laying down of cutlery. The pair remained silent, which had the effect of causing me to continue.

'I don't know who he is, actually. I'm here to find out.' I sipped my wine, waiting for one of them to speak but they didn't. 'Creg-ny-Varn is my father's...' – I sipped again, as if to erase my mistake – '...*was* my father's house. It was my childhood home.' This information elicited raised eyebrows and Lewis puckered his lips, folding his arms.

'You've come back to have a look at your old home then?' He was satisfied with his assumption.

'Not exactly.' They knew too much already. I laughed and turned to Liz. 'Nude women?' I wanted to change the subject again but they were both busy puzzling over my intentions and ignored my question.

'I can ask at the Post Office.' Liz shrugged her

shoulders, perhaps realising how little she and Lewis knew about the nearby estate's new owner. 'The woman there knows everything about everyone.' She smiled. 'Too much, I sometimes think.' Then she received an elbow in the ribs from Lewis.

'No, really. You needn't bother.' My covert mission was spilling from between my fingers like ice melting in the sun. Soon there would be no mission because everyone would know my business, including Ethan Kinrade. 'I'd like to hear more about your photography.' I peeled apart the layers of potato and melted pecorino. The good food, warmth and company made up for the awkwardness of trying to conceal my situation.

'So aren't you technically trespassing by staying in the beach cottage? It belongs to Kinrade's estate.' Lewis tried to sound affable but the nature of his question caused the back of my neck to prickle. To defend myself, I would have to reveal more of my story.

'Not exactly,' I began. 'I'm aware that the cottage belongs to Creg-ny-Varn. I used to spend many hours playing there while my father fished or mended his lobster pots.' I hesitated, ate more food and drank more wine, but Lewis and Liz were attentive listeners. Nothing short of an earthquake would have distracted them from what I was saying. 'My father died a few months ago. I haven't seen him for over a decade.' I paused again, bowing my head and hoping they would urge me not to continue my painful story. They didn't. 'I'm here to find out who's living in my family home. Simple as that.'

'To find out who has stolen your inheritance, you mean.' Lewis was stirred by the inkling of a legal case. He blew out through tight lips. 'That's a tough one. You really need to see a copy of the will before you go steaming in there.' He poured more wine. 'You have no idea if Mr Kinrade is the rightful owner?'

I shook my head and tried to prevent Lewis from filling my glass yet again but he ignored my protestation.

'That could explain why no one around here ever sees him,' Liz said. 'Perhaps he's a fraud!'

'The thought hadn't crossed my mind,' I said rather too sarcastically. 'I spoke with the gardener at Cregny-Varn earlier today, hoping to get some information about the man.' I omitted the bit where I'd been caught red-handed peering through the kitchen window and certainly didn't tell the story of how we ended up in Kinrade's bed together. 'He told me that Mr Kinrade is away at present so I'll have to bide my time until he returns. Perhaps I could research the will, as you suggested, Lewis.' I smiled, grateful for his input.

'That's funny. I swear I saw Kinrade driving out of the estate gates when I went to buy the paper earlier. I was walking Nog to the village.' Lewis served himself more salad, frowning as he pondered on what he had seen.

'I doubt it was him,' I said. 'The house didn't show any signs of anyone being around other than the gardener when I was there earlier.' I smiled inwardly as I replayed snippets of my earlier fun with Dominic. It was most likely that he had used Kinrade's vehicle to run an errand for the estate. He was in charge of the property, after all.

'So that's why I'm here, anyway. I'd appreciate it if you didn't mention my presence in the beach cottage to anyone. I'm not doing any harm living there. If anything, I'm improving the place.' I smiled as I wrapped up my mission in a little packet and handed it to them. Having to dredge through my family history, explaining why my mother and I were forced to leave the island in the first place, was not something I relished. 'And please, Liz, I want to hear all about your interesting job.' I leaned forward on my elbows and clasped my hands under my chin while Lewis cleared the plates and Liz regaled me with tales of how she had first got into glamour photography.

'You must think we're a dirty pair,' Lewis said as he carried a tray of coffee into the cosy sitting room. 'Is Liz telling you the story of how we first met?'

I smiled up at Lewis from my position on the floor by the fire. I was growing to like the couple and their simple lifestyle. In spite of their full-on careers in London, they managed to maintain a contrasting life on the island. Old Bridge Cottage betrayed nothing of Lewis's fast-paced legal firm and I would never have guessed Liz's connection with glamour models. Photography, maybe, as the whitewashed cottage walls contained a patchwork of framed black and white pictures, although mainly of artistic coastal and harbour scenes.

'I was about to,' Liz said. 'And I was going to give the *clean* version.'

'There is no clean version.' Lewis settled onto the sofa next to Liz. 'It's a mucky story however you tell it.'

'Don't feel you have to censor it on my behalf.' I thought I might have been overstepping the mark, especially as I hardly knew the pair – well, not in person anyway. The food, the wine, the waves of heat on my back from the fire made my senses hum with pleasure. Despite a few tricky questions, I was having a wonderful evening. I would have written it all up in my diary later, if it hadn't been stolen. A brief surge of anger and panic set in as I wondered where it was, or more to the point, where Steph was, the wretched girl from the ferry. But I forced such thoughts from my head for now, along with the prospect of walking home alone, and continued to enjoy the evening. Studying Lewis and Liz together, the way they exchanged glances or placed a hand on the other's thigh, shared minute details that only they – each half of an indomitable couple – could notice, well, it made me realise how much I wanted to be a half too.

'She was taking pictures on a film set. A *porn* film set.' Lewis cleared his throat but then grinned at Liz. 'It was all very up-close and personal.'

'Were you there?' I asked.

'Good heavens, no. I happened to see Liz's pictures in an advertisement for the movie in the back of a men's magazine.'

'And?' I didn't want to prompt too hard but Lewis's story seemed to fizzle out.

'I felt compelled to get in touch with the photographer to get the full, well, picture. I found out her name through the advertising agency.' Lewis dropped a log onto the fire but I still wasn't sure his story was complete.

'Why?'

Lewis gave a sigh and a laugh, and glanced at Liz. She nodded. 'Because it was my fiancée in the pictures. Naked. She was the star of a kinky movie that I knew nothing about.' He let out a brief snort.

'Darling, it was the three men eating her out that really set you off.' Liz giggled. 'Don't worry, Ailey. It was years ago and they were totally incompatible. My pictures saved Lewis from a life of jealousy and turmoil.'

'And you two would never have met otherwise.' They were nice people and deserved a happy ending. I drained my coffee cup and glanced at my watch. 'It's late. I've got that awful walk back and –'

'Nonsense. You can't possibly attempt to go home tonight. Have you heard the rain outside?' Lewis settled back in the sofa and grinned in a way that reminded me of the intent yet delirious expression he wore while I was spying on the pair the previous night. 'The guest room's all made up. We insist you stay the night, don't we Liz?'

'Absolutely.' Liz slid off the sofa and onto the floor beside me. To my surprise, she placed a hand on my thigh and very gently slid it towards the zip on my jeans. Then she leaned forward and, her lips brushing in my hair, whispered, 'Besides, you'll be able to see better from here.' Then that giggle again, somehow seeming silly although charming coming from a woman in her early thirties. It was just a tiny dose of flirting, barely detectable, and, of course, if I had mentioned watching them through binoculars it would simply have made my embarrassment tangible. I held her gaze for a moment before making up my mind. However bad the weather, I really wanted to get back to my cottage. The rain pelted the windows, lashing in from the west, and I could hear the wind roaring down the chimney and rattling the front door behind the heavy curtain.

'Really, I'll make it back just fine. It's only a bit of rain.' I didn't sound particularly convincing but when I stood, stretched and began searching for my coat, Lewis and Liz took my intentions seriously. I noticed a flash of communication between them, a moment of disappointment.

'Then I shall walk you home,' Lewis said, reaching

for his own waterproof coat. 'I can't possibly allow a young woman out alone at night.'

I glanced at Liz to gauge her reaction and, though my judgement was hazy from the wine, I did notice her eyebrows raise and her lips swell to a thoughtful pout. Perhaps even her cheeks flushed although that could have been the sudden blast of cold air as Lewis and I stepped out into the noisy weather.

'Thanks again,' I shouted above the wind. I kissed her on each cheek, secured my waterproof against the rain and followed the cone of light from Lewis's torch as he marched off down the road.

He set a quick pace and while we tried to talk, it was virtually impossible to hear anything other than the rain pelting my hood. The walk along the road was the easy part but when we reached the rocky track to the beach, Lewis made a point of taking my hand and channelling the torchlight along the ground.

'The rocks are slippery,' he called out. 'Watch your footing.'

I cursed myself for not accepting their invitation to stay. I imagined another couple of hours talking by the fire, more wine and then retiring to a cosy bed and perhaps an audible sample of lovemaking from Lewis and Liz.

Finally, we made it to the beach cottage, which was barely visible in the torchlight and sheeting rain. I hurled my weight at the front door, which gave immediately with a creak. Inside, I was relieved to feel a glimmer of warmth. The huge log that I had put on the fire earlier was still glowing.

'Thanks so much,' I said, feeling guilty that the poor man had to make the journey back again. 'Would you like something to warm you up before you go? I have some supplies.' I grinned and, for silly some reason, I winked.

'What've you got?' Lewis took off his waterproof, ruffled his fingers through his wet hair and made himself comfortable in one of the armchairs. I lit three candles and stoked the fire with another log.

'I could boil some water for tea or I've got some Glen Broath from the local shop or Spanish brandy perhaps?'

'The whisky sounds fine.'

'Here, sorry about the mug,' I laughed. 'It's clean though.' Earlier, during my hasty spring clean, I'd found a few items of dusty crockery and swilled them in the sea. It would have to do for now.

'Damn, no reception. I hope Liz doesn't worry.' Lewis snapped his phone shut and went to the window to peer up at his house. He cupped his hands around his eyes and pressed his face to the glass. 'I think she's still up because the lights are on. Can I use these?'

'Sure,' I said, bowing my head. I took a large sip of Glen Broath as Lewis peered up at his house through the binoculars. He stood motionless, the lenses fixed to his face, for several minutes before lowering the glasses and exhaling, half sigh, half laugh.

'She's still up, all right.' Lewis held out the binoculars to me but didn't move away from the window. 'Take a look at this.'

He stood behind me as I found the cottage lights and adjusted the focus. I caught my breath as the window came into view. The small square of light was filled with Liz's naked body and she was performing a slow, provocative dance. Her hands swept over her skin, lingering on her breasts before slipping down between her legs. I could see that her eyes were closed and her head swayed in time to whatever music accompanied her moves.

'You should go back to her,' I said, although my voice barely worked. Spying on Liz's erotic act with her husband didn't seem right.

'Nonsense.' Lewis's voice faltered too and it was then that I felt something firm press into the small of my back. 'She'd love it if she thought we were watching her. Take another look and tell me what she's up to now.' He slipped his hands around my waist and trailed his fingers around the top of my jeans. 'Why don't you flash the torch at her to let her know you're watching, like you did last night?'

I swallowed and realised that I couldn't pretend any more. Liz and Lewis knew I'd been spying on them. 'Are you cross? I didn't mean to –'

'Cross? Liz loves being watched. You made our evening sizzle!'

'I did?' I held up the binoculars again and saw Liz teasing her body. 'She's still there.'

'Doing what?'

'She's touching herself.'

'Like this?' Lewis pressed a hand between my legs and I let out a little moan – a cross between surprise and pleasure. Then he took the torch from his pocket and signalled a series of flashes to his wife.

'Are you sure she won't mind?' I somehow gasped and sighed at the same time, quite unable to comprehend what was happening. It was as if the contents of my lost diary had somehow become reality.

'She especially wouldn't mind if she thought she was turning us both on. I could tell her how she had driven us wild and we simply couldn't help ourselves.'

I heard the amplitude of the waves increase as the wind and rain whipped up into a sizeable storm, similar to the thoughts and feelings racing through my body. What was Lewis implying? I shuddered as his lips pushed through the mass of my hair, searching for the skin on my neck. He was a big man and the size of his face, the intensity of his breath on my skin, the strength of his hand as it pushed deeper between my legs weakened any resolve I had to protest that it just wasn't right. I turned slightly and he took the opportunity to smother my mouth with a deep kiss that rocketed to the pit of my belly.

'Take another look at her and describe what you see.' His words slipped down my throat and I could barely hold the binoculars steady. Then, 'Do you think she's beautiful?'

'Oh yes,' I said. 'You're a lucky man.' I realised the implication and so did Lewis.

'You like women?'

To share my thoughts, to give them form and voice, was comparable to wafting the pages of my diary at Lewis. For many years I had fantasised about touching another woman's body and even a coy glimpse at an aroused woman would have sent me spiralling with delight. I was convinced that witnessing Liz pleasuring Lewis the previous night had been the cause of my reckless tryst with Dominic earlier. Quite simply, every cell in my body had been awakened by their performance, heightened by the possibility that the display was entirely for the stranger signalling from the beach cottage. Even now, my yearning wasn't entirely sated.

'I think so.' It was hard to be honest. I could barely be truthful with myself. Only my diary. 'I've never, you know...'

'Never made love to a woman.'

I shook my head.

'Would you like to try?'

'Perhaps.' I felt my cheeks flush and hoped Lewis would think it was the glow from the fire colouring my skin. My shyness did something to him though because he emitted an unintelligible reply that seemed to get stuck in his throat. 'I wouldn't know what to do,' I added.

'It would be easy. Just do to her what you like having done to yourself.'

There was a sudden lightness around my waist and I realised that Lewis had unfastened my jeans. He turned me to face the window again and told me to tell him what I liked most about Liz. Her fingers were teasing her breasts, lingering on the defined circles of dark brown nipple as the rest of her body swayed to the music I assumed she was playing.

'Her breasts are so...' I faltered, wondering how to best describe Liz's full body. 'I just want to reach out and hold them, to feel the weight of them.' Dizziness from my admission made me wobble but Lewis steadied me by pressing his body against my back. The stiffness was still there, still straining. I had never been so candid and the rush was even better than the whisky.

'She would love it if you felt them.' And to mirror my desire, Lewis wove a hand beneath the layers of my clothing and located the small rise of my braless flesh. The coldness of his fingers transformed my nipples into trim points while his other hand slipped deftly within my jeans, eager to find a path to the heat that had already produced wetness in my panties.

'Being a glamour photographer, surely Liz has had plenty of offers?' I was strangely disappointed at the thought.

'Sure, plenty of offers from some of the most beautiful women in the country.' Lewis plucked at my nipples, making me whimper and my knees bend. 'But she's never accepted any. It's her ultimate fantasy and she's saving herself for the right person. Someone that I approve of.'

Was I being examined as a potential candidate? Was I being vetted as a suitable plaything for Liz? What if I didn't pass examination? I tensed briefly as Lewis's finger finally found the groove that would lead him to the lips of my eager sex. Another thing: how had this happened to me twice in one day?

'Take another look at Liz,' Lewis rasped in my ear. His forefinger slipped easily between my lips and began to draw a slow, deliberate line from the tingling nub of my clitoris down to the fullness of my sex. 'Is she doing this to herself?'

'Yes,' I answered as I viewed Liz trailing her finger in the same way Lewis was teasing me. Liz was leaning forward slightly with one arm supporting her on the window frame. Her head was bowed and her knees bent a little so she could watch her lips spread as her fingers worked between the folds. Her sex was covered with a light spray of blonde hair, such a contrast to the cherry-red tips of her fingernails. 'She's doing just what you're doing to me.'

'And would you like to do this to Liz? Would you like to feel the softness and sweetness of her pussy?' Lewis's words contained a rhythm, as if he was already pounding me in his mind.

'Oh, yes,' I whispered. 'I would give anything to touch her there.'

'So if I promised that you could have Liz, that you could do to her whatever pleased you, would you let me fuck you right now, here, with Liz above us on the cliff top?' The beat and tempo of his voice increased and it seemed that if I didn't agree, he would have some kind of verbal orgasm just to satisfy the image he had created in his head of Liz and me writhing in tangle of legs and breasts while he watched.

'Yes, I want that. You can have me, if I can make love to your beautiful wife.' Barely before the agreement was complete and certainly before I was able to comprehend that I had been promised the body of a woman all for myself, I felt Lewis grappling with my clothing. In an instant, he had removed my boots and jeans and for the second time in a matter of hours I was standing naked before a virtual stranger. How I was beginning to love the quest for my inheritance!

'Oh, Liz will adore you. You have just the figure she craves.' Lewis knelt in front of me and swept his large hands from my shoulders, across the small buds of my nipples, down my flat belly and into the space between my legs. 'I want you to watch her while I taste you.'

I reached for the binoculars again but nearly dropped them as Lewis's tongue pushed warmly into my furrow. He nuzzled and licked me with the skill that only an older man would possess, knowing exactly when to slow and tease, and to my absolute delight, when I spied on Liz again, I saw that she was pleasuring herself with an unfeasibly large vibrator. I told Lewis.

'You can do that to each other,' he promised. 'But first, I have you to deal with.'

Before I knew what was happening, Lewis had me on my back in the chair with my legs spread open over the cushioned arms. He shed his jeans and entered me so swiftly that I barely had a chance to notice what his erect cock looked like. In several accomplished strokes, Lewis had inserted himself deep within me, leaving me to guess at his length and colour and taste. As he dragged himself up and down my body, devouring the feeling of my sex gripping his shaft, I imagined Liz doing the same with the vibrator and longed for the time, however nervous I would be, that I could help her.

When Lewis came, he unwittingly catapulted me into an orgasm that made me forget what an extremely bad girl I was for having two lovers in the same day. He caused all the worries about my lost journal and Ethan Kinrade and my stolen inheritance to roll up into a neat ball and be tossed onto the fire along with the absolute wickedness of having sex with someone else's husband, whether they minded or not. I dug my fingers into his tense shoulder muscles and felt the fibres of his body slowly unravel.

'Oh,' I gasped, rather pointlessly. Perhaps a token breath of guilt although laced with an undeniable amount of relief and pleasure. 'That was nice.'

'Mmm. Very.' Lewis withdrew from me and hoisted me onto his lap while he sat in the chair. 'Liz will be delighted with my choice. I saw the way she was eyeing you up all evening. I think she's already decided herself that you're the one.' He gave my small breast a gentle lick and cradled his arms around my body when he noticed my shiver. 'Quite a productive evening for you then, Miss. You've got yourself a lawyer *and* a willing partner to satisfy your naughty little fantasies.'

'You'll really help me fight to get my home back?'

Briefly, I felt angry with myself that on the first day of my mission I had been swayed so far off course. I was a lightweight dinghy cut loose in the raging sea. However freed I felt, perhaps because I had exchanged the usual routine of daily life for dangerous and unknown waters, it was imperative that I remain on course to launch a wholehearted assault on Kinrade.

Lewis nodded and I kissed him tenderly on the neck. He left to walk back to his wife and within minutes I slipped into a deep sleep.

4

I recognised him immediately, from behind, stooped over counting eggs into a basket, his back and head swathed by a dark green waterproof jacket. It could have been anyone but it wasn't. I knew it was *him*. It was the voice, the rich tones that were as earthy as mountain water filtering through peat, that caused tiny goose-bumps all over my body. I caught a whiff of whisky mash, barley, yeast and smoke, reminding me of the smell he always wore after visiting his father at work deep inside the Glen Broath Distillery. Connor stood up straight and carefully placed his chosen eggs on the counter and it was then that I could see he was now a man, not the teenager I still cradled in my head.

I stood only three feet behind him as he placed his groceries in a bag. Idle conversation with the shopkeeper provided a constant and evocative flow of his voice, filling me with memories of days spent tumbling together in the springy, moss-covered fields and weekends clambering over slippery rocks on the beach. We were happy children, would perhaps have become lovers, maybe married, if it hadn't all ended. I swallowed and blinked back awash with tears. Connor turned to leave and walked straight into me.

'So sorry,' he said and began to sidestep around me before stopping and studying my face.

'That's OK.' I bowed my head, a part of me desperate for him to recognise me but the sensible side of me screaming that enough people already knew of my presence on the island and one more could undermine my mission.

'Ailey?' he said. 'Ailey Callister, is that you?' Connor leaned back as if to get a better view of the unlikely person he saw standing before him. 'It's been years!' His final declaration told me that he had deduced that it was definitely me.

'Yes, hi,' I said meekly. The shopkeeper was tuning into events, ready to pass on juicy titbits to the next customer – the parochial equivalent of a buy-one-get-one-free. 'Fourteen years, to be precise.'

'Where have you *been*?'

I slowly looked up at Connor. His face had widened; it was no longer that of an eager, skinny youth. His bones had thickened into those of a man used to heavy work and the skin on his face had roughened from a smooth palette of tentative, boyish freckles into a ruddy, experienced expression.

'Away,' I replied.

'Well, where away?' Connor reached out a large, lightly-haired hand and touched my shoulder. All those giddy feelings that once kicked up in the pit of my belly as a young girl came swirling through my body again although this time with the honesty and power of a woman. 'Look, are you free? How about coming back to Glen Broath for a bit of a warm up? You can fill me in on all the missing time.'

It was better than standing in the shop broadcasting my private life to the village via the shopkeeper. I nodded and flung the few groceries that I needed onto the counter. Besides, Connor would most likely have come by car and I wasn't keen on the walk back along the coast road in the twilight and drizzle. I paid and joined Connor outside the shop. He was holding open the door to a beat-up Land Rover and took my bag of shopping as I climbed in.

'It's all tins,' he said with a laugh as he dumped the bag at my feet. 'Your mother was always fanatical about healthy eating.' He grinned and yanked the stubborn gear lever into first. He glanced at me quickly before looking back and pulling out. 'So what's your story, Ailey Callister? Why'd you disappear on me?'

I wanted to reach out to the strong hand that gripped the wheel. I wanted to touch his neck, where his black scarf had come loose. I wanted to take time back fourteen years and make deep holes in the sand and catch mackerel on Peel Harbour wall.

'My parents got divorced. My Mum moved away and took me with her. That's it really.' He'd either know the shameful truth about my mother or not. I was taking a risk.

'You could have written to me. Let me know you were OK at least.'

'We ended up living in Spain. I went to university in Granada.'

'I wouldn't have thought to look there.' He glanced at me again and smiled, but only as long as the winding coastal road would allow. 'I missed you.'

We drove in silence for several minutes, the usually interminable walk flashing by in the bumpy Land Rover. It was my third visit to the local grocery shop since my arrival on the island. I'd been lying low after my evening with Lewis and Liz, mostly because I wanted to allow my presence to die down but also because I was nervous of repercussions from the evening's rather unusual end with Lewis at the beach cottage. I only had Lewis's word that Liz would approve of our antics. With that in mind and the striking teen-to-man transformation of Connor sitting beside me, my mind was in a spin once again. I was beginning to think there was something in the mountain water.

'And I missed you,' I replied but too late so that the mutual impact was lost. Connor sighed and swung the vehicle through Creg-ny-Varn's imposing gates and headed up the driveway, past the magnificent façade of the main house and into the separate courtyard of the Glen Broath Distillery. I didn't need to ask if he had taken over the running of the business from his father. He had grown up knowing how to malt barley, mash the grist, manage the fermentation vessels and procure the finest barrels for ageing. It was logical that he would take over as manager of Glen Broath. No, it was imperative. Connor would never have been able to do anything else and he'd known that since we were kids.

'Nothing much has changed.' I scanned around the courtyard at the L-shaped grey slate buildings. Somehow they managed to blend into the heavy, low sky. Even on a sunny day, I remembered, the single tall chimney would reach up to tie land and air together. Glen Broath was as integral to the Isle of Man as Snaefell or the Laxey Wheel.

'Oh, yes, it has. I've dragged the business into the modern world.' Connor grinned and led me across the courtyard, a patchwork of cobbles and flagstones glistening from the fine mist that was part cloud and part rain. 'In here.' He guided me into what used to be my father's tasting room but now looked more like an office and wasted no time in reaching for one of the amber bottles that ran the circumference of the room on a high shelf. He studied it briefly and then poured two measures. 'Enjoy,' he said. 'Fifteen-year-old single malt aged in barrels from Armagnac. Most of this goes to the US market.'

'You export to the States?' I sipped and raised my eyebrows. Glen Broath certainly had been dragged into the modern business world. My father and Connor's father would never have considered shipping their whisky overseas. If they want it, let them come and get it, they would have said. Marketing was not their forte.

'Exports make up about eighty per cent of our business.' Despite his hands-on appearance, Connor was obviously a shrewd businessman. 'Sit,' he said and pulled out a beat-up wooden stool from under his desk. He sat on the other side so that it suddenly felt as if I had come for a job interview.

'So where are you living now?' I asked.

'In the estate cottage, where my dad used to live.' Connor viewed me from over the rim of his glass as he thoughtfully drew in the whisky between his lips. I wasn't sure if he was enjoying the flavour or sizing me up as I sat nervously rotating the glass between my fingers. 'Dad's in Peel now. In a home.' There was a tinge of remorse, as if he had given up on the old man, but also gratitude that at least his father was still alive. 'I'm so sorry about Patrick. It was a shock to us all.' Connor bowed his head briefly.

'I only found out recently.' I knocked back half of my whisky. How much further should I go? 'By accident.'

'No one told you that your father had died?' Connor frowned, causing several gentle furrows to appear at the top of his nose. A few freckles still remained on his forehead, allowing me a glimpse of the boy that used to chase me around the copper mash tuns.

'I read the obituary.' Again, I was being drawn into revealing too much. But then I had put myself in a situation where questions would be asked. Short of wearing a disguise and remaining a recluse at the beach cottage, I had to be prepared to reveal my story with whatever level of honesty I felt appropriate.

'Well, I do hope that Mr Kinrade has made you welcome. It must be strange being a guest in what was once your home.' That same intent stare again, to gauge my reaction as he refilled our glasses. It was distraction enough for me.

'Whoa, or I'll be in no fit state.' I made a futile attempt to cover my glass but allowed the whisky to cascade from the bottle. I was clearly going to need all my courage. 'This really is a fine malt. It's strange to think that it began life just before I left the island.' Somehow, talking about the past seemed safer.

'I'm relieved that you've returned to taste it.' Connor removed his jacket even though the temperature in the small room wasn't much above that of outside. A black, long-sleeved T-shirt with a frayed hem was revealed and he pushed up the sleeves to show forearms that appeared very different to the ones I remembered. He noticed me looking. 'You've changed too,' he remarked. 'You're thinner and your face, it's...' He squinted and gave me a look that I would expect if he was about to kiss me. 'Well, you're a woman now. A beautiful one. I feel like I've lost a part of you.'

'Lost?' I said. I didn't understand. I was here, wasn't I, in his office, feeling as if he had touched my breast for the first time, as if we were awkward adolescents?

'Lost as in the last fourteen years. It's not just the physical you that I've missed, Ailey. It's all your thoughts, dreams, your hopes, *our* hopes. Do you remember how badly we wanted to be king and queen of the island?'

I laughed. 'We would have done anything. My mother never did find out what happened to the velvet curtains that I made our royal gowns from.'

'They're probably still down in the beach cottage where we used to reign.'

'I've not seen them there.' Then I stopped, realising what I'd said.

'You've been to the beach cottage?' Connor leaned forward on his hands.

'I'm *living* down there,' I whispered. There. It had been said. Now the questions would follow and I would attempt to explain.

The fire had gone out and an extra-high tide had deposited weed and froth virtually on my doorstep. The brisk westerly stung my cheeks and my boots were wet from slipping into a rock pool on the scramble across the beach. Connor had grabbed my wrist, as he would have done when we were younger, but he was too late to save me from plunging ankle-deep in seawater.

'Yuk,' I said, pulling a face. I took off my boots, emptied the water from them and wrapped my feet in a towel. 'I'll get the fire going then we can have tea. Oh, and I do the best seared mussels around.' I grinned up at Connor who was already stacking the fireplace with kindling. 'Thanks,' I said to his back, wishing we had lived here together since we were kids.

'You'll be warm in no time.' Connor sat next to me. 'Just like old times, eh?' There was a look, a connection of understanding that if one of us moved, tilted forwards by just an inch, there would be a kiss; a slow, time-defying kiss that would erase the void of the last fourteen years and transport us back to where we left off.

I stood. 'Wait here. I'm going to fetch something.' I couldn't afford to complicate my mission further. Getting involved with Connor, however much I was drawn to him, would not be wise. I skipped from the room, my feet chilling once again on the bare stone floor, and went into the room at the rear of the cottage. I rummaged through the wooden chest that contained my father's old fishing sweaters and summer table linen from when my mother brought picnics down to the beach and insisted that we eat at a table, not on the sand. Finally, buried beneath memories and a strong smell of damp and the ocean, I found them. Folded and faded at the edges, I took our robes to show Connor.

'Hard to believe they were ours,' he said, reaching out and touching one as if we might be transported back in time. I could almost hear our childish songs as we danced about in fancy dress. 'Look how short they are.' Connor held one of the robes up against his body. 'I've grown about two feet!' It was true. Connor was a tall man and he towered above me as he handed back the robe, pressing it against my body. 'Good times,' he said. 'Now, sit and tell me about yourself. I want to know everything.'

The evening curled itself around the cottage as if a blanket was being tucked under the eaves. We sat and talked, occasionally rising to stoke the fire, to make some tea to accompany the whisky Connor had brought, or to unpack the groceries when the conversation became tricky. One part of me wanted him to know everything about my life, while the other part was determined to keep quiet, at least until I had found out more about Ethan Kinrade. While I didn't want to use him, I knew that Connor would most likely be able to answer my questions about the wretched man.

'Do you see him much around the estate?' I cupped my mug of hot tea between my hands.

'Kinrade? Hardly ever.' Connor leaned forward and sighed. 'He's only visited the distillery about three times since he took over the estate and one of those was to stock up on whisky. I do think that a man with his responsibilities should get more involved with the day-to-day running.'

I thought carefully about what he had said. Already a picture of Kinrade was forming in my mind. Not a physical image but an impression of his character. Ethan Kinrade was supercilious, aloof, ungrateful, scheming, smug and, worst of all, undeserving. I felt the muscles in my neck contract and tighten around my bones, causing lines of pain to stretch between my shoulders. I must have unconsciously expressed my discomfort because Connor's arm slipped casually along the back of the chair and his fingers began to stroke my tense muscles. He had never quite found the confidence to do this as a teenager.

'What does he look like?' I should have slipped out of range but really, Connor's touch was doing no harm.

'Tallish, dark hair I think.' Connor blew out and pulled a face. 'It's hard to remember because I've seen so little of him.'

'I've heard he's away at the moment. Does he leave the estate often?' Knowing Kinrade's movements would be useful.

'Then you've heard wrong. I saw him from a distance earlier today, walking across the courtyard with the dogs.' Connor was becoming impatient. I don't think he wanted to talk about his elusive employer.

I pondered what he had said. Could it be that Kinrade had already returned from his trip? That would be a major blow. I was hoping to begin my new position as maid without him being around, allowing me to snoop into his personal affairs and papers without interruption. I'd only need a day at the most. And with the prospect of being alone in the house with only Dominic to occasionally check up on me, I was already wondering how I could procure a naughty maid's outfit instead of having to wear jeans and boots for my first day at work.

'Ailey?' I felt Connor's hand brush my cheek. 'You're miles away.'

I blushed and shook my head, perhaps trying to dislodge the multiplying thoughts of Dominic. Connor would be shocked if he knew that I had slept with Creg-ny-Varn's gardener. I've always thought that Connor wanted me for himself and even now, I suspected, he somehow believed that I would be his and his alone.

'I was thinking.' I perked up and smiled, trying to twist ever so gently away from his arm. He raised his eyebrows. 'About my new job.'

'Really?' The hope in his voice confirmed my suspicion. Connor was desperate not to lose me again. 'Where?'

'You'll never believe it.' I swallowed. I was taking a risk but he would find out soon enough anyway and I was beginning to believe that Connor and I were on the same side. 'At Creg-ny-Varn. I'm going to be a maid.' I smiled as I introduced my new career and waited for a reaction. He stared blankly at me, unblinking, his face paling slightly as he took more tea.

'You're going to work for Ethan Kinrade? As a servant? In your own home?'

'Yes.' I glared at him, willing him not to ask more.

'Why?' Incredulity spread across his face.

'Because I need to...' I stopped myself. Trusting anyone, even Connor, would be a mistake. 'Because I need the money. It'll be strange but I'm big enough to cope with my emotions.' My head dropped of its own accord, perhaps to hide the skim of tears that began to pool.

'Are you big enough? Or are you on some kind of masochistic mission, determined to rub your own nose in what could, sorry, *should* have been yours?' Connor stood and walked to the window, hands in pockets, elbows jutting from his slim hips. He stared out to sea and I wondered if he noticed the glimmer of light on the cliff top that was Lewis and Liz's cottage.

'It's just a job, for heaven's sake. I'll do it for a few weeks and then use the money to go back to Spain.'

He turned abruptly, his full features accentuated by the flames. I reached out and prodded the blaze, sending a rain of orange sparks up the chimney. I knew what he was thinking.

'You'd never consider settling on the island again.' It wasn't a question although it should have been. Connor should have taken me in his arms, pressed his body against mine, nursed my confused head against his shoulder and allowed his lips to seek a kiss. Instead, he stood with his back to the fire, shaking his head in disbelief that someone he had once thought of so highly could behave so recklessly.

'I've lost everything I ever wanted anyway. My father's gone, my home has been taken over by an impostor and ... and...' I wanted to mention the feelings that were stirring within me since seeing him again but they would have given a tense, unnecessary edge to the evening, an evening that I wanted to be filled with memories of us both as happy, irresponsible kids.

'Where's your fight gone? Do you honestly believe that Kinrade has any right to your family home? Have you heard about his gold-digging mother yet?' Connor splashed large measures of whisky into our tea and continued with his rant. 'The man obviously has no morals or shame. He kicked his mother out barely before the funeral was over.'

Then, as the extra whisky rushed through our veins, he kicked down a gear. He squatted beside the flames in the only truly warm spot in the cottage and blew out, laughing and shaking his head at the same time. I was tired of thinking about Creg-ny-Varn and almost wondered if it was worth the bother. Did I really have any right to undo my father's wishes?

'Will you really go back to Spain?' He was virtually sitting at my feet, his expression earnest, his intentions all right.

I nodded. 'It's my home now.'

'Tell me about your life there. Why Spain?' Connor pulled himself up to sit next to me, this time not risking any contact.

I sighed. 'Why indeed. It wasn't like I had any choice in the matter. My mother and father, well, they split up.' I wasn't going to regale him with the story of how my mother had been kicked off the island in an explosion of shame and debauchery and that by association I wasn't welcome either. No doubt he would have heard his own version of events anyway. 'And my mother eventually met the love of her life.' I smiled, trying to sweeten the story. 'He's a much younger man, a Spanish man who took us back to his home village in the mountains of Southern Spain.'

'What an adventure.' Connor was a good listener.

'I hated it at first. I didn't understand a word that anyone was saying. I just wanted to come back to my dad and you and Creg-ny-Varn.' I shrugged, to indicate that things were OK now, that life was good and I was happy. Despite the strong link that I now felt with Connor, the link that had probably been there all along and been stretched to infinity by distance and time, I also had a link to my Spanish home. I was suddenly overcome by a feeling of ingratitude and betrayal. My mother had struggled to do everything right for me and, under impossible circumstances, had given me a good life.

'Is there a man back home?'

The question made me jump, as if I had jolted from a dream, and Connor misread the half-smile that made up for my lack of a simple answer. His eyes lost their shine and he stared at his feet.

I didn't know what to say so filled my mouth with the remains of my tea. Yes, there was a man and yes, he was waiting for me back in my village and yes, I missed him but no, he wasn't *the one*. Marco was my anchor and my friend and my lover and the person I shouted at when things went wrong. He was there when I needed to be with someone but equally adept at keeping out of my way when I craved solitude.

'No one as special,' I said.

That one word, the insertion of a single syllable, caused Connor to look up and believe that we had a future together. I don't know how it slipped in; I don't even know what I meant by it. I only know that it was true. There hadn't ever been anyone *as* special as Connor. And there probably wouldn't ever be.

'You look cold,' he said and dragged the chair, with me on it, closer to the fire. He invited himself into the dusty nest of cushions, squashing up close to me and hauling my legs over his. He unfurled the sleeping bag and draped it over us and I immediately began to feel my body warmth mingling with his. It felt as natural as the waves outside as the tide crept up the shingle. It felt as if we could have been nestled together for the last fourteen years.

'Now tell me all about him. I want to know how he got to you, like I would have done if you hadn't disappeared.' Connor made no attempt to touch me. What with the feeling of his thighs beneath my legs, the strength in his shoulder as our bodies were pressed together and the sweet whiff of whisky on his breath, it was almost as if his lips were exploring every part of me. I was torn between two worlds: the place that I had called home for the last fourteen years and the magical island that was recorded deep within my heart, however faded the etching had become. To translate my feelings I would need to show him the very core of my mind. Connor deserved this much.

'I've kept a journal for as long as I can remember,' I began. 'From the day my mother and I left the island, as my home floated into a misty line on the horizon, I wrote down my thoughts and feelings. Much of it's childish ranting.' I snorted, briefly recalling detailed yet improbable Christmas lists and gripes about my mother's new lover. I drew pictures and glued in photographs and cuttings in the early editions. Even at that age, my diary was a part of my existence. I twisted sideways to face Connor. 'It's funny. When I was about fifteen, I became fiercely protective of my journals and locked them away.'

'Ahh,' Connor said slowly. 'You began writing about boys.' He grinned.

'Would it shock you if I confessed that now my entries are mostly about sex?'

'Not at all. It's natural.' I noticed the quick swallow, the brief clench of his jaw.

'It's not so much about, well...' It was my turn to swallow. 'Not about the act so much as the thought of the act and who with and why and what if –'

'Your deepest, darkest fantasies, you mean.'

'Yes.' I fiddled with the sleeping bag's zipper.

'You know, by writing down your desires you're taking the first step to making them happen.' Connor reached for the Glen Broath and held the bottle fondly between his palms.

'I am?'

'Every thought you have can become reality if you give it a place in the world.'

I mulled this over as Connor tipped a little more whisky into my mug. I reflected on my encounter with Dominic and the unnatural role I had taken by tying him to the bed. Lewis and Liz's desire to include me in their sexual games haunted my mind as I began to consider that Connor might be right. Had my desire for sexual risk, having been given a place in the world in my diary, reached critical mass and finally become a reality? Was my life to unfold similarly from now on?

I sighed. 'But I've lost it.' And I wondered if this was why. 'My diary,' I added to allay Connor's look of puzzlement. 'Or it was stolen. I think it might have been taken by someone I met on the ferry.'

A grin to match any I had seen when we ran

through the gorse with a couple of stolen cigarettes or netted a lobster the size of two house bricks peeled across Connor's face. He wiped a hand over his chin as if to extinguish his amusement. I noticed the stubble, a day or two's growth of copper blonde hair that had transformed my best friend into a man.

'I'm glad you think it's funny. If you knew just how deep this book went, how I had stripped myself bare, then you might even consider helping me get it back.' My clipped tone deleted his remaining smile.

'And what would my reward be if I located your journal?'

'That's simple,' I said rather too recklessly. 'I'll love you forever.'

The pause between us, the empty space devoid of words, breath or any thought that wasn't about loving each other, could have spanned a thousand years. It was Connor who regained consciousness first.

'Well, let's get searching then.' He pretended to stand up but I placed a hand on his arm. 'Just kidding, although seriously, I know someone who works for the Steam Packet. I can find out if your diary's been handed in and make sure it's safe.'

'Thanks. It's very important to me.' I placed my head on his shoulder and again wondered if he was right. Had the unusual events of the last couple of days been brought about by the loss of my diary? Were my innermost thoughts out there, manifesting, shaping my life?

During the next few hours Connor barely said a word. He moved only to fetch another log or open a can of soup that we heated on the fire. He arranged the faded cushions behind my head and rubbed my cold feet and hands, while all the time listening greedily to every word I said. I had returned to the island as a pencil drawing and he was attempting to colour me in by fathoming every minute of my fourteen-year absence.

'When I returned from my first year at Granada University, Marco was still living in our little village. I thought that he would have wanted to travel or study too but he seemed content working on his father's farm. It never occurred to me that he would find someone else while I was away.'

As I recounted the story, I stared into the flames that were as hot as the summer when I had arrived home on the bus from university. My body had buzzed with anticipation as if it was filled with the cicadas that speckled the mountainsides. Seeing Marco after nine months apart was going to be like iced water in a drought. Of course, we had spoken on the telephone and written, especially early in the academic year when our parting was still raw. I'd decided to stay in Granada for Christmas to save money travelling but also to sample the elaborate celebrations that I'd heard of. My new friends had told me of the spectacular *Hogueras* on the shortest day of the year and I was keen to witness the madness of young men jumping through bonfires in order to ward off illness. After so many years of country living, I was enjoying the thrill of such a beautiful, vibrant city.

It appeared that Marco had made new friends as well. Once I had dumped my belongings in my room and greeted my mother and reminded myself why I loved my home so much by taking stock of the stunning mountain views from the cool veranda, I went in search of Marco. My plan to surprise him by arriving home a day early certainly achieved a level of shock I had never anticipated. When I couldn't locate him in the olive groves or in the tapas bar, I walked to the casita that he rented on the outskirts of the village. As expected, the flaking wooden shutters were closed against the white-hot sun although the wrought-iron grille that secured the front door was open. Smiling to myself and with my heart pattering as if a butterfly chrysalis had burst open in my chest, I stepped into the cool, dark hall and padded silently through the tiny house looking for Marco.

I smelled it first. The undeniable tang, although I tried to convince myself it was something cooking or a scent from a rare flower that had blown in on the breeze. The pungent flavour of sex-marinated bodies hung in the air like a dirty morning mist. I should have stopped. I should have forced my legs to turn and carry me back home so that I would never know the source of the smell but it drew me on like a starving person seeking food.

The door to the bedroom wasn't quite closed and as I walked silently down the dark, windowless passage I began to hear voices, or rather noises, that fuelled my curiosity. I didn't dare open the door any further in case the hinges creaked but the six-inch gap was enough to take in the tangle of bodies that thrashed on the bed. With a white cotton sheet twisted and wrung out around them, Marco and a beautiful Spanish girl – to this day nameless – were violating each other's bodies with an intensity I had never seen before.

I found it impossible to move. My feet had welded themselves to the terracotta floor and my eyes were drawn inextricably to the scene as if I, too, was one of the lovers. Marco withdrew his face from between the girl's legs as she rocked on all fours, perhaps signalling that she wanted more. He wiped his mouth before peeling apart the lips of her sex with his thumbs and taking a close look at his work. Even from where I was standing I could see that he had engorged the hairless slivers of mahogany flesh with his kissing and transformed them into overripe plums. Marco lowered his head again and thoughtfully tilted it to the side before opening his mouth wide and taking a large bite of the fruit.

I knew what he was doing. I could feel it between my own legs as I stood gawping at the scene. Many times Marco had hoisted me into that position and devoured me from behind, always insisting that I shave myself before we began so that he could tease my lips with tiny, fragmented yet torturous licks. As I watched him doing it to someone else, I touched myself, more for consolation than anything although my fingers noticed that, remotely, I was beginning to respond.

My breathing had become, I thought, audible as my disbelief translated into short, painful gasps. I steadied myself by leaning on the cool wall but remained quite unable to walk away from the scene. Marco ordered the girl to lie on her back and she moaned something unintelligible back but obeyed his orders. It was then that I saw the full beauty of her body contrasting with the hard lines of Marco's work-honed muscle. She was soft and full and had dark breasts that spread out across her chest as she lay back. Marco kneaded them back into place and instructed her to keep them in position while he jammed his erection into their softness. Within moments I could see the tell-tale signs on his familiar body that told me he was going to come. Marco was a selfish lover with a greedy appetite for pleasuring himself. The veins on his neck stood out of his deep tan skin like blue rivers and the way his mouth thinned and tightened told me he would orgasm at any time.

As I placed a hand on the cotton of my panties, just to prove that I was still capable of feeling, Marco ejaculated on the girl's breasts and wasted no time in sliding off the bed and stepping out onto the veranda for a cigarette. The smell of smoke wafted through to where I was standing and it was all I could do not to cry out in surprise as the girl stared directly at me, opened her legs wide and brought herself to orgasm.

'Did you and Marco split up?' Connor's arm ventured further around my shoulder. He thought I needed comfort.

'For a while, yes. But being at university for the next few years made any kind of relationship difficult.' I felt ashamed that I had never confronted Marco about his infidelity. I had excised my pain with many diary entries and much support from several of my girlfriends on campus. 'To this day, Marco doesn't know that I watched him having sex with another woman.'

'So you indulged yourself with lots of other boyfriends and forgot all about the scoundrel.' Connor let out a laugh that tried to say he didn't care but I knew from the transparency of it that he did.

'No, not at all. Marco is the only man I've ever been...' I stopped and flushed scarlet as I suddenly remembered that Marco wasn't the only man I'd been with at all. In fact, in the last three days I had trebled the number of sexual encounters I had ever had although I wasn't about to announce that to Connor. On the one hand it seemed rather unadventurous having had only one lover at my age but then again, I didn't want to announce my recent frolics and be branded easy. Also, I knew that with a couple of flirtatious sentences and a provocative rearrangement of my position next to him, I could have quadrupled my headcount and included Connor on the list.

He sighed and smiled and unfurled himself from the chair. 'I'd better go. It's late.'

'And I've got work tomorrow.' I was going to Cregny-Varn in the morning to start my new position. There was no point delaying things. If I carried on like this, Kinrade would know of my presence in no time.

'I shan't interfere, Ailey. It's your business. If you want to allow Kinrade to languish in what's rightfully yours then –' He stopped and shook his head before fastening his jacket. He kissed me once on the cheek and opened the front door. A cold, salty wind fanned the flames in the fireplace and the noise of the waves obliterated my reply as Connor strode awkwardly across the pebbles and rocks.

'I'm going to fight for it, Connor. We can still be king and queen.' But my words were dragged back out to sea.

5

It was still dark when I got up although I could see that it was going to be one of those winter days when, if you didn't venture out, you could truly believe it was summer. The western sky was littered with constellations and I took a few moments, despite the chilly wind, to calm myself with a mug of hot tea outside on the beach.

I had already boiled some water and washed and dressed in clean clothes. I'd pulled my long hair back into a neat pony-tail and smudged a minuscule amount of kohl under my eyes, topped off with mascara; I intended to apply lip gloss before I left. I wanted to look my best, both for Dominic and to appear professional in my new role, however menial the job.

An hour later, the first slivers of orange appeared over the cliff top and the usual morning rush hour of gulls swooped around the beach for scraps and dead fish. My aim was to be at Creg-ny-Varn before nine o'clock so even while the sun was still spilling over the horizon, I picked my way across the wet rocks to the track that led to the cliff top road. My guess that it would be a beautiful day was correct. The egg-yolk yellow of the sunrise paled and gradually transformed into a cool turquoise, the colours separated only by a wispy band of cirrus.

The walk along the cliff top road seemed shorter than usual. My pace kept time with my quickening heart as I anticipated the possibility that Ethan Kinrade could indeed be at Creg-ny-Varn, if Connor really had seen him the day before. I resolved to remain courteous, dutiful and, if necessary, servile. It would be one of the hardest things I had ever done but essential if I was to gather precious information about the man. He was my new boss and I was his maid. I would look after his needs while at the same time securing mine.

Before entering the long driveway, I squinted at the house through the pale winter-morning light. It was going to be a clear day but the sun hadn't fully touched the island. I looked for lights in the house but saw none. Either Kinrade wasn't home or he was still in bed. As a new employee, it wasn't necessary to skulk through the field and enter the estate furtively so I marched down the drive, which was lined with chestnut trees under which Connor and I had once gathered conkers like hungry squirrels, and pulled the chain of the front-door bell. A shiver of memories ran the length of my spine as I heard the ghosts of our spaniels barking and my father calling out for someone to answer the front door. We had been happy once.

I rang the bell again and, when no lights flicked on, I decided to rouse attention at the rear kitchen garden door. I rapped as hard as I dared on the brittle Victorian glass but again no one answered my call. I was about to give up and see if there were signs of life at the distillery when two Labradors came bounding across the herb beds, emitting half-hearted barks and wagging their tails.

'Ready for some hard work?' Dominic strode around the corner with a chain of keys jangling in his hands. His expression was business-like, with none of the warmth and satisfaction he exuded at the end of our last meeting.

'Good morning to you, too,' I said, unable to help the grin that I hoped would remind him of our encounter. 'I'm ready for anything you like.'

Dominic ignored my comment and proceeded to unlock the rear door. He shooed the dogs outside and ushered me into the kitchen, which was filled with the warmth of the Aga and the smell of coffee and toast.

'He's home then?' I asked, my eyes scanning the spotless kitchen.

'Like I said, Mr Kinrade won't be back for some time. Your job is to keep the place immaculate and prepared for his return. I want every room cleaned thoroughly, all the fireplaces cleared and stocked with logs and each bed made up with fresh sheets.' Dominic dropped the keys on the table, causing my already raw nerves to prickle with fright.

'No problem but –'

'And certain areas are off limits. If the door's locked and there isn't a key that fits, then keep out. Understand?'

I nodded. My curiosity about who had been drinking coffee and eating toast suddenly seemed inconsequential. I allowed my eyes to quickly flick up and down him. He was obviously dressed for work, and I couldn't help it that my gaze lingered just below his waist and feasted on delightful memories. 'What time do I finish?'

Dominic allowed a slow smile to cross his face. Not the kind of smile that invites further conversation or even a smile in return. No, it was a leer that continued to fill me with uncertainty about what I was doing; an expression that drove home the fear I thought I had overcome.

'You're finished when you're finished,' he replied and walked out of the kitchen, calling the dogs to heel.

I stood alone, gathering my thoughts and fighting back tears as the same ghosts that had met me at the front door filled the room. Being alone in the house, *my* house, and preparing to clean it from top to bottom while searching for clues and weaknesses about its owner, battered my senses more than I had bargained for. And I didn't understand why Dominic was being so petulant, especially after the last time we had met. If he had been instructed by Kinrade to employ a maid then he should be welcoming my presence, not trying to scare me off.

I located a box of cleaning materials in a store cupboard and decided to begin my work at the top of the house. I had to search every room methodically, to gain hard evidence in the form of my father's will or solicitors' letters as well as build up a profile of the man I would soon be fighting in court. The third floor contained three attic rooms, which belied nothing of the fourteen years that had passed. Each piece of furniture, every storage box containing old toys and clothes and hoarded birthday and Christmas cards, remained as my parents had left them. I rifled through the contents of a couple, determined not to waste time on ancient memories, and consoled myself that there would be plenty of time for reminiscing when I moved back into Creg-ny-Varn. I opened all the windows, swatted away strings of cobwebs and brought order to the rooms by rearranging the twenty or so cartons neatly. It was evident that Kinrade had never bothered to use the top floor so, as quickly as I could, I began work in the main bedroom.

I was surprised to see that the bed was unmade,

probably just as it had been left when I untied Dominic and slipped away from Creg-ny-Varn with a delicious tingle warming me. I began by stripping off the sheets and dropping them into a pile on the floor but not before pressing them to my face to inhale the remains of my masterful session with Dominic. I was surprised to find that the cotton was still strongly impregnated with the aroma of his body. I would have thought that by now only a trace of our sex would remain and that the sheets would have turned as cold and dank as the rest of the room. I shrugged and continued my work, throwing back the heavy drapes to reveal the bright, low eastern sun. Unfortunately, the light disclosed just how dusty the room was and I wondered if Ethan Kinrade had ever used the master suite since gaining possession of the property.

I uncovered the beautiful antique furniture that my father had cherished so much and applied polish to all the surfaces. Then I drew in a deep breath and opened the doors of the Jacobean carved oak wardrobe to take a good look at what a man like Kinrade would wear. I expected to see rows of tailor-made suits and designer shirts, all neatly pressed and hanging in colour order. I knew that a man in his position would want to impress with fine garments so nothing could have prepared me for the basic display, in fact hardly any clothes at all, that hung limply off two wire coat hangers.

'Who would have thought...?' I said to myself in amazement. A ripped pair of jeans slid to the floor of the wardrobe as I reached out a hand to make my first physical contact with the man I hated most in the world. I noticed a crust of mud around the hems as I hung them back up. Two thick shirts shared another hanger while a well-worn sweater languished at the back of the dusty cupboard. 'Money a bit tight, eh?' I asked an imaginary Kinrade. 'Can't afford any pretty clothes now you've got this place to look after?' I laughed, already feeling one up as I remembered my father constantly worrying about paying the bills. I shut the doors and turned to the mahogany chest that I assumed would be filled with neat rows of underwear. I was wrong again. Aside from a silk cravat and a couple of mothballs, the drawers contained...

I gasped and my thoughts slewed to an abrupt halt. I actually closed the chest and reopened it just to make sure that what I saw was real. I might have taken the empty box and tossed it in the rubbish bin or even ignored it completely had the picture on the carton not been of an erect penis strapped up in a kind of horse's bridle. The faceless male model stood proudly beside a scantily dressed blonde woman who held a lead connected to the leather penis strapping by a metal ring. I had never seen the likes of such a contraption and had I not been desperate to find out anything I could about Ethan Kinrade, I would have shut the drawer in fright.

'Good heavens,' I whispered in disbelief and picked up the box, thankful that the contents had been removed. 'Who *would* have thought?'

The leather cock harness, as the box boasted, wasn't the only unusual item to be found in the chest. A pair of handcuffs graced the next drawer down, along with several black leather straps that must have been used for many spanking sessions, judging by their frayed edges. I picked one up and ran the split ends of the leather between my fingers. I tried to imagine who had held the studded handle and across whose flank the leather had slapped. I brought the implement to my face and inhaled the smell, trying to garner its history. The raw odour coupled with the mystery of finding such an object sent shivers through me as I envisaged the thrills it must have delivered.

But it wasn't the role of recipient that excited me. I walked over to the bed and raised my arm high above my head, bringing the strap down with full force onto the sheets.

'*One*, Mr Kinrade,' I counted, 'for being such a dirty, low-down scumbag.' I ran the leather between my fingers again, my eyes narrowing as I prepared for a second swipe at the imaginary man's ass stripped bare by my own hands. '*Two*,' and I lashed him again, 'because I want to chase your sorry behind off the island and *three –*'

'Three – because you'd like to whip and tease your poor, helpless boss before fucking him senseless?'

I spun around, my arm raised high ready to deliver another blow to my imaginary Kinrade's smarting skin and was confronted by Dominic standing in the doorway, hands on hips wearing that same smirk as if it hadn't yet left his face. I froze for a second, maybe two, but then began beating the bed for all I was worth.

'Can you believe the dust in this place?' I said with a smile. The lump in my throat and the sudden dryness of my mouth made it hard to speak. A dizzy cloud of dust motes shimmied through a shaft of sunlight that struck across the room and for a moment I was hopeful that Dominic believed I was intent on airing the bed. 'But don't worry, I'll have it ship-shape in no time.'

'You don't look the type,' he said. His slow advance was even more menacing than if he'd strode up to me and yanked the strap from my grasp. A sparkle, like sunlight on the sea, glinted in his eyes. 'A slender girl like you wielding a harsh instrument with such force seems unlikely.'

'Well, when there's cleaning to be done,' I chirped and raised my arm for another lashing but Dominic grabbed it in mid-arc and squeezed my wrist so hard that I had no choice but to let the leather fall to the bed.

'You don't strike me as the dominant kind but then you don't look much like a maid either.' He reached for the strap and held it in front of my face. I cowered, afraid he would be angry with me for prying in Mr Kinrade's belongings and punish me with the leather. 'Having said that,' he continued, brushing the implement over my lips and down between my breasts, 'you do have a certain way with this.' To my surprise, he replaced the strap in my hand and tightened my fingers around the handle. He sat down on the bed, the weight of his body sinking into the messed-up quilt. 'Don't let me stop you,' he continued. 'I only came by to tell you that I've left some cut foliage in the kitchen that I thought you could arrange to brighten up the place.'

Now I was confused. The harsh tones, the scowl and disapproving manner had disappeared. Dominic was talking about foliage and sitting on the bed looking as if he had nothing better to do although the glint in his eyes remained, suggesting that he was lingering with intent. Still clutching the leather strap, I began to unfold the new sheets in a futile attempt to appear busy, when something stirred inside me: an early warning of latent thrill that I had only ever explored within the pages of my lost journal. Was Connor really right in his assumptions? Had my secret yearnings been tipped into reality? Was this why the moisture between my legs had not stopped seeping since the moment I arrived on the island?

It took me a moment to comprehend that it was I who had caused the loud snap as the leather connected with the wooden bedpost. I waited for Dominic to stand up in disgust and order me to get on with my work but he didn't. He shifted uncomfortably and offered a small smile when I trailed the tool up his muddy jeans, over his chest and under his chin.

'Lie down,' I whispered and then brought the strap down hard on the bed, missing him by only an inch. 'Now!'

Trying to understand the thrill of Dominic obeying my order was pointless. There were many things I couldn't comprehend in my life so I decided to allow instinct to overcome reason and made a promise to myself that I would seek the return of my diary as a matter of urgency, to halt any further incidents of irrational behaviour. When I had finished with Dominic, that was.

'Unfasten your jeans and turn over.' I wasn't sure where this was going. All I knew was that my mind had been set alight by the imagined sight of Ethan Kinrade's bare ass on this bed and me administering a damn good thrashing. A substitute would have to suffice and if that meant venting my frustration, sexual or otherwise, on Dominic then I was prepared to face the consequences. And besides, he appeared to be doing exactly as he was told.

'Pull them down to your knees.' The spectacle of him writhing on his front exposing his tight ass cheeks gave me delicious palpitations. He turned sideways but I flicked his face away with a deft lick of the strap. 'And don't even think of looking at me unless I tell you to.' Dominic buried his face in the quilt and wrestled his jeans and shorts to his knees, his pale flesh quivering in the runway of winter sun that crossed the bed.

I began to salivate as I realised what I was about to do. My nipples burned within my bra and half of me wanted to strip naked, locate Dominic's cock and work it into a frenzy before lowering myself onto his erection. But I knew I had to stay in control and rid myself of the pent-up feelings that had accumulated over the last few days – if I was to be of any use in my mission against Ethan Kinrade, anyway.

I screwed up my eyes and brought the leather strap down on Dominic's naked flesh as hard as I dared. He emitted a little groan and I noticed his fingers curl around a pillow. A very pale pink line bloomed across his skin and I couldn't resist slipping a finger inside my bra to dissipate the electricity pulsing through my breasts. I didn't care who it was lying on the bed. All I knew was that the thrill of administering a sharp slap across virgin skin was both cleansing and exhilarating.

Smack – another lash from the leather and Dominic moaned even louder, this time following his pain with a buck of his hips. Was he enjoying this? I certainly hoped not. Five more slaps, each one increasing in strength, and he was crying out incoherent noises that were a muddle of pain, humiliation and arousal.

'Stop moaning and lift up your hips.' What made me say that I don't know, but I was desperate to see his balls dangling underneath his smarting ass. I slapped him again, the hardest yet, and watched in delight as his balls swung free at the base of what I could only assume was a full-blown erection because, from my angle, his penis was not visible. 'Did I say you could do that?' I thrust a hand between his legs and made a grab for the hard line of his erection. I would never have believed that a man could become so stiff from pain. 'Do you think I'm doing this just so you can come all over the bed?'

'No.' He sounded nothing like the Dominic of a few minutes earlier and nothing at all like the man who had caught me red-handed snooping around the garden. The transformation was barely believable and all because of a leather strap.

I began to pump his cock, nothing gentle about my actions – in fact it was the roughest I'd ever been with anyone, and from this angle, snatching him between his legs and tugging him downwards, I was sure he'd cry out in discomfort.

'If you mess the bed, I'll have to beat you again.' I was using language that I'd only ever dared use in my journal and the tightness that braced my chest felt exactly the same as when I'd scrawled a similar imaginary scene in desperation to experience something sexy and wild. Dominic moaned and ground against my firm hand. 'I'm warning you –' But it was too late. I felt the warm viscous honey spreading between my fingers as Dominic was unable to control his body. He immediately went limp.

'I'm sorry.' His body fell forward onto the bed and I couldn't have been more outraged.

'I don't make false threats,' I said. 'But before I give you ten lashings, you can clean up this mess. I pushed my wet hand in front of his face and Dominic stared at me with dark, eager eyes. Rather than offering him punishment, it seemed I was giving him a treat. His tongue came out and began lapping at my palm, weaving between my fingers and around the silver ring that was a gift from Marco, as if it had no limit to its length. So sensual were the strokes that I couldn't help feeling aroused in my knickers and wishing that he hadn't already come.

Dominic finished by drawing tiny wet circles on the inside of my wrist, quickening the pulse that lay beneath, before I pushed him back on the bed for his promised spanking. He took it like a man, strawberry-coloured welts rising across his trim buttocks, and, as I watched him silently fastening his jeans afterwards, I wished I'd had the courage to make him try on the cock harness, which would have looked both stunning and dangerous on his once again erect cock. The thought of it nestled within his jeans would have added sparkle to my cleaning duties.

Dominic retreated to the doorway, wearing the same disapproving expression that he had entered with, and spoke seriously, unable to look at me directly. 'Like I said, please arrange the cut foliage.'

'In case Mr Kinrade returns?' I was hopeful for information. 'Although I've heard that he's back already.'

'Mr Kinrade is a very private man.' Dominic trod the plush carpet on the landing, barely making a sound as he descended the ornate staircase, leaving me desperate for both knowledge and sex in equal measures.

I made a point of replacing the items in the chest of drawers exactly as I had found them. I cleaned and aired Kinrade's bedroom with the detail of a maid at a five-star hotel and swiftly worked my domestic magic on other rooms of the house. My enthusiastic cleaning came not from a desire to hold down my temporary job but rather as a way of masking what I had just done to Dominic. I couldn't rid my mind of the sight of his bare bottom quivering helplessly beneath the leather. The ass of such a formidable man, too.

In fact, it was that particular thought that lingered more than anything else: I had brought him down from a towering figure of masculinity to a quivering apologetic specimen, only to have him rise once again and return to his original, indomitable stature. I spent the rest of the day wondering if it was me, the leather or a combination of both that had caused the event. Either way, it made me smile through my duties.

I didn't see Dominic again that morning, apart from when I spied him trudging across the lawn pushing a barrow of compost through the skim of mist that had collected underneath the sunshine. The two Labradors trotted faithfully beside him, unaware of what their temporary master had recently been up to, while he deposited piles of leaf mould at the base of pruned shrubs. I watched for several minutes, studying his hefty shoulders and supple back as he shovelled the crumbly soil onto the beds.

And then it occurred to me. Dominic was masterful. Of himself mostly, in the way that he carried himself with sustained importance and an air of superiority. He was masterful of his domain – the beautifully kept gardens and well-managed land were a credit to his position as devoted estate manager and, when Ethan Kinrade was away from home, Dominic was in charge of Creg-ny-Varn entirely. But the most masterful trait about the man was, ironically, his ability to lose control and become the victim of his own imperious actions. Dominic knew exactly what he wanted. I wasn't sure that I did.

By lunchtime, I'd found very little to convince myself that anyone actually lived in Creg-ny-Varn.

Fourteen years had been well preserved beneath the dust sheets that shrouded the house, and little but spiders and occasional inspections by Dominic had disturbed its history. Every piece of furniture, each heavy drape and richly woven rug remained in the same position as my fragile memory allowed me to recall. I almost expected to see ancient relics of out-of-date food in the pantry when I searched for something to eat, and was surprised to find a small stash of foods typically bought at a delicatessen. Several tins of lobster bisque and turtle consommé were racked up behind a box of water crackers. Dried pulses and beans were arranged neatly in sealed packets beside sun-dried tomatoes, anchovies and black olive pesto. My hungry eyes scoured the other ingredients, concerned that if I ate anything from the carefully arranged store, Kinrade would know I'd been helping myself. Aside from his kinky bedroom habits, the man was obviously a lover of fine food.

The picture I was building of Ethan Kinrade was certainly an interesting one, if not highly unusual and perhaps – I hated to admit – somewhat alluring. I had searched comprehensively and was unable to locate a photograph of him or indeed any clue as to his appearance. My best source for that, I decided, would be Connor, although I already knew he would not want to talk about his elusive boss. He seemed more intent on securing his place in my future than on furthering my desire to overthrow Kinrade.

'Looks like it'll have to be cheese.' I peeked in the small refrigerator and, surprised to see that everything was still within its use-by date, retrieved a piece of Manx cheddar. 'You can't have been gone that long then, if your food's still edible.' Again, I found myself conjuring an imaginary Kinrade as I tucked into the cheese while wiping an apple on my sleeve. It appeared home-grown with its unwaxed skin and several fresh leaves still attached to the stalk. 'Thanks,' I said, showing him that I had only taken a small amount of food. 'I'm starving after all my hard work. Surely you don't mind?'

My make-believe Kinrade shook his head and grinned. He was better looking than I'd given him credit for – tall with slightly messy, Viking-blonde hair and pushed-up sleeves revealing strong forearms with just the right amount of hair. His teeth were straight and sparkled and his trousers hung from slim hips, just skimming the gentle curve of his groin. When he spoke, his voice filled the room but not in the domineering way I had expected. Ethan Kinrade was welcoming me, telling me to help myself to as much food as I wished.

'My home is your home,' he said.

'Damned right it is!' I crunched the apple and walked around Kinrade, thoughtfully assessing how much of a threat he presented.

A large one, I finally decided, as my imaginary adversary dissolved into thin air. He looked like the type to take a fight to the end and I didn't like it one bit that he blew me a kiss as I forced his image from my head.

I'd been saving the best until last. I decided to finish up for the day, after an extremely unproductive start to my mission, by flicking a duster around what was once my father's library, where I remember him keeping all his papers and estate documents. If I didn't locate anything of use in there, then I was not only baffled by the lack of information but also completely stuck. I needed something, *anything*, to help Lewis put together a case for me. It was all beginning to appear rather hopeless.

I carried a tin of beeswax and a soft cloth, along with the vacuum cleaner and the set of keys left for me by Dominic in case the room was locked, as was usually the case when I was a child. My body ached from cleaning and carrying basket-loads of wood for the fires so I didn't really intend to spend much time in the library other than from to locate vital information. I turned the brass door handle and, as I had suspected, it was locked. I tried key after key in the old lock but none of them slid home and allowed me entry. Puzzled, I tried the entire set again in case I had missed one but the result was the same.

I recalled Dominic's warning: *If the door's locked and there isn't a key that fits, then keep out.*

My heart skipped. Ethan Kinrade had something to hide and Dominic had been instructed to see the library remained secure in his absence. My hands trembled as I withdrew the last key, wishing I knew how to pick a lock. I bent down to take a peek through the keyhole but something was blocking my view — most likely the key in the other side.

'Well, Mr Kinrade. Don't expect me to give up easily. You've shown me you have something to hide and I'm going to find out what it is.' My words skittled unheard down the corridor, echoing amongst the remains of my childhood memories. Instead of Kinrade's image haunting my thoughts, I was suddenly filled with recollections of happy times when Connor and I had charged around the house playing tag and hide and seek and anything else noisy that we could get away with.

'You're on!' I squealed to Connor, who darted as

skilfully as the shoals of mackerel we used to catch. I turned to flee, steaming down this very corridor before bursting into my father's library, breathless and dizzy with excitement. I slammed the door, panting against it for barely a second before I realised that my father was working at his leather-topped desk. I prepared for a telling-off.

'Looking for a place to hide?' he whispered, a mischievous grin expanding from his usually tight mouth. I nodded, desperate at nine years old to beat Connor at something. To my surprise, my father peeled back a small rug a few feet away from the bay window and plucked a metal ring from the floorboards. Before I knew what was happening, I was being packed down creaky wooden steps beneath a trap-door hatch which, from the chink of light available, seemed to lead into a pitch-black chamber.

'Don't make a sound,' he instructed, allowing the trap door to fall shut. I was terrified but exhilarated and hardly dared to breathe the fusty, cold air but rejoiced when fifteen minutes later I heard Connor's bored voice admitting that he gave up. I sprang from the hidden cavern like a jack-in-the-box, revealing myself to Connor with a grin, and, as we sloped off down the corridor again, I told him about the secret place beneath the library floor.

I laughed as I stowed the vacuum cleaner and polish back in the store cupboard but then stopped motionless, my hands strung with cable, as the memory came back. Several days after I'd hidden beneath the library, when my father had become bedridden with flu, Connor and I ventured where we knew we shouldn't. We even packed a bag of food and an extra sweater along with all the candles I could lay my hands on.

We set out on our journey beneath the floorboards

like a couple of adventurers and spent a good few hours exploring the tunnels and cave-like rooms that networked beneath Creg-ny-Varn. Looking back, it was the point at which I learned to see Connor differently. However young we were, the way he took control, the determined look that set into his face, made me feel safe and secure – that he would protect me from whatever monsters we might meet along the way.

I hastily shoved the cleaning stuff in the cupboard and grabbed a torch, thankful it contained live batteries. 'Right, Kinrade. Think you can beat me in my own house?' I paused as if he might reply. 'Well, you can't. I bet you don't even know anything about the tunnels.'

Remembering every thrilling moment of that morning with Connor, our sheer delight as we surfaced among rakes and pitchforks and strings of crispy onions in the gardener's hut, my mind was made up. I flicked off the house lights and picked my way cautiously through the kitchen garden to Dominic's shed. As long as he wasn't present, I would enter the coal chute inside the lean-to shed and make my way into the library that way. Then I would find out exactly what it was that Kinrade was trying to hide.

I clamped my arms around my body. It was cold and I'd left my jacket in the house. Even at this hour, only a few minutes before two o'clock, the light fell on the island as if a heavy shawl had been draped over the low winter sun. I approached the shed, half expecting Dominic to slap a hand on my shoulder and arrest me as he had done several days before. But there was no sign of him or the dogs, who would have certainly noticed me skulking. I turned the handle of the old door and sighed with relief as it gave and allowed me entry to the gardener's domain. Knowing I would have to be quick – Dominic would most likely return for a forgotten implement or his flask of whisky-stoked coffee – the urgency made my heart jump and skip with the sheer thrill of getting one up on Ethan Kinrade.

I moved sacks of apples and onions and shifted aside an old chair, finally revealing the secret entrance to the tunnel, and pulled back the wooden doors of the coal chute. Fortunately, it was empty although I remember returning to the house as a child looking like a coal miner from crawling across the heap of fuel that was used in the ancient boiler rumbling beneath our feet every winter.

Finally, I was in and walking by torchlight towards the library. I had to stoop to avoid the floor joists above, reminding me just how much time had elapsed since Connor and I made the same passage as children without the need to duck. Brushing cobwebs from my face, I located the wooden steps easily. Strange, how the magical network of tunnels now seemed nothing more than a dull basement.

I gripped the torch against my shoulder like a telephone and pushed up on the trap door. It took a moment for my eyes to adjust to the low sun that spilled across the floor but when I was able to see clearly, when the shimmering dust motes had settled and I had taken a sweeping glance around the library, I wasn't entirely sure if my scream was prompted by what I saw or by the hand that clamped around my arm.

6

I ran across the courtyard, following my nose, following my senses. I held back the tears – mostly from frustration – as I burst through the door of Connor's office, praying that he would be somewhere within the Glen Broath distillery. I breathed in deeply, trying to settle my racing heart as the sweet aroma of maturing whisky, malt and peat fires caught in my throat. It took me a moment to realise that Connor wasn't in his office so I began to search the distillery, desperate for his comfort and understanding.

Several workers eyed me suspiciously as I walked briskly past but none challenged my presence. I was just about to approach a female worker, the lines of whose rough brown boiler suit flared gently over her curvy buttocks and hips, when I saw Connor striding along a metal walkway about fifteen feet above.

'Connor, down here.' I stuck up my arm and sighed with relief when his face widened into a grin.

'This is a nice surprise,' he said as we sat in his office. 'But you look anxious.' Connor wiped his hands down his thighs, pulling the canvas of his work trousers taut around his groin for a moment. As I watched him pour two shots of Glen Broath's finest, it struck me again just how much time had been lost between us. It would be easy for me to succumb and catch up – and I knew that Connor was willing for that exploration to occur, both mentally and physically – but I wasn't sure if I was. To me, maintaining a steady course and securing my inheritance were paramount and if I analysed it truthfully, any involvement with Connor would throw me off-track. It was easy to justify my out-of-character actions with Dominic and Lewis and Liz. They were casual flings and a source of experimentation and release, although my involvement with Dominic smacked of something more sinister. It was true to say, too, that I believed Connor was right: by giving life to my sexual desires in my journal and subsequently losing it, I had effectively made my dreams come true. A kind of sexual magic spell.

Why, then, was I sitting in Connor's office, sipping his whisky and wanting nothing more than to bury my face in the warm crook between his neck and shoulder until he felt compelled to stroke my back and neck, push his fingers through my hair and tilt my face to his for a lasting kiss?

'Thanks.' I raised my glass. 'I'm sorry to have interrupted your work.'

'I don't count a visit from you as an interruption.' Connor perched on the corner of his desk, tapping his foot and eyeing me thoughtfully. 'Gut instinct tells me there's something you want to get off your chest.'

I nodded, then wished I hadn't. I didn't know where to begin or even where to end. My eyes were still smarting from what I had just seen in the library and my arm was still burning from Dominic's tight grip. And, if I got past all that successfully, would I be able to continue with tales of how I'd left pink stripes on the estate gardener's buttocks or tied him to Ethan Kinrade's bed and ridden him in return for what proved to be useless information? And then there was the tale of Lewis and Liz, jangling in my mind like the promise of delicious candy.

'I don't know what's happening to me, Connor.' I

closed my eyes, partly punctuating the beginning of my confession and partly to prevent him noticing my welling tears. 'Since I came back to the island, well, it's like I've been...' I paused. There wasn't a word for how I felt.

'Transformed?' Connor suggested. 'Released?'

'Kind of.' He was close but hadn't quite caught the essence of my emotions. 'I thought that I'd only ever loved one man.' I couldn't look at him while I spoke. I wasn't sure where this was leading or what at all it had to do with the shocking goings-on in the library.

'Marco?'

'Yes, although I somehow always knew it wouldn't be forever. It's like I've been in transit.' I messed with my hair, hoping that chunks of it would fall over my face, allowing me some relief from the pain of speaking so honestly.

'But you've been with Marco for years. It's been a long transit, don't you think?'

'Exactly. And that's why all *this* is happening.' I was even confusing myself and was unable to prevent several tears spilling onto my cheek. Connor approached me and I honestly thought he was going to wrap my head and shoulders in his arms and rock me gently. All he did was remove the empty whisky glass from my hand.

'Don't say another word. Just get in the Land Rover.'

And, better than cradling my confused head, Connor drove us the short distance back to his home.

Being within the thick stone walls of a traditional Manx cottage soon soothed my befuddled head and I immediately felt comfortable as Connor invited – no, instructed – me to sit in the oversized sofa that virtually filled the snug sitting room.

'We'll have complete privacy here.' He didn't attempt to conceal what this statement implied and I couldn't imagine what else, apart from something very intimate, would require so much solitude. 'You can cry all you like.'

'Don't worry. I'm not about to break down like a helpless female and sob the afternoon away.' I looked up at him as he stood in front of the wood-burning stove, holding his hands behind his back to soak up the heat. 'You must think I'm pathetic.'

'I never have and I never will.' There was something timeless about his remark. I believed him.

'I had a bit of a shock earlier, at Creg-ny-Varn, and it stirred up some other feelings that I've been trying to make sense of.'

'What kind of a shock?'

I paused. Did I really want to string Dominic up in the feelings that spun like spider silk between Connor and me? The fragile cobweb of trust, respect and something way deeper that could so easily be swiped away? I didn't entirely trust myself not to lash out with a denying hand and dust down our emotions. I took a deep breath.

'I wanted to clean the library, you know, where my father used to work. Well, it was locked and I was so intrigued by what Ethan Kinrade might be hiding that I decided to get in from the basement. Do you remember the tunnels under the house?'

Connor loosened at the memory, grinning and nodding, his silence urging me to continue. I faltered for a moment though enchanted by the fire that lit up his powerful features, making him appear god-like, with an orange corona burning behind him.

'I never even got as far as going into the library. All I did was poke my head up through the trap door.' My heart began to skip and jump as I recalled what I'd seen.

'And?' said Connor impatiently.

'It was indescribable. Like a scene from one of those kinky movies.' I felt tiny prickles of perspiration on my back. It was so warm in the cottage, quite unlike my temporary beach home, and the recollection of the transformed library made me even hotter.

'People were having sex in there?'

'Not exactly. I've never seen so much leather and metal and other quite incomprehensible bondage equipment. The library looked nothing like it did when we were kids. I couldn't even see any books as all the walls had been draped with red and black fabric.'

'Are you sure it's just not Mr Kinrade's attempt at unusual interior design? Perhaps a project that went wrong.' Connor's defence surprised me but then I noticed the slight smile, the quiver in his voice.

'There was even...' I paused, secretly thrilled by what it meant. 'There was even a cage suspended from the ceiling.'

'Perhaps he has a bird.'

'It was big enough for a human and that's what worries me. Who is he planning to lock up?'

Connor sighed and sat down beside me. 'Is this what's caused you to be in such a state?'

'Oh, no. My biggest shock came when the gardener caught me red-handed. Again.'

Surprisingly, Connor said nothing but instead retreated to the kitchen, shaking his head, and I soon heard pots and pans clattering. It wasn't clear whether he had left the room ashamed of my behaviour – for taking the demeaning job in the first place and then getting caught snooping around – or if he retreated in quiet thought to help me form a plan. Connor had always been secretive about his feelings and even now, with the pair of us grown up and mature and worldly-wise with the freedom to say what we believed, that was still the case.

'What are you doing?' I joined him in the small kitchen, just in time to see him sliding a terracotta dish into the oven.

'You look like you haven't eaten properly for weeks. I'm making you a meal.' Connor wiped his hands on a tea-towel and, when he locked me against a wooden bench with his arms pinned either side of me, I truly believed he was going to kiss me. An involuntary gasp caused my chest to rise and I briefly closed my eyes, waiting for the initial contact.

'And I'm not keen on you staying down at the beach cottage by yourself. It's so remote and you don't even have running water.'

My eyes burst open and I was thankful that he couldn't see the tingling in my expectant lips. I blushed, having no choice but to stare directly into his face. I saw day-old stubble littering his jaw as I noticed the single swallow he made when he realised my thoughts. But the moment was gone.

'I like being down there. There's something about the seclusion, the nearness of the sea.'

Connor shrugged and stepped away. 'You always contested everything I said. Why did I think you'd have changed?' He offered a glimmer of a smile, indicating that he wasn't angry with me for being so stubborn. 'I was going to suggest that you could stay here. At least you'd have a bathroom and a proper bed.'

The tingling began again at the thought of being so close to Connor when I was bathing or he was undressing at night. We would perhaps meet on the landing, each requiring the bathroom, our toothbrushes together on the basin, our discarded towels mingled together on the floor. A tight feeling knotted my stomach and I wasn't sure if it was from hunger or fear or a signal of how much I wanted Connor.

'I'll be OK where I am. But . . .' – perhaps I was being cheeky, perhaps it was a hidden invitation – 'but I wouldn't mind taking a hot bath now. If you don't mind.'

Connor held up his hands. 'Be my guest. There are fresh towels in the cupboard on the landing and help yourself to anything else you need.'

We were both silent, trying to guess what the other was thinking. I wanted to reach out and hold his hand, even brush my fingers down his stubbly cheek.

'Maybe then you'll be able to tell me exactly what's on your mind and why Ethan Kinrade has got to you so much.'

'Deal,' I said, knowing that it would take more than a soak in a bath to purge my mind.

I allowed my hands to drift from my breasts, across my half-submerged stomach, down my thighs and back up again, each slow stroke of my bubble-covered body a sheer delight. It had been nearly two weeks since I had taken a bath, although I'd been able to keep myself clean by taking showers and by makeshift washing in the beach cottage.

Submerged up to my neck with my long hair pinned up loosely, I was reminded of the first time I'd met Marco. I'd been in the bath then and splashed about like a cat thrown into water as he burst into the bathroom in search of soap. He'd been fixing my mother's ancient car and needed to wash his hands. His expression, when he saw me in the bath, was tattooed irrevocably on my mind just as his needy love-making was later stitched into my body. For many years, Marco was integral to my life, the selfish link that held us together as much a part of me as him.

As I fished for the soap in Connor's bath, I smiled and I remembered how I'd naughtily told Marco that if he wanted the soap he'd have to find it. He never did locate the bar but he did find his way from my ankles to the top of my legs and beyond, his dark and grimy hands a contrast to my much paler skin. It didn't take him long either, to strip and join me in the tub, the already high water level sloshing onto the tiled floor as he lay on top of me, grinding himself into me and bringing the tepid water back to near boiling point.

It was like that with Marco. We rarely had sex in bed at night. If he could hitch up my dress in the alley behind the tapas bar or bend me over the misshapen trunk of an ancient olive tree in the heat of the summer, then he would. Once, on the walk back to my house from the town, we overtook a bus-load of German tourists who were hiking in the sweltering valley. Marco virtually dragged me up the hill to get five minutes ahead of the crowd. Without a word about his intentions, he tore my flimsy panties from beneath my wrap skirt and leaned me over the rough stone of a baking-hot wall, the thrill of the approaching foreigners fuelling his need for risky games. The softness of his mouth on my pussy and the late afternoon breeze cooling my flustered skin brought me to a helpless climax just as the first tourist came into sight.

Marco wiped his mouth, hauled me upright and clamped an arm around my waist as if we were sweethearts admiring the view. Men and women, panting from the incline, nodded and smiled at us, while Marco's huge erection strained beneath his clothes. When they had passed, he put me back into position and satisfied himself by pumping me greedily from behind. I'm surprised that he even bothered to conceal his lust or my exposed body from the tourists.

I decided I might as well take the opportunity to wash my hair and so unleashed my tresses into the sudsy water. I pressed my fingers against my ears – I'd never liked the feeling of water gurgling in my head – and slipped further down the bath and tipped back my head so that my hair got a good wetting.

I know I heard something because the sound reverberated underwater but registered only as a dull noise. I paused, still submerged, and then continued to soak my hair until I heard it again. It was Connor calling up to me, most likely to tell me that food was ready and, not wanting to cut short the chance to get really clean, I yelled out from beneath the water.

'Yes, OK.' Without full hearing, it was difficult to know how loud I had shouted but it was obviously loud enough, although undeniably the wrong reply, as I felt a sudden draught of cold air across my exposed breasts.

I pulled myself out of the water into a semi-sitting position in time to see Connor standing in the doorway, unsure if he was delighted or shocked at what he saw.

'Oh, I'm sorry.' He was motionless, his hand still on the door knob, and I half expected him to ask for the soap as Marco had done years before. 'I asked if I could come in and you said "Yes, OK".' Connor bowed his head and looked to the side but didn't leave the small, steam-filled bathroom.

I clamped my hands around the hillocks of my wet,

bubble-covered breasts, concealing them easily in my palms, but my sopping hair dumped all over my face and I could barely breathe let alone speak. I risked exposure again to clear my face and, as if his eyes had thoughts of their own, Connor snatched an ill-timed glance at my body.

'I didn't mean to –'

'Can you pass me a towel?' I made no attempt now to conceal my nakedness. In fact, I *wanted* Connor to see me. That he hadn't made a move on me, or even hinted that he found me attractive since my return to the island as an available woman, cut deeper than I wanted to admit. I could let him off his teenage shyness and clumsy attempts at compliments as we chased each other and tumbled around Creg-ny-Varn as kids. I could even allow for temporary shock following my unexpected return, and of course there was the possibility that Connor was involved with someone else. But even if that was the case, he could have still offered a token advance or ambiguous comment to let me know what might have been. Or perhaps I was too dumb to see it.

'Thanks.' I took the towel from his outstretched arm and stood up, making no attempt to wrap it around my body. Water flowed from my elbows and drizzled down my back and buttocks as I stood in the bath with the soft towel pressed to my face. When wet, my hair was longer by an inch or so and I could feel the damp tendrils reaching down to my nipples, which had risen from the draught and Connor's presence. I wondered: if I hadn't been thinking of Marco when Connor burst in, would I be feeling like this? I answered immediately, almost audibly. Yes.

'Connor, look at me.' My body shuddered, as if I had absorbed the spirit of someone determined, sexy and unconcerned with respectability. There was no going back. 'Connor?' What did he want me to do, physically turn his head in my direction? I noticed how his chest deepened and his fists balled at his side, as if he was fighting something unfathomable. 'I want you to look at me.'

Very briefly, although the moment seemed like a lifetime, Connor allowed himself a glance at my nakedness. His jaw tightened, his pupils dilated and there was that swallow again, as if he was forcing his feelings back down inside. Several slow blinks marked his sweeping appraisal and his gaze left my body where it had begun – just below my navel, where the tiniest of curves dropped away to the small, dark triangle that I knew would be glossy from the bath.

'Is that it? Can't you bear to look at me any longer?' Disappointment drenched me as quickly as the water spiralled down the waste pipe. I tossed the towel on the floor, my body studded with water droplets. 'Do you think I'm beautiful?' I felt as if I was asking for a Christmas present or demanding a piece of jewellery for my birthday. What was wrong with the man? I was standing naked and wet in his bathroom, begging him to look at me, and all he could do was maintain a steady gaze at the toilet seat.

'Ailey, don't. You're shocked and distressed.' Again, as if he'd done a quick deal with the devil, Connor stole a look at me. As his eyes drew level with my breasts, I noticed the slight parting of his lips and the way he had to wipe his fingers over his top lips to rid himself of the perspiration that collected there. 'I've always thought that you're beautiful. Even when I believed you were lost for ever.' He paused, refuelling with a deep breath. 'If I look at you, properly, and then lose you again...' He couldn't find the words and so to end the sentence he left the bathroom, telling me not to take long because the food was nearly ready to eat. I towelled myself dry, pulled Connor's robe off a hook and wrapped my body in it. It seemed like the only way to get close to him. I trod the creaky stairs like a skulking cat and padded into the kitchen where he was serving roasted vegetables and salmon.

'Feel better now?' He spoke brightly, as if nothing had happened, and I nodded, stealing a bursting cherry tomato.

'Ouch!'

'What did you expect? It's come from the oven.'

What I actually expected obviously hadn't entered Connor's thoughts and so I pulled a mask over my mind and began the process of denial – something I had become expert at over the years. Don't like it? Then pretend it didn't happen. Simple as that.

'You're good to me,' I said, wishing that he would be.

We ate with trays balanced on our knees and our conversation was spiked with apprehension, despite my efforts to obliterate the moment in the bathroom. I actually felt relief when Connor brought up the subject of my earlier shock at Creg-ny-Varn.

'I'm a bit confused about what happened. Explain again.' Fortunately, he was smiling and I'm not sure he knew it but the descending sun set a glint in his pale-grey eyes that gave him the look of a man intent on whipping up mischief.

'It was simply awful. To see what that despicable Kinrade has done to my father's library. If the wretched gardener hadn't come snooping and caught me, I'd have gone in and resurrected the room.'

I replayed the words privately in my head, just to make sure I hadn't really said: *As punishment, I shack-*

led the gardener to the wall and worked him to a frenzy with my mouth before leaving him dangling, spent, satisfied. No part of me could admit to Connor that my pulse had quickened at the sight of the library's unusual contents. I hadn't got a clue what most of it was for but my immediate thought was: *I'd like to learn.*

'To be honest, I wasn't even aware that Kinrade had hired a gardener. I don't tend to have much to do with the running of the house. All my time is taken up with the distillery.'

'The man's everywhere at once,' I said, meaning Dominic. 'I can't seem to find out anything useful about Ethan Kinrade and if I'm to make a case against him, to get back my home, then Lewis needs something concrete to work from.'

'Lewis?'

'My advocate.'

'Which firm?'

I shrugged, realising that I didn't even know Lewis's surname. I'd got more knowledge about his body and the sexual preferences of his wife than I had of his professional qualifications. Suddenly, my stupidity tugged me back to the root of my emotions. There was no getting away from the rush that swelled inside and, really, it was appropriate that Connor help me sift through my feelings. I was doubtful about his willingness to become involved with me so, much as I hated to admit that this bothered me, I didn't see that I had anything to lose by confessing.

'I've been having fantasies, Connor.' I was completely changing the subject and to punctuate this, I put my knife and fork together and slid my plate onto a side table. A sudden gust of wind, heralding the onset of another bout of westerly low pressure, buffeted the side of the house, rattling the small-paned window. The fire flared within the stove as the current disturbed the draw.

'That's normal.' Connor mirrored my action, his appetite obviously sated by my confession.

'You know what you were saying about my diary? Well, I believe you're right. And now that it's lost, I'm choosing reality rather than fantasy.' I fiddled with Connor's gown. It smelled of sleep and cologne I didn't recognise. 'Something's happening to me.'

'I asked at the ferry company, by the way, and no one's handed in your journal.'

I wanted to tell him that I already knew that; that somehow, as long as my thoughts were roaming free in the universe, my desires would continue to materialise, as indeed they were. It was a kind of karmic accident, in which need and probability had combined in the most unlikely of ways on the most unsuspecting of people.

'I *have* to get it back. The last year of my life is in that diary. It's a part of me.'

'I understand,' Connor said. For a moment, he sounded fatherly. 'I'll do what I can but first, it sounds like you have a more immediate problem in the form of Ethan Kinrade and his over-protective gardener. Have you thought of just confronting the man, stating your intentions?'

'What, and give him time to defend himself?' I realised that I sounded naïve and I'd never felt so lost or helpless but I knew for certain that laying my cards on the table in front of Kinrade would be the hardest thing I'd ever done. 'I should probably just go back to Spain and forget about it.'

'Forget about Creg-ny-Varn? You know that's not possible. And besides, that would mean forgetting about us.' Connor's eyes paled in the light of the fattening sun as it spread on the horizon like a deflating beach ball. He stood and snapped the curtains across the small window, the unusual light causing him to squint. 'As kids,' he added in case I thought he was referring to our present situation.

I sighed. 'God knows, I've tried.' Again, I caused Connor to become motionless. I knew that he thought I was trying to forget us – now or then – but I didn't make any attempt to put him right. As self-preservation, I needed him to believe that I didn't feel anything for him – and how could I, anyway, in such a short time? It had been fourteen years, and my longing for him back then had simply been the need for a pillow fight or for someone to help me lug my homemade go-cart back up the driveway. I'd encountered him only twice since my return. Hardly cause for infatuation; barely time to recognise each other.

'Then why come home?'

I bit my lip so hard I thought it might burst. My hair was beginning to dry and, so it wouldn't form wiry strands or unruly clumps, I mussed my fingers down its length. Besides, it gave me time to think. Connor watched as I tugged at a knot.

'Does he have a wife? A lover?' I decided upon a new tack.

'Not that I've seen. We may, however, get the chance to find out.' Connor's expression promised information. What he showed me filled me with both intrigue and fear. He reached out to the oak mantelpiece and retrieved an envelope, passing it directly to me. I slipped out a gold-edged card and read.

'What is he playing at? Who does he think he is?'

'Lord of the Manor, perhaps?'

'He's ingratiating himself and fawning to Manx

society, that's what he's doing. It's nothing more than a vain attempt to secure a firmer hold on my inheritance.' I wanted to toss the invitation onto the fire but found myself gripping it tightly, a new link to Kinrade.

'It's a Christmas party, Ailey. Not a plan of war. I was wondering if you'd like to be my guest but obviously if you feel that strongly about –'

'No, wait. I'd be honoured.' I read the words again, another step closer to the workings of Kinrade's mind. He was going to have a party.

'Something tells me it's not my company you'll be after.'

'How right you are. Any chance to wear a silly costume.' I ran my finger under the last line of the invite and showed Connor. 'Did you realise it was fancy dress?' I said with a smile. In other circumstances, it would be fun.

'Leave it to me,' he laughed. 'I know exactly what we can wear.'

Connor opened a bottle of wine as the afternoon drifted into evening. I wasn't sure if we'd eaten a late lunch or an early dinner but I didn't care as I began to relax and the wine worked its magic on my thoughts. Despite having received the invitation several weeks ago, Connor knew little more about the party.

'Everyone who works at the estate received an invite as well as most of the island's elite society.'

'I didn't,' I remarked sourly, then I quickly realised that my employer didn't even know of my existence yet, having entrusted the running of the house to Dominic. That in itself seemed strange, a gardener fulfilling such a role. 'It should be *me* hosting this party, not Kinrade.'

'Has it ever occurred to you that it was your father's wish to leave his estate to Ethan?' Connor's direct question, a plain truth that I had been avoiding since I had learned of my father's death, sank a wedge as thick as the cottage walls between us. Whose side was he on?

Connor raised his eyebrows at my lack of response. I could see he wasn't entirely approving of my battle. 'I came to call for you the afternoon that you disappeared.' He leaned forward on his forearms, the skin once again exposed by pushed-up sleeves. I could see their strength, how he had changed from the young boy that once struggled to land a fish. 'Your father said nothing to me. He just pointed out to sea. When I turned to look, he closed the door and when I asked my father or the other villagers what had happened to you and your mother, no one would talk. Not to a young boy, anyway. I soon learned not to ask and I still don't know the truth.'

'My mother,' I began, surprising myself with my clipped tone, 'had an affair. Lots of affairs, actually.' My mind began to gallop back to the past, a place I really didn't want to visit. 'My father found out and kicked her off the island.'

'How could he do that?'

'He shamed her in every social circle from Douglas to Peel. You know how gossip travels around here. In those days, my mother would never have survived without a constant stream of invites and functions to attend. But I was a child and knew little of what was going on. All I remember is that one day my life was turned inside-out and the people I loved most in the world were gone. And then she ended up running off to Spain with a much younger man.'

'Is she happy?'

'Deliriously.' I grinned on my mother's behalf. We had carved a life for ourselves in the sunburnt country and nestled within the community as if we had been there all our lives. As a teenager, I all but forgot the Isle of Man and its dank climate. I was too busy enjoying the thrills that accompanied being a young English girl amongst hoards of sexually hungry Spanish boys. But I couldn't tell Connor this. 'And I was happy too. I love my mother and know that she did the best she could at the time. That's no reason to resent a person's choices.'

'You said that you *were* happy. Has that changed?' Connor shifted uneasily, perhaps expecting me to admit to restlessness.

'I'm not happy that I'll never see my father again. Somehow, I always believed that one day I would return and get to know him again. Sadly, I didn't feel able to do that until I'd made something of myself.' I sighed, allowing my arms to rise and fall heavily. 'I wanted to impress him and now it's too late.'

'Is this why you're so intent on getting back your home?' Connor paused and cocked his ear to the window, like an alert dog sensing the arrival of his owner.

'Perhaps. And perhaps it's just because I can't bear the thought of a stranger living within the walls of my memories.'

I watched Connor peel back the curtains and then shrug. 'Thought someone was out there,' he commented and then there was a sharp rap at the back door, proving him right. He excused himself, relieving me of having to explain my motives further. Would he truly understand that the more I learnt about Ethan Kinrade, the more I wanted him out of my home?

I heard voices in the kitchen, one of them a girl's, the hairs on the back of my neck prickled.

'Come in and get warm,' Connor said, the voices getting closer. 'It's no evening to be out. Drink?'

'I'd love one. It's nice to be back. I'm exhausted.' By this time, the voices were in the small living room and I turned, annoyed at having an intimate moment with Connor disturbed – especially as I was still wearing his robe – and welded my eyes to the girl's face until it slowly dawned on me who she was. She was draped around Connor's neck, giving him a kiss as they came into the room.

'Ailey,' Connor said to me, 'this is Steph. She's here to learn some new production methods at the distillery.' He then turned to the fragile young creature that clung to him, brushed a strand of white-blonde hair from her face – *he touched her face* – and said, 'Steph, this is Ailey, my best friend from when we were kids.'

Did he have to say 'when we were kids'? Was it a temporary role that I'd fulfilled and now I was unable to be named as his best friend? Just because I'd been away for fourteen years, did that make me surplus to his emotional requirements? I was already jealous of Steph, and confused too, my brain scrabbling to thread together the bits of information that were spinning around my mind. It was rather like gathering up beads from a broken necklace. Instinctively, I held out my hand. Steph didn't take it.

'Steph's been travelling around Europe for the last few months. She's come to visit for a couple of weeks. It's been ages, hasn't it?' Connor gave her a squeeze and I thought she might break. Even beneath her winter layers, she would weigh no more than seven or eight stone, and standing next to Connor, who towered over her, only emphasised her petite body. I had all these thoughts before I realised who she was.

'Did you mention a drink?' she giggled, her pretty Scottish accent turning up at the edges. I still gawped, failing to move up as she joined me on the sofa.

'I've just had a bath,' I said stupidly, tugging at Connor's robe. Steph looked at it briefly and then clinked glasses with Connor. He had forgotten to refill my glass so I got up and did it myself but when I returned from the kitchen, he was sitting next to Steph, laughing and pawing at her tiny leg with his sturdy hand.

'Well, I'm going to get dressed and then I'll head off,' I said. My attempt to drain my newly filled glass in only two mouthfuls exploded in a spray of realisation as I heard Steph say *'great sex'*, after which she dissolved into helpless giggles. It was the intonation in her voice rather than her looks that finally joined the fragments in my mind. I didn't even have time to consider why she was talking about great sex to Connor.

'Steph, we met on the ferry. Do you remember? We were the only two not being sick? I fetched you a coffee and...' – I hesitated, breathing in – 'and then you stole my pocket-book as we were disembarking.' As I stuck my hands on my hips and positioned my feet in a stance that planted me firm and tall in front of Steph and Connor, I had no idea that the robe had come apart and my left breast was partly revealed.

'I'm sorry,' she said, her half smile obviously suppressed in an attempt not to embarrass me, 'but I don't think we've met before. And, er, your...' She pointed a slim, painted fingernail at my exposed chest and might as well have hurled an ice dagger at me.

I tugged the towelling back into place, the shock of revealing my breast considerably less than the surprise that I felt at Steph denying having met me before.

'You *must* remember,' I continued. My voice faltered but I refused to let this go. 'You came and sat next to me as I was writing up my diary and virtually every other passenger was being sick except us. We had a brief chat and then you took out a book and began to read.' I paused, desperately trying to think what she'd been reading. '*To Kill a Mockingbird*,' I said triumphantly. 'That's what you were reading and then you told me about your trip to Paris and the good, sorry, *great* sex that you'd had there.' If nothing else, I hoped that would turn Connor off her.

I could see Connor shifting uncomfortably next to Steph, probably wondering if I'd had too much wine. 'Ailey, why don't you tell Steph about your life in Spain? She'd love to hear.' A poor attempt at changing the subject and it didn't prevent me from raising my eyebrows at Steph and waiting for her reply.

'Nope, sorry,' she said vaguely. 'I'm sure I'd remember if I'd seen you. I'm sorry that you think I stole something of yours.'

'Ailey's under a bit of pressure, aren't you Ailey?' Connor's voice hardened and, while I was in his home and drinking his wine and wearing his robe, I decided to remain civil. 'She doesn't mean anything by it. A case of mistaken identity, I think,' he added, while I nodded in agreement.

And as a result, my outburst caused two things: enormous self-doubt – perhaps I was going mad – and then Connor placing his hand on Steph's upper thigh, leaving it there for the next twenty minutes while I regaled her with tales of life in Spain. Both ways, it hurt.

'And what about you?' I asked, tired of talking about olives and mountains and university life in Granada. Was it all so foreign to them? 'What are you doing during your stay on the island?'

'Work experience in the distillery mainly. Glen Broath has such a fine reputation.' My stupid question caused Steph to drool adoration all over Connor and he returned an equally sickly-sweet look that told me he enjoyed the flattery. 'Then I'll be going back to the Highlands to help my father in his whisky business. I have no brothers.' Steph and Connor then entertained me with stories about the whisky business and what a struggle it was to keep afloat in the shadow of massive companies. It seemed that Steph's family business was a few years behind Glen Broath in terms of world trade and Steph was here to learn. Then it struck me that the female figure I had seen earlier in Glen Broath, when I'd sought out Connor in my distressed state, was Steph. It seemed strange that Connor hadn't mentioned her before, especially as they appeared so close.

'Like I said,' I repeated. 'I'd better be going. It's a long walk.'

'Nonsense,' Connor barked, finally levering himself away from Steph. He stood and took my elbow. 'Sit and talk and drink more wine and forget your silly walk back to the beach at this hour. Have you seen the weather?' Connor briefly exposed the night by tugging on the curtain. It was as if someone was squirting a hose pipe at the window.

'OK,' I said with a smile. He still cared then. 'I'll stay a while longer and hope the storm passes.'

'No, you'll stay the night with us and not say another word about it.'

It was as if someone had suddenly opened the window and the hosepipe spray was hitting me directly in the face. A cold, relentless spike of water pounded my forehead and washed away all rationale. The only thought I had was of the word *us* and it rang through my head like the tolling bell on an ocean buoy.

'Steph is staying with you?' I think it was a question. Connor could have taken it either way.

'Yes, of course. Where else did you think she would be staying?' The last time I'd seen that look was when he was eleven and he'd hidden a naughty magazine in our stables. When it had been discovered and presented to my father, Connor denied all knowledge but sported the same mischievous look as he wore now. Was it only me who realised the implications? Two women, equally attracted to one man, spending the night together. It was the unspoken promise that was alluring. The potential of the night more provocative than the reality.

'I'll have to take you up on the offer. The thought of climbing over those rocks in the dark fills me with fear. And the tide will be in about now.'

'Sense at last. You two get to know each other for a bit. I have to make an important phone call. Do help yourselves, ladies.' Connor slid the bottle of wine across the table in no particular direction and went into the kitchen, closing the door behind him.

I could feel Steph staring at me even before the waft of breeze that Connor left in his wake had dissipated. The fire crackled and spat behind the glass door but I opened it anyway and nestled another log within the flames. It was something to do other than glare at Steph.

'Sorry I denied knowing you. I didn't expect to see you again. I've read your diary.' She curled her legs up underneath her and rested her head on a brown velvet cushion with the most self-satisfied grin I have ever seen on anyone. 'It's quite shocking really.'

'I could report you to the police for pickpocketing.'

'What, and risk me handing over the evidence?' She laughed.

'I want it back.' This was playground banter except there was no teacher to tell.

'And what if I haven't finished with it yet? We're about three quarters of the way through.' Steph twisted around on the sofa, her feline movements showing me just how slight she was.

'We?' My heart thudded as I poured more wine.

'It's been great bedtime reading. I would never have thought that such an innocent-looking person could have such deliciously wayward thoughts. Have you ever actually, you know, done what you've written about?' Steph twirled a strand of silver-blonde hair around her tiny finger and, with widening eyes that were already too large for her small oval face, failed to suppress another giggle.

'I demand that you give it back now! It's personal property.' I stomped about the living room, opening drawers and cupboards looking for my journal. I could barely believe that I'd inadvertently stumbled across the wretched Steph – although that's the Isle of Man for you – let alone comprehend that my diary had most likely been read by Connor. She said *we*, didn't she? I would never be able to face him again and the prospect of anything happening between now us had been irrevocably dashed.

'Sorry, I can't. It's not here.' Steph unfurled herself as Connor returned from the kitchen. 'But tell you what, I'll drop it round to you. Connor can tell me where you're staying.'

And that was it. I knew I wouldn't get any more from her and didn't want to cause a fuss in front of Connor. I stared at the floor, unable to look him in the eye in case he realised what we were talking about. I wanted to scream at him and thump him for not confessing that he had read my journal. He couldn't feign ignorance either, as the book had my name clearly written on the cover and he was aware that I had lost my diary. I mustered courage and turned to his warm, smiling, irresistible face, pretending for all I was worth that he was a repulsive traitor. It didn't work.

'How *could* you?' I whispered. The spitting fire behind me and the steady trickle of water on glass were the only other noises in the breathless room. 'Connor, how could you?'

And I gathered my belongings and ran out into the rain.

7

Athol Street clicked with the heels of the lunchtime scurry. Dark suits ducked and twisted with mobiles pressed to their heads in the race for a table at the most popular bistros and café bars.

'Sorry,' I said as a young woman in a trouser suit knocked me with her briefcase. I walked along the street, the financial heartbeat of the island, staring up at the immaculate facades of the Victorian buildings that were peppered with more modern constructions where space allowed. It was hard to acknowledge the change that had taken place over the last fourteen years; the memories I had of Douglas, the island's capital, while on shopping trips with my mother bore no resemblance to what I now saw.

Banks filled with offshore accounts, advocates' brass plaques and firms of accountants ran up the entire length of the street and spilled into neighbouring streets too, by the looks of the workers that flooded from their offices to wheel and deal over lunch. I made my way, against the flow, to the prestigious building of Macaulay & Fisher Advocates Limited, where I was greeted in a plush reception area, decorated mainly in gold and green, by an immaculately dressed woman in her thirties. Suddenly, I felt very out of place in my walking boots, jeans and waterproof. I caught sight of myself in a gilt-framed mirror and ran a finger beneath my dark-rimmed eyes, while my other hand worked through the mess that was my hair. Judging by my appearance, which was usually fresh and sun-kissed, my mission to reclaim Creg-ny-Varn was taking its toll. I was tired, fed up and, having discovered that Connor already had a girlfriend and had no doubt been reading my journal, I was ready to go home to Spain. I was only keeping the appointment with Lewis because he had shifted other clients around to make time for me.

'Ailey, you found us.' His rich voice calmed me and I took a deep breath and stood, blushing as he kissed me slowly on both cheeks in front of the receptionist, who would have been wondering why her boss would want to make contact with someone who looked as if she lived on the street. 'Come into my office and have some tea.'

Tea sounded good. Proper tea, boiled in a kettle and brewed in a pot with a cosy and stirred with a spoon. Drinking tea from a cup and saucer would be a treat, a biscuit or two a bonus. Lewis didn't let me down.

'Thanks,' I said, the china cup rattling in its saucer. 'I've been dunking teabags into barely hot water that tastes of smoke. As for milk, well, that's a luxury.'

'You're welcome to spend time with us at our place. Liz would be delighted.' Lewis pushed back his unruly hair. Even dressed in a shirt and trousers, although without a tie, he managed to appear ready for a fishing trip or a day digging the garden. I noticed how his shoulders strained beneath the striped cotton. Then he winked and leaned forward across his desk, his slightly stubbly chin resting in his hands, and whispered, 'Liz has been very keen to see you again since I told her about our encounter at the beach cottage.'

'You told her?'

'Of course. She could hardly contain herself. She wanted to know everything that we'd been up to and

I was awake all night describing every detail. She was especially thrilled that we'd spotted her at the window.'

'I see,' I said and took a sip of my tea. 'And she wasn't –'

'Jealous? Not at all. She's been desperate for this for ages.'

'This?'

'Another woman, silly. For me to find another woman for us.' Lewis was stretched across the huge leather-topped desk, his elbows spread wide on top of a stack of files, and the glint in his eyes told me that work on my case was far from his mind.

'Us?' I was beginning to sound silly with my monosyllabic replies that curled up at the edges like autumn leaves.

Lewis glanced at his watch. 'We've got about twenty minutes and she'll be here. Did you enjoy your shopping spree?'

Lewis had kindly driven me into Douglas earlier that morning and dropped me in the shopping area of the town. I had wandered the narrow streets, meandering through expensive boutiques and high-street stores with only enough spare money to buy a plastic cup of hot chocolate. The money that remained in my purse was for food, and the wages from my cleaning job, although I had yet to see any money, would be my return fare home.

'Yes, thanks, although I didn't buy anything.' I had walked slowly up to the offices of Macaulay & Fisher, hoping to use up some of the time Lewis thought I desired in the shops.

'That certainly doesn't make sense,' he joked. 'Liz can't go near a clothes shop without having the urge to strip and try everything on. And you can guarantee that she'll step out of the changing cubicle in skimpy undies just to ask me something pointless. She's not happy unless she's had at least three strangers see her body each day.' Lewis grinned and leaned back in his leather chair, perhaps uncomfortable from the tightening within his trousers. 'Once she even took me back into the changing rooms with her and leaned over a stool while I –'

My shocked expression interrupted him. He began to rifle through the papers on his desk and located a clean notebook. He cleared his throat.

'Right, tell me everything you've found out so far about Ethan Kinrade. Any detail, however small, may be useful.' Lewis looked me straight in the eye. 'Although I have to tell you honestly, Ailey, I don't hold out much hope. If your father's wish was for his estate to go to Mr Kinrade then –'

'I understand,' I said. 'Let's get to work.'

Picking over the bones of what I had discovered about Kinrade was, after fifteen minutes or so, proving fruitless. While Lewis was patient and took notes about everything I revealed, none of the information was particularly useful when it came to putting together a case.

'Is there anything else you can think of? Anything that may go against his character?'

'There's the library,' I offered and pulled a face. 'He's pretty much turned it into a kinky bondage room.' I was saddened that the beautiful room had been desecrated but also secretly wished that I'd had the chance to mess around in it with Dominic when he'd caught me spying in the basement. Plenty of time yet, I thought.

'I'm not sure there's a law against that unless he had a hoard of young beauties tied up against their will.' Lewis pushed back in his chair and ran the end of his pen along his lips. 'Ailey, if I were you, I'd simply confront the man and talk to him about how you feel. I really don't think you have a case for kicking him out of his home but you may appeal to his humane side if you voice your feelings to him.'

'A possibility, I suppose, but the wretched man's always away from the island.' Lewis was right. Seeing the flimsy facts about Ethan Kinrade spread out in black and white made me realise how futile it all was.

'I'm not sure that's true. I saw him again today. He was buying the newspaper at the local shop when I went out to fetch milk.'

'Kinrade?'

'He said good morning to me. So you see, introduce yourself and in all probability you'll find yourself as a guest at Creg-ny-Varn with Mr Kinrade behaving perfectly reasonably.' To indicate just how serious he was about his suggestion, Lewis closed his notebook and pushed it aside. The intercom buzzed.

'Your wife's here, Mr Macaulay. Shall I send her straight in?'

Lewis grinned and rose from his chair, confirming that his wife should join them. When he greeted Liz, I noticed the expensive cloth of his suit trousers pull snugly around his well-shaped bottom. His shirt, too, stretched across the sheets of his back muscle as he wrapped his arms around his wife's body, squashing her large breasts between them. They kissed without a care for my presence, a deep kiss which implied an urgent need that wouldn't wait.

'Ailey, how nice to see you again.' Liz smiled and allowed Lewis to relieve her of several shopping bags from designer boutiques.

'Anything nice?' Lewis took a peek into one of the

bags and looked up grinning. 'Hmm,' he said. 'You got me a present.'

'Would you like to see?' Liz didn't wait for an answer nor, it seemed, was she particularly aware of my presence any more because she dashed into Lewis's private bathroom and returned only a minute later virtually naked.

'Whoa!' Lewis steadied himself on the desk.

Liz was wearing the sexiest, most alluring lingerie that I had ever seen. Personally, I was used to wearing simple white thongs or perhaps a black one in the evening and I often went braless. My entire wardrobe consisted of little more than loose skirts – many of them see-through for Marco's benefit – and a few tight-fitting tops that emphasised the neat shape of my breasts. In the cooler months, I snuggled within soft sweaters and jeans.

But what Liz was wearing had not only taken Lewis's breath away and most likely any thoughts of the afternoon's work, but had also rendered me motionless, aside from my quickening pulse, as I realised that I wanted to be the one who peeled off the delicate slivers of lace and replace them with my mouth.

'That's so pretty,' I offered in an attempt to break the silence as Liz posed before us. 'I love the colour.'

'The fabric's beautiful too. Come and feel the quality.' Liz beckoned me over and I quickly realised that refusing would result in her insisting and then I would look silly and shy if I didn't, and besides, my fingers were tingling at the prospect of a small touch, perhaps just below her breast or around the rim of her panties. I remembered my diary and realised that it was happening again. I wondered if every time I found myself sexually mixed-up since my return to the island, Connor and Steph were reading through the pages of my journal. It was entirely possible and gave me both pleasure and pain to think of them engrossed in each other's bodies after an extra dose of my fantasies. But while my writings had brought them together and opened up a new world of sexual possibility for me, Connor seemed further away than ever.

Slowly, I approached Liz and raised my hand to her ribs. I connected with the lilac chantilly of the lace-up corset, feeling the warmth of her skin beneath the delicate panels. She was right and even I, who was not familiar with such items, could feel its beauty. Her beauty.

'It's under-wired as well, to keep me in place.' Liz took my hand and slid it under the weight of her breast. 'Feel how it lifts me.' She took both of my hands and cupped my palms around her soft, round flesh.

I heard something from Lewis, a small moan of approval, and Liz too made a throaty noise when I allowed my thumb to wander up to the brown outline of her nipple, barely visible through the lace. I'd seen all this before in print, of course, in women's monthly magazines left behind by our British lodgers. Sexy women in unattainable lingerie had always intrigued me: not because I wanted to strive to become them, as many young women aimed and usually failed to do, but as an inspiration for lust. A brief need for their bodies to be within reach. I wanted to touch and explore and do the things to them that Marco had done to me. I wanted to know what I felt like.

As my thumbs lingered on the dark circles of her breast, the buds of her nipples pushed up and out, causing a tiny rise beneath the patterned lace. I traced a line along the scalloped edge of the bra cup, leading up to the satin shoulder strap. Liz was wearing a velvet choker in deep purple and a cluster of gold chains with a glittering cross dangling between her almost spherical breasts.

'Was it expensive?' I whispered because I knew my voice would fail me.

'Terribly,' she giggled, eyeing Lewis for a second.

I stood back, causing a brief flash of concern to spread over her face, but when she realised I was simply appreciating her from different angles, she began to pose and show off her new extravagance. I stepped behind her and was pleased to see that her bottom was as full and rounded as her bust. Liz had a tiny waist, which emphasised her curves perfectly. She possessed a typical hourglass figure set upon pretty legs, dressed up with an ankle chain and mauve suede court shoes, the heels of which brought her a couple of inches below my height. I reached out and rested my hands in the small of her back, just above the band of skin between the edge of the corset and the hairline strap of her thong. Slowly, I brushed my hands over her skin and its barely-there covering of blonde hair, and passed around to the sides of her ass-cheeks – the flawless expanses of flesh that I longed to nibble and bite.

'The thing about pretty lingerie, though,' Liz said as I cradled her buttocks, 'is that it never lasts very long. It took me all morning to choose these items, the stockings included, and I'm certain that Lewis will rip them off me in a matter of seconds later on.'

'What makes you think I'll wait until later?' The male voice was obtrusive in what should have been an entirely female exchange.

'Typical,' I replied, grinning. 'You look absolutely gorgeous and deserve to be worshipped and adored for hours.' I briefly touched her corset, her panties, her stockings. 'I'd love something like this.' With that, I let go of her bottom and came to her side, reminding her how drab and practical I looked in my outdoor clothes and tied-back hair. 'For now, this is what I'm stuck with and I barely feel like a woman. I was lucky enough to take a bath yesterday but that was the first in a long time. How I would love to straighten my hair and wear tarty red lipstick and dress up in underwear like yours!'

I only said all this because I was thinking of Connor and Steph entwined in front of the fire, my journal between them and their bodies ready to act out my secret fantasies. I was turning into that person again, the one who ends up in naughty, unthinkable trouble.

'Then you must go back to our house with Liz and be pampered from head to toe.' Lewis stood and adjusted his trousers. Without doubt, I noticed a bulge behind his zipper. It was strange to think that he had buried that same erection within me, while his wife made do with a vibrator and the hope that we were watching her. It was an unspoken tease.

'Yes, Ailey, come home with me and let me give you a treatment you'll never forget.' Liz squealed at the suggestion and went back into the bathroom to dress. I was slightly disappointed that my brief touches hadn't lured her into a naughty display for Lewis's benefit but settled upon the promise of being pampered back at her house.

'I have a meeting to go to but then I can get back early. Liz can give you a –'

'Let's get you back to my place, young lady, and give you a good going over.' Liz emerged from the bathroom in her clothes again.

'You took the words from my mouth,' Lewis said. 'I'll join you ladies later. Have fun in the meantime.'

And then I was being driven across the island with the promise of much girly pampering making my heart skip beneath all the layers of my clothing.

I didn't wear my dirty boots in the house. These were the first things to leave my body in a muddy heap by the door. My socks weren't much better, although I had been washing my underwear in boiling water from the fire and scrubbing them with a bar of soap. I left my heavy jacket on the hook in the hall and began to relax as I entered the living room and warmed myself by the fire that had obviously been stoked earlier in the day.

'Go straight upstairs,' Liz suggested. 'There'll be plenty of hot water and I've loads of lovely body scrubs and lotions in the bathroom.' She escorted me up the narrow stairs and retrieved several cream towels from a cupboard along the way. She showed me into a bathroom with low beams and a wooden floor and, in the middle, a cast-iron bath with lion's-claw feet. There were dozens of candles and tea lights adorning the window sill and shelves and Liz meticulously lit each one. The warmth and glow that filled the bathroom made me want to shed all my clothes and never leave the room again. Liz turned on both taps, pulled the cord of the window blind and flicked off the main light so that even before I had taken off my clothes, I was drenched in sensual lighting.

'Let me help you.' Liz was tugging on my sweater and fiddling with my belt. 'You're so tense,' she said as she trailed her hands down my body after discarding my woolly layers on the floor. 'You can take a hot bath and then I'm going to give you an all-over massage. I'll use aromatherapy oils to get you in the mood.'

'The mood for what?' I asked stupidly, feeling that I wouldn't need anything to help me except Liz's hands.

She didn't answer but raised her eyebrows instead. 'Go on, get them off.' The slight nod of her head indicated clearly that she was waiting for me to discard my T-shirt and underwear and I knew that refusing out of stubbornness or shyness would be silly. Besides, not knowing when I might get another, I really wanted to indulge in a hot bath.

'You win,' I mumbled as I stretched my arms above my head to reveal an expanse of tanned skin left over from the Spanish summer. I dropped my shirt to the floor and reached to my back to unfasten my bra but Liz had already wrapped her arms around me, our bodies pressed together, and she was fiddling with the catch.

'You're so slim,' she commented. 'Do you ever eat?'

'Like a pig when I get the chance.' But I needn't have replied because she wasn't listening. Liz had deftly removed my boring plain cotton bra and cast it aside before transferring her attention to the little hillocks of flesh that were my breasts.

Just as I had done to her half an hour before, Liz cupped her hands beneath the mounds and weighed up my size in her palms. 'Isn't it odd,' she said, 'how we're all shaped so differently and coloured in with different shades.' I nodded, hardly able to keep my thoughts focused as she pushed my breasts together. 'But we all feel in the same way, don't we?'

I nodded, knowing this was how my touch had felt to her.

'And can you imagine what Lewis would be thinking if he was watching us?'

I nodded again and a smile spread across my face. It was all in their plan, I realised. It was all written.

Liz ducked her head and brought her mouth down around my left breast. The sensation of her soft, wet lips on my skin was like nothing I had ever experienced and even as I stared at the top of her cropped, blonde hair it was hard to believe that it was another woman making me feel like this. I longed for my diary and a chance to record such a fantastic sensation. She looked up at me with heavy-lidded eyes. I felt sure she wanted more than a quick suck of my breast.

'The water,' I said, noticing how high the level had risen in the tub. Liz turned off the taps and then lingered over the withdrawal of my plain white knickers. She delighted in the revelation of the soft triangle of hair at the top of my legs and I secretly willed her to investigate further although I suspected that she would be getting to that.

'Climb in,' she said after swishing her hand in the water to test the temperature. She took a lavender-coloured bottle from a shelf and drizzled in a long stream of something that smelled divine, rather like the fresh herbs in the kitchen garden at Creg-ny-Varn. She swished again to create a thick layer of bubbles.

I lifted a leg over the enamel roll-top edge of the tub and let loose a flicker of a smile as I saw Liz devouring the sight of my parted thighs. She placed a hand on my bottom, perhaps to guide me, perhaps to do as I had done to her in Lewis's office, and allowed her touch to slide up my body as I sat down in the sudsy hot water.

'Mmm, two baths in as many days,' I said, lying back and closing my eyes. The bubbles didn't quite cover the spread of my breasts as I settled in the deep bath and I lifted one leg out of the water to run my hands down its length. 'What luxury,' I said and Liz stroked my forehead with her wet hand. She began to gently massage my temples, dispersing the tension that had been building up over the last few days. Even discussing my apparently futile case so briefly with Lewis had sent tight, aching lines through my head, neck and shoulders.

'I don't think I'll ever get my home back,' I said with my eyes closed, while Liz's fingers worked magic around my eyes. 'I'm just going to have to accept that Kinrade's there to stay and the closest I'm ever going to come to my inheritance is by being its cleaner.'

'Sshh, don't think about that now. I can feel you tensing up.' Liz's voice dropped a couple of tones and even her words helped to soothe me. She walked her fingers down my face and onto my shoulders before stroking around my breasts and I knew, without even looking, that my nipples would be peeking out from beneath the bubbles.

'I'm going to wash you first and then you can come and lie beside the fire and I'll massage you all over. Sound good?'

'Wonderful,' I said, 'but what about you? You must be stressed from all that shopping.' I opened one eye and giggled. 'Did you see how Lewis was looking at you in your new lingerie?'

'Did you see the massive hard-on he had, more like,' Liz replied. 'Like most men, he's a sucker for sexy undies.'

Briefly, I thought of Marco and his simple and basic desire for a naked body. The less clothing the better, in his opinion. And if he was able to ravage his naked lover in the sunshine or beside a lake or, and this was his favourite, with the risk of being caught then he was a happy man. That was why, I supposed, I had never bothered buying lacy knickers or bras or even considered anything as extravagant as Liz's new lilac lingerie.

'Do you have a lot of naughty undies?' I asked, hoping she would have something to fit me. I fancied experimenting.

'Drawers full and it all comes from the little boutique in town. They import it from France.' Liz's hands were resting on my stomach. 'I bet we could find something for you to put on after your bath. She dragged her hands down my tummy, spreading out and avoiding the bit I wanted her to touch most and then down my legs to my ankles. 'You have lovely long legs. I wish mine were this slim.' Liz glanced down at her body, still clothed, and sighed.

'You have a gorgeous figure and like you said earlier, everyone's made differently.'

Liz took my compliment to as a cue to stand up and remove her blouse and short skirt, hanging each item carefully over a chair. Again I was faced with the sight of her in her new corset, thong and sheer stockings but more intriguing than this, way more delectable than the expensive lingerie, was what Lewis had said to me in the beach cottage: that Liz had already decided that I was the one. I was her ultimate fantasy.

'I decided to wear it home. It makes me feel so . . .' – Liz looked at the ceiling for a second – 'so indecent!'

I sat up in the bath so that my face was level with the tiny triangle of sheer lace that disappeared between her pale thighs. How I wanted to lean forward and plant a tiny kiss on the barely visible strip of dark hair that nestled behind her new panties. How I knew I would never dare do such a thing.

Liz took a large natural sponge and added a dose of

rose-scented body wash. She began with my back and lathered up and down my spine, her fingers brushing against the sides of my breasts as her strokes swept under my arms.

'That feels so good. You have no idea what aches and pains I have from sleeping on a bed made from a couple of ancient armchairs.' I dropped my head back and hugged my knees as Liz rubbed my back vigorously. Gradually, she worked her way over my shoulders, down my arms, across my stomach, although very gently, and up and down my legs with brisker strokes again.

'Lie back,' she instructed. 'I can't reach all of you if you sit like that.' She guided me back into the nest of bubbles and discarded the sponge in the water. Then both her hands began to slosh water over my breasts and she fondled them tenderly, making sure she drew my nipples into hard buds once again.

This is fine, I thought. One woman tending to another's needs. It's a feminine thing to do. This is OK, I convinced myself, but I couldn't help the little gulp of air in my throat as a hand slipped between my legs and ever so gently began to knead my inner thighs. I felt her wrist brushing against my mound and she even parted my lips once or twice unintentionally as she reached deep down to give my buttocks a playful squeeze.

'You like that?' she asked as I whimpered again. I nodded, not sure if I wanted her to go further.

Suddenly, our matching fantasies – to be intimate with another woman – seemed a dangerous game to play. True, I had never felt so comfortable being naked in front of a woman before. True, too, that I knew she harboured a desire to experiment specifically with me. What I was worried about was that I would let her down, that I wouldn't be able to satisfy her in the way that Lewis could.

Then the answer to my worries called out from downstairs.

'I'm home.' Lewis approached, every footstep a second nearer to him witnessing his wife with her hands between another woman's legs, and, spurred on by her husband's approach, Liz dared to ease a finger into the groove between the lips of my pussy. With the warm water and Liz's foreign touch, I knew that nothing short of several orgasms would settle the unreal feelings that enveloped me as thoroughly as the water.

The door opened and Lewis was standing, hands in his pockets, peering through the steam and attempting to focus on what was going on. He half smiled, half-frowned when he noticed where Liz's hand was nestled.

'You couldn't wait?' he asked, approaching his wife from behind as she knelt beside the bath. He admired how the lace of her new lingerie decorated her skin and delivered two sensual kisses either side of her neck before peering into the bath. 'You dirty little thing,' he said to me. 'Make sure you get her sparkling clean, Liz. That way it'll take us longer to make her filthy again.'

Lewis and Liz exchanged glances and Liz continued to probe with her slender fingers between my pussy lips. I couldn't prevent my hips from rising and falling in the water, causing her fingertips to rub my bubble-filled cleft. I wasn't sure who I wanted most – Liz and her unfamiliar yet gentle way with my body or Lewis, who I knew was capable of filling me up and levering me to an incredible orgasm. As I bathed in the bubbles and the sensations from Liz's fingers, I decided that both of them would be nice.

'How exactly do you propose to make me dirty?' I asked them.

'Shouldn't be too hard,' Lewis commented while playing with Liz's short hair. 'I think you're a natural when it comes to being grubby. What about your behaviour the other evening, for instance? Liz, I'll have you know that it was all Ailey's fault that I came home to you spent and satisfied.'

Liz turned and looked up at Lewis, winking at the same time as running a finger neatly between my lips, prising them apart in the water. I arched my back at the fragility of her touch. No man had ever dealt with me this lightly.

'Little hussy,' she directed at me. 'Messing about with my husband, huh?' I nodded shamefully, going along with their game. 'I had to work extra hard to get him aroused all over again. I was so desperate for him to come home and when he did, he smelled of you.'

'Liz already knows what you taste like,' Lewis added. He clamped his arms around his wife's body and burrowed two fingers beneath her flimsy thong, searching for something warm and moist. I could see the needy tremble in his arms as he worked, the same urgency mirroring in his face as the prospect of having two women to deal with dawned on him. Lewis's fingers never did find the treat they were seeking because Liz pulled away and fetched a towel off the heated rail.

'Time to get dry.' She held out the soft towel and gestured for me to stand up. Lewis looked out of place in his work trousers and shirt and would no doubt have willingly shed his clothes but stood motionless, gawping at the sight of his sexily dressed wife attending to my needs. He was silent as Liz helped me from the bath, the bubbles sliding from my clean skin, and remained that way as she dabbed and patted me to remove the excess moisture. She didn't, however, attempt to dry my breasts or between my legs and I shivered as the air cooled my wet skin.

'Lewis, you see that the fire is stoked so that Ailey doesn't catch her death while I dress her up into a little treat.'

The implication was, as far as I could discern, that I would become a kind of edible fancy for the adventurous couple. That they were older, more experienced and obviously far more daring than me made me suspect that even if I had not been a willing party, I would have found it nearly impossible to prise myself from their tempting lair. I was their prey. I was excited. I followed Liz into her bedroom and watched as she pulled item after item of exotic lingerie from a drawer.

'Ah, here they are.' Liz carefully placed a tiny pair of scarlet panties on the bed and then began to sift through her wardrobe. 'And this will get his blood pressure soaring.' A flimsy red and black garment slid off the hanger and joined the matching panties while Liz grinned at me. The towel was draped loosely around my body and apart from that I wore nothing but a widening smile and a bemused expression that hadn't really left my face since the day I arrived on the island.

'Is that our aim?'

'He's going to need a paramedic by the time we're done.'

'Done?'

'Put these on,' Liz instructed, answering my question with an exaggerated pout. 'And get yourself in the mood.'

I didn't intend to argue with her. While my conscience wasn't entirely clear – I still had Connor rattling in my mind – I instinctively knew that in a couple of hours I would be feeling as delicious and outrageous as I had when I'd bound and spanked Dominic. If only I could convince myself that none of it was my fault, that my stolen thoughts were responsible for my irrational behaviour, then I would feel a whole lot better about slipping into the garments that lay on the bed.

I stared at the sheer red fabric. I felt certain that Connor would be poring over my diary with Steph nestled beside him. The thought made me even more determined to play Liz and Lewis's games although I couldn't help wondering what Connor would think of me if he discovered what I'd been up to. An ache gripped the pit of my belly, a needy, desperate ache that would exist as long as Connor wasn't mine. I hoped he would be jealous as hell.

'Oh, Connor,' I said out loud, my imagination noisily crossing the boundary into reality. But I quickly realised that messing about with Liz and Lewis had no bearing on whether Connor was attracted to me. It was thankful distraction, especially as he was most likely spilling himself into Steph at that very moment, while I was considering how I'd look in Liz's little red baby doll number. 'I love it,' I said, hoping she hadn't heard what I'd said before. I forced and jammed and kicked Connor out of my mind. I couldn't quite close the door, though.

I stood in front of the full-length mirror, balancing on my toes. Liz had said that ideally I should be wearing high heels, but hers were a little too small for me. While she sought out some make-up, I admired my new appearance. It felt strange wearing someone else's panties but I enjoyed the feeling of the thin strap running between my legs and couldn't help admiring the way the band of lace pulled up high on my hips, emphasising the length of my legs. I didn't think I needed heels at all.

'Lewis bought that for me last birthday. He'd love to see you in it.' Liz approached me with a scarlet lipstick and carefully streaked it on my lips. I'd never worn such a vibrant colour and if I hadn't been adorned in the naughty lingerie I would have felt ridiculous. As it was, I was beginning to realise why men loved all this stuff so much.

'Let me fix your hair.' Liz had to stand on tiptoe herself as she swept a brush through my long hair. The bathroom steam had added waves and gloss and the darkness of it against my pale face and scarlet lips made me feel as if I'd been touched by the devil.

Suddenly, greedily, I wanted Liz all for myself.

'Let your hair fall forward, like this. It looks really sexy.' She pressed against me, the fullness of her breasts melding around my back, her voice slow and winding like smoke curling from a winter bonfire.

'Do you think so?' I played with my hair but found myself turning away from the mirror and facing Liz. 'Do you think I'm attractive?'

'Lewis will adore –'

'Do *you* think I'm attractive, I said.' For some reason, my eyelids felt heavy and my cheeks flushed strawberry as I realised how provocative I was being. The new, impulsive me, when faced with the thrill and danger of Dominic at Creg-ny-Varn, had acted impetuously and without a care for the consequences. Now, more practised in the art of spontaneous seduction, I quickly plotted and considered how I could charm Liz and keep her all to myself. One thing was certain: I wanted to make love to her more than anything. Even more than Lewis had told me she wanted me.

'You are as beautiful as the sea,' she said, smiling, her rich voice again filled with experience and poise. She dabbed beneath my lip, wiping away smeared lipstick. 'And in that naughty little get-up, you're irresistible.'

I glanced down at my body. My breasts just showed through the gossamer weight of the scarlet fabric, appearing larger for some reason, while my still damp stomach was exposed through the deep slit up the front, allowing a clear view of the tiny panties I was wearing. I'd never felt so sexy.

'Touch me, if I'm irresistible.' To indicate where I'd like Liz to touch me, I lifted up the fine net so that it shrouded my face like a veil. I closed my eyes. For a moment, I felt nothing and imagined that Liz was staring at me blankly, her open mouth a sign of her shock, truly believing that I was shameless. If only she knew how far from the truth that was. I was simply tumbling through an adventure, initially fuelled by my lost inheritance but now powered by far more potent emotions.

Her open mouth came down upon the tanned skin of my belly, just below my navel, sketching a wet line down to the top of the tiny knickers. I drew in a breath and held it for safekeeping, capturing the loveliness of the moment for ever. Liz moved slowly, pressing her tongue into my skin as she dropped lower so that finally her lips and teeth nipped at the rim of lace decorating the thong she had dressed me in. My breath escaped in an encouraging whimper.

'Get on the bed,' I heard someone say and then, as Liz went to lie on the quilt, I realised it must have been me. I touched where her mouth had been and then followed her to the bed. She looked stunning in her expensive French lingerie with her breasts vying for space beneath the lace and her misty eyes drawing me closer. She lay on her back, her fingers resting on the teasing expanse of naked skin between her corset and knickers, and I couldn't help folding myself around her legs and letting my mouth do what she had just done to me.

But unlike me, who had let out a breathy gasp in a vain attempt to hide the desire I harboured for another woman, Liz quickly began to pant and moan in response to my kisses and licks. She rocked her hips as I peeled aside the fresh lacy triangle at the top of her legs to reveal a neat patch of blonde hair that dissolved into her creamy skin.

I gazed at her, my eyes dizzy from the sight and my mind woozy from her scent. The very core of another woman was inches from my face and I don't know how long it took me to lower my mouth to the dainty pout that she offered up, or even how I separated her soft lips with my tongue. But I do remember the first taste of her juice as clearly as my first sip of an exotic cocktail. Liz was blended to perfection with just the right amount of musk to send a tremble of need down my spine and plenty of sweetness to make me salivate for more. As my tongue flicked through the delicate groove of her pussy, I realised why men desired women so much.

I thought of Marco and his rough search of my body every time he took me in the heat of the day; I recalled how Dominic had slipped his fingers inside me as he told of Ethan Kinrade's loneliness, their presence an indication of his boss's need. I recalled, too, Liz's own husband as he had taken me so suddenly in the beach cottage and realised that if this was what a man experienced each time he explored a woman, then it was a wonder our bodies weren't constantly being looted.

I removed Liz's panties completely, allowing her to spread her legs wide and offer a total view of her pussy. Lying beside her, as her fingers brushed tenderly through my hair, I began to take small, interested laps from the tip of her mound down to the gentle spread of her bottom as it melded into the quilt. Never before had I seen another woman at this close range. I was fascinated and driven wild by the possibilities. At that moment, I didn't want Lewis to spoil our fun and I didn't even want Connor or Dominic or Kinrade to invade my head with the complications that each of them presented. I just wanted to devour Liz — although she had other ideas, which included her being allowed a fair share of me. After all, it was her fantasy in the first place that drew us together and as I lay amongst the pillows, with Liz taking her turn on my body, prising open every possible place with her fingers and tongue and driven forward by my little moans of delight, as all this was happening to me, I became more determined than ever to fulfil the mission that I had set out to achieve.

The orgasm that unexpectedly crashed through me, with the power of the insistent breakers on the beach, sealed my resolve not to give up. But first, before I committed to my final assault on Kinrade, I wanted to make Liz feel as delicious as I did.

8

When Steph arrived at the beach cottage, she was all fizzed up and excited. Having met her only a couple of times previously, I should have found it difficult to tell if her behaviour was typical, but such was the force with which she bounded across the rocks and such was her agitation, in a positive way, that her enthusiasm was unmistakable.

'It's going to be just like Cinderella's ball,' she squealed, catching her ankle on a sharp rock but ignoring the pain. There was no 'hello', no explanation for her behaviour two days ago at Connor's place when she brazenly informed me that she had stolen my diary. I glanced at her hands to see if she was returning it but I didn't make out that she was carrying anything. Steph approached me, as I was collecting mussels from the rocks, as if she had known me all her life. I stood and stretched, my back a little sore from the harvest and also from the contortions Liz and I had performed yesterday. I gave a little smile at the thought.

'Hi,' I said. 'Did Connor tell you where I was staying?'

Steph nodded, her almost white-blonde hair frothing in the sunlight. The day was blessed with a hint of warmth from the winter sun. 'How do you manage down here?' Her zeal was temporarily halted as she raised her hand to her brow and squinted at the low, weathered walls of my cottage, her mouth curling into an expression of what I believed to be distaste.

'Just fine,' I replied. 'Apart from having to lug fresh water down here daily, I get by very well.' I knew what she was thinking as she glanced at my thoroughly wrapped-up body that showed no shape whatsoever beneath the six or so layers I had put on earlier. 'If I keep the fire going, I stay toasty warm and the shop is within walking distance.'

'Are you going to invite me in, then?' Steph exuded impertinence, especially from the smile that had hardly left her face since she came bounding across the beach.

'Of course,' I said and gathered up the mussels in one of my mother's old tablecloths. 'Come and have tea.' I was hoping that she might be tempted to deliver my diary and also give away details about her relationship with Connor. It still bothered me immensely.

Once she had finished poking about the cottage, which she evidently saw as a cute plaything rather than my home, she settled in an armchair and watched while I made tea.

'Do you have it, then?' It was my diary after all. 'My pocket book,' I added when she appeared perplexed.

'Yes, yes, I'll get to that. I want to know what you think about the Christmas party up at the big house.'

'Creg-ny-Varn?' I said stupidly. 'Connor has asked me to go with him but I'm not sure if I will.' I waited for the change in her expression, watched for the downturn of her pretty almond-shaped eyes and the barely-there lines of a frown when she realised that Connor had asked me to the ball rather than her. It was obviously a token gesture on Connor's part but unfortunately the only ammunition I had.

Steph continued to grin. 'Aw, you must go. He'd be devastated if you didn't. It must be just about the most exciting thing to happen on the island in a long time and I can't say that I've ever been to a masked ball at such a fine country mansion.'

'Devastated?'

'I doubt if he'd go alone. Connor's not big on socialising. If you don't go with him, I will.'

I swallowed. 'A masked ball, did you say?' There were simply too many things to take in at once. My life in Spain was uncomplicated, quite unlike the emotional rush that had swamped me since my arrival on the island, and now all of a sudden I was facing new relationships, however serious or permanent, legal battles and a desire for someone I hadn't seen for fourteen years.

'Such a fun idea, don't you think? Apparently Mr Kinrade himself thought it up, but I've never met him so I have no idea what it will be like.' Steph's excitement was incessant. 'And I have nothing to wear.'

'That sounds fitting,' I said, not really to Steph but more to myself as I mulled over the implications.

'Huh?'

'The secrecy, the elusiveness. Sounds like Kinrade, all right.' I handed Steph her tea and she didn't even notice that it wasn't exactly boiling and that the milk was in short supply. 'Biscuit?' I offered her a packet of chocolate digestives and she took several.

Why I was being civil to the girl, I didn't know, although her enthusiasm was infectious and rapidly attaching itself to me. I began to experience symptoms of anticipation like hers. Going to Kinrade's ball with Connor – for I saw no other way to gain access to what I presumed would be a strictly controlled event and it would at least prevent Steph from being his date – would be my initial and perhaps only chance of contact with Ethan Kinrade. How I would react to his presence, I didn't know. It could go to either extreme: I could fall mute and be so intimidated by his presence that I wouldn't utter a word of protest or, and I suspected that with the build-up of anger inside me this was the more likely, I would hammer my thoughts into the man and demand that my case be heard. Either way, worrying about what to wear to the event was far from my mind.

'There's a shop in town that specialises in ball gowns and cocktail dresses and has some wild fancy dress outfits.' Steph was unstoppable. 'You are the only other woman I know on this entire island and I absolutely *demand* that you come with me to help me choose a costume.'

'Sure,' I said absentmindedly, unaware of what I had let myself in for. My head was a soup of thoughts and for the first time I actually realised that I was soon to come face to face with Ethan Kinrade. 'I would love to help you choose a costume. I'll need one myself.' And I grinned almost as brightly as Steph.

It was nearly an hour later when Steph finally ran out of things to say about the party. Her desire to meet the elusive Kinrade was almost as great as mine, although for strictly different reasons. Steph, it seemed, was on the lookout for any wealthy, good-looking bachelor going and Kinrade fitted her criteria almost perfectly. I felt a pang of jealousy on Connor's behalf. The woman was obviously brazen and had no morals. I was sure Connor, on the other hand, would be a loyal partner. I wondered whether to tell him about Steph's interest in other men but decided that Connor was big enough to make up his own mind. It did, however, give me some hope that Connor and Steph might not be the inseparable couple I had first thought.

'I'm destined to be an old maid,' she said and then confessed to being only twenty-three. What she really meant was that she hadn't had good, sorry, *great* sex since her Parisian escapade. Steph was in love with the idea of seducing a powerful man in possession of a large fortune and currently saw herself as Lady of the Manor, even though Kinrade might look like one of the limpets clinging to the rocks outside my cottage. 'If I don't get it soon, I'm going to have to hire an escort.'

I breathed a sigh of relief. Did that mean she hadn't slept with Connor yet? I was by then thoroughly used to Steph's frankness and laughed at the thought of her being escorted by a paid-for stranger, most likely to the nearest bed.

'So you've been staying with Connor for a week now.' I was thinking out loud, trying to work out the probability of them having had sex based on the number of nights they'd been together.

'Yes,' she replied casually. 'He's such good company.'

All I did was nod slowly and bite my bottom lip. My gaze ended up focused on the shore and I watched the frothy breakers tease the black rocks. I would just have to be honest with her, hoping she would reciprocate.

'And, you haven't ... you know, got a thing for him?'

'Me and Connor?' she asked incredulously. 'Nah.' Her reply was quiet and unconvincing, as if she was holding something back. The short flicks of her hair as she shook her head didn't persuade me. In fact, the very way that she purported to be uninterested in Connor told me she was madly in love and besotted with the man. 'You like him, too?' she added.

Too? I was right.

I shrugged. 'We go way back. We've known each other since we were kids.' I hoped that would seal my claim on the man we both desired.

'Yeah, so have we.'

I had to put this out of my mind, at least until I had confronted Ethan Kinrade. Connor and Steph would have to wait until after the party.

'My diary,' I said, attacking the other pressing matter. 'You have it?'

'That's the thing,' Steph said, giving me that mischievous look again.

'The thing?'

'I thought I'd slipped it in my jacket pocket before I left but...' She raised her arms and dropped them to her sides before slurping her tea. 'Sorry. It must still be back at Connor's house.' A little pout gathered her lips and she gave a tiny shrug of her shoulders, which caused some tea to spill on her fingers, and then she was yelping because she'd burnt herself and I was finding a cloth to mop her and so it was a little while before we were talking about my diary again.

I sighed, not quite sure where to begin. I wanted my diary back, possibly almost as much as I wanted Connor and Creg-ny-Varn, but I had to handle the volatile Steph carefully. Even though I didn't know her very well, I'd already deduced that she was a wild card. Besides, I was missing my evening ritual of writing up my fantasies and, for the first time in my life, there had been *real* events to record. It didn't seem fair.

'It's very personal, Steph, and I'm pretty angry that you stole it from my pack.'

'It just kind of slipped out.' The way she hung her head and her eyes closed momentarily convinced me that it hadn't slipped out at all.

'I definitely recall wedging my diary deep inside my bag. You stole it.'

'Well, you'd been writing about me.' She stood and paced about the small room. 'I'd every intention of handing it in to the ferry company when I'd read it. I guessed that you'd call their lost property number. I just haven't got around to it yet.'

'Has Connor read it?' Aside from getting it back, that was a major concern.

'Maybe. Not sure.' She shrugged and squinted out of the window as the low sun caused spangles to bob on the waves.

'Well, we're going to get it back. Now!' I stood and retrieved my jacket and stoked the fire so it would still be burning when I returned. I was determined to have a night of comfort and warmth and smiled inwardly at the thought of playing catch-up with my journal. I'd already bought supplies from the shop and had treated myself to a bottle of Glen Broath. Drinking something Connor had produced made me feel a little nearer to him.

'Couldn't we go via the fancy dress shop to get our outfits? They're bound to be in short supply as virtually the whole island's going to the ball. Do you really want to go looking like that?' She gestured at my jeans and walking boots. Steph had a point. 'Please? And then you can have your diary back. Promise.'

I glanced at my watch. If we didn't go soon, the shop would be closed. If I didn't get an outfit, I couldn't go to the ball. If I didn't go to the ball, I wouldn't be able to confront Kinrade in the totally demeaning way I had planned and Connor would probably take Steph as his partner instead.

'You have a car?'

'No, but I can borrow the Land Rover. It's up at the

distillery.' Steph began bouncing around the cottage, animated at the prospect of choosing a costume.

We'd virtually run up to Glen Broath, our excitement showing as shots of hot breath in the still winter air. Steph had briefly asked Connor for the keys to the Land Rover and he agreed, insisting we return by six as he had some errands to run. Steph drove to Douglas as if we were about to miss a flight and all the while she was muttering about masks and bodices and what colour suited her best. I didn't care what I wore as long as it got me into the party.

The tiny boutique, which smelled of lavender and mothballs, was stuffed with an overabundance of gowns and ludicrous costumes ranging from court jesters to dominatrix gear. Steph was drawn to the traditional, Cinderella-type gowns and pulled several off the rail.

'What do you think?' She held up a scarlet dress that puffed out from its tiny waist in an explosion of voile and crumpled silk and another jade gown with a slim-fitting design.

'Beautiful,' I agreed. 'But they both look a bit too big for you.' Steph was a size eight at most.

'I mean for you, dummy.' She pressed the dresses against me so that I had to take them and then she began rummaging in a rail of what looked like vintage gowns. Something had caught her eye as she began panting and stuttering at what she had found. The shop assistant watched.

'Heavens, he'll adore it.' Steph was breathless as she held up the gown.

'Who will?' I asked perplexed.

She didn't answer. 'You must try this on.'

I didn't need much convincing. While the ball was a nerve-racking necessity, it was also a chance to see Connor under conditions that might at least procure a dance or some intimate conversation. I wanted to look my best, especially when I confronted Ethan Kinrade, which I planned on doing in an entirely public display of revenge.

I stepped out of the changing cubicle with my cheeks flushed and my small breasts heaved to new heights by the boning in the bodice. Both Steph and the shop assistant were speechless. I turned and stared into the mirror, thinking that someone had stepped in front of me because I simply didn't recognise the reflection. My entire body was encased in swathes of faded toffee-coloured lace, while ruffles of scrunched net skimmed my shoulders in a provocative but not overstated way. The cream bodice clung to my ribs so that I hardly dared breathe in, every little hook beneath the magnificent trim of leaves and snowdrops tying me into this masterpiece.

'Nice,' I said, knowing that was not the way to describe such a unique gown but lost for any other word. 'Is it expensive?' The skirts tumbled and swished around my legs as I turned to the shop assistant. As she was checking the price, Steph spotted a cream feather mask and handed it to me to try.

'Fabulous! If you don't wear this dress, I'll –'

'One hundred and seventy five pounds. But I'll include some shoes and the mask.' The shop assistant snapped her price book closed.

'I only wanted to hire a dress, not buy one.' I shrugged at Steph.

'That *is* the price to hire the gown. If madam would prefer something from the budget rail...' The woman gestured to the other side of the boutique before glancing at my muddy walking boots that peeped from beneath the gown.

'We'll take it,' Steph interjected, pulling her purse from her pocket. 'You go and change again, Ailey, while I find something for myself.' It wouldn't be until the night of the ball that I would discover Steph had picked out the most beautiful shimmering tiara for me to wear in my hair as well as a pair of impossibly high-heeled shoes.

'I had no idea, really.' Connor held my diary by his side, his strong fingers wrapped around the leather cover as if he would never let go of it. His expression was serious, the complete opposite of the frivolities contained within my journal. Was I to believe him? Sensing the tension between us, Steph had left the office muttering some reason why she needed to return to Connor's cottage.

'Then why is it in your desk drawer?' I stood my ground, my feet planted wide and my gloved hands thrust deep into the pockets of my jacket. Connor didn't reply. He sighed heavily and predictably poured two shots of Glen Broath. 'I thought you were driving?'

'My errands can wait.' Connor perched on the corner of his desk and eyed me almost dolefully but also with a deep, serious appraisal, as someone might look at a thoroughbred horse they were thinking of buying.

'I'm sorry. I just don't believe you.' I turned and walked to the far side of Connor's office. I trailed my finger over his bookshelves, which were stacked with whisky-related volumes and numerous trophies he'd won for his finest malts.

When I turned, Connor had my journal in front of him and his thumbs between the pages, as if he was about to open it. It felt as if he was holding a gun to my head.

'It's personal,' I said, trying to hold my voice level. 'Steph had no right to take it and you certainly have no right to read it either.' At that moment, I wished I'd never written the damn thing. I should have known better. I should have realised that such provocative writings, in the wrong hands, could change my life. *Had* changed my life.

'What you said a few days ago at the beach cottage, about my thoughts becoming reality.' I paused, giving him time to remember. 'It's true. Things that I've wondered about for years are beginning to happen, like I'm a simmering pan and my lid has finally been lifted.' I was deliberately vague. How could I tell Connor, the man I wanted to impress most in the entire world, that I had indulged in kinky shenanigans with my nearest neighbours? Would telling Connor about my involvement with Dominic deter him from ever loving me? It was a risk I couldn't take, even though I had jeopardised my future by muddling my life with these sexy risks. It wasn't like me at all.

'Then do you really want your diary back?' Connor's large hands, laced with precise veins and tipped with clean, trimmed nails, gripped my diary and held it in front of his chest like a prayer book.

He had a point. Did I want to continue simply writing down all my hopes and desires for the rest of my life or would I rather live my dreams? I took a long, warming sip of whisky and stared at the ceiling. A layer of tears skimmed my eyes and I begged for it not to burst free.

'Have you read it?' This time my voice definitely betrayed my emotion.

'I told you. I didn't even realise it was in my desk

drawer. Steph must have put it there.' Connor exhaled and shook his head. 'You'd think she was at school still, the pranks that girl plays.'

I could imagine. Connor, Steph, pranks – and my diary fuelling their naughty games.

I was strangely convinced by the depth of honesty in his eyes, the way he approached me and placed a hand on my arm and then brushed his fingers against my cheek. If Connor had read my diary, he would know that I'd never forgotten about him, that I'd wondered what kind of man he'd grown into.

'It's up to you,' he said. 'But expect your life to change again if you keep your thoughts to yourself. Symbolically, you've already let go.'

'Connor The Shrink.' I laughed and wiped away a stray tear as it fought for release. I would never know if he was telling the truth, if he really hadn't read my secrets. A part of me hoped that he had at least taken a peek at the bits that included him, the anticipation I had written about as I returned to the island. Perhaps that was why he leant forward and placed a kiss on my cheek.

'Things are hotting up at Creg-ny-Varn.' Connor gestured towards the house. 'Caterers, florists and musicians have been coming and going all day.'

'Any sign of Kinrade?' I still wasn't sure that he was even on the island let alone capable of organising such an event.

Connor shook his head. 'I've told you. The man keeps himself to himself. It's a wonder that he's hosting this party. I expect he's trying to ease himself into the island's social scene.'

'What about his mother? Will she be attending?' I had a sudden urge to talk with the woman who was most likely the last person to see my father alive. That somehow made her special to me, even though she and her son had robbed me of what was mine.

'I expect so, although she doesn't live here any more. Ethan manages the estate himself.' Connor sounded sympathetic, which made me pull away from his touch.

'Such a burden,' I remarked sourly. 'Several million pounds worth of property. How does he cope?' The Kinrades would get little sympathy from me. 'Anyway, I shall find out more tomorrow when I go to work. I expect I'll get caught up in the bustle of preparations.' Connor appeared bemused and I knew what he was thinking. 'It's not like I *want* to be a cleaner,' I added. 'Don't you understand?' He had completely the wrong idea.

'Ailey, my love, I don't think I've ever understood you.'

And he approached me again, as if our differences had been bridged by the very fact that we were dissimilar, and delivered another kiss, although this time I closed my eyes and parted my lips because I knew it was aimed at my mouth. It never quite happened.

'Ted's got big problems!' A draught of cold air wrapped around our ankles as Steph lunged into the office. 'One of the machines is, well, broken.' She shrugged but froze with her shoulders up around her ears as she realised what she had interrupted. 'Oh God,' she cried and ran out of the office with her hands over her face.

'Great,' Connor said and ran to the door. 'Steph!' But she was gone and nothing Connor could say would erase the brief swipe of his lips against mine that she had witnessed. 'I'll have to see what's up with Ted. We were having problems with pressure in one of the tanks earlier. Coming?' He replaced my diary in his desk drawer and left his office a troubled man, one incomplete kiss having produced immeasurable problems.

I nodded and followed Connor into the depths of the Glen Broath distillery, which was pungent with the special smells and the mystery it had held for me as a child. I was filled with admiration for Connor as I realised what a vast responsibility the business was for him. We found Ted crouched beside a series of copper pipes and gauges.

'I'm not sure the cut didn't come too late, Mr McBryde, or possibly there's something wrong with the hydrometer.' Ted, a weathered but healthy-looking man in his sixties, straightened up and stared at me. 'You leave it with me, sir, and I'll get it sorted.' He grinned, displaying a row of crooked teeth. 'I told that young Stephanie not to bother you but she seemed determined you'd want to know.'

'I trust you entirely, Ted, and you're right. There was no need for me to come.' Connor turned to me and spoke as if he barely knew me, let alone had just tried to kiss me. 'I'd better find Steph. Let's go.'

When the girl couldn't be located, Connor insisted on driving me back to the cliff top, but instead of offering to escort me across the dangerous beach, he supplied me with a torch and a pleasant but brief 'goodnight'.

'I guess I'll see you tomorrow then, at the party.'

'OK,' he replied casually, dipping his headlights as another car passed. 'See you tomorrow about eight.'

And that was that. The tail lights of Connor's Land Rover disappeared into the thick sea fog that was blanketing the coast. The locals referred to such mists as *Manannan's Cloak*, when the island's ancient sea god swathed the shores in fog to protect the land from unwanted visitors. What it was doing now was preventing me from watching the last glimmers of Connor as he drove home to Steph, as well as making my passage to the beach cottage even more treacherous than usual. To make matters worse, tears cut hot grooves down my cold cheeks.

As I stumbled down the track to the shore and made my way across the precarious rocks by torchlight, I thought about tomorrow night. In a little over twenty-four hours, I would have asserted my claim on Creg-ny-Varn and made public just what a scoundrel Ethan Kinrade was, in front of the very people he wished to impress. I would look stunning, I promised myself as I hurled my body against the jammed front door of the cottage, in my hired gown that was safely stored in Steph's room at Connor's house, although I wondered now if she might cut it to shreds. The arrangement had been for me to pick it up after I had finished work in the morning, but preparing myself for such a social event without running water worried me somewhat, not to mention the trek across the beach in my multi-layered skirt. I daren't think of the cost if I damaged the dress.

I bundled myself into bed, although not without a glimpse through the binoculars at Liz and Lewis's cottage, and retired, disappointed, with another large dose of Glen Broath to help me sleep.

I dreamed of Connor and gowns and feathered masks and the sea mist and whips and handcuffs and woke to a screeching seagull and the brush of Connor's faint kiss still on my lips.

'Over there!' Dominic barked at several young men who were wheeling stacks of velvet upholstered chairs through the echoing hallway of Creg-ny-Varn. 'Do you need instructions too?' He turned to me, his harassed face descending into a shade of deep burgundy.

Until he snapped at me, I was beginning to feel sorry for him. Kinrade had evidently left most of the ball preparations up to him, which was asking rather a lot of a gardener.

'No, I don't. I shall clean the Grand Hall until it's sparkling. Is Mr Kinrade here?' It wasn't that I wanted to see him yet, I was just curious.

Dominic halted midway through firing instructions at the florists, his pupils dilating and his breath quickening. 'Yes, he is here but he's not available until later.' The stammer was barely noticeable.

'I can wait.' And we exchanged glances that meant something more than I could put into words. Perhaps it was because we both remembered our last meeting.

'Is Mr Kinrade's bedroom still ship-shape?' I asked, alluding to our encounter. I felt like Steph with my cheeky grin and confrontational tone.

'Of course,' he snapped. 'The man's not been home so how could it need cleaning so soon?'

'Speak to me like that again and I'll see to it that you don't sit down for a week.' I flicked Dominic's shoulder, buried somewhere beneath his dark green jacket, with my feather duster – the only implement I had for immediate punishment – and gave him a look that suggested if he was at a loose end...

'I'll hold you to that,' he said and strode off down the tiled floor to admonish someone who, judging by Dominic's roar, was doing something very wrong.

The Grand Hall had been used regularly when I was a child. Virtually every month, my parents would treat the island's social set to an evening of gourmet food and entertainment. I remember my mother assigning a theme to every event and the meticulousness with which she chose the menu was verging on obsessive. The spring dining table would be laden with young minted lamb and tender new vegetables from our own garden and the Grand Hall would be decorated with spring flowers. Everyone was told to wear a certain coloured outfit, perhaps yellow or forget-me-not blue. Autumn was my favourite and I still recall the smell of roast pheasant and chestnuts with candied orange and baked plum pie waiting in the kitchen. Many times I had sneaked downstairs and spied on the dozens of adults in their garish costumes and listened to grown-up talk that I didn't understand. I would virtually jump out of my skin at the shockwaves of laughter that exploded from the party, usually led by my father when he'd drunk too much Glen Broath. Wild games and dancing would follow the meal and often I would wake in the early hours and the frivolities would still be in full swing.

Then there was the time, mid-winter, with the Grand Hall decked for Christmas and the food at its most sumptuous, when I woke to the shrieks of my mother. The house, eerily silent apart from her wails, had been cleared of guests and no one knew that I crouched in the gallery and watched as my mother, dressed only in her underwear, sobbed her life away.

Words that meant nothing to me then – big, venomous words, full of pain – floated around my head that cold, empty night. My mother and I left the island the next day. The memory of my home slipping into dots of light on the horizon, coupled with my mother's shame and anger, manifested in many ways but never directed at me, marked a turning point in my life.

Everything familiar was gone. Everything new was an adventure ripe for exploration. And I recorded it all in my secret diary.

The Grand Hall, many years on from those outrageous parties, had taken on a strangely familiar air. When I had searched around the house several days earlier during my first cleaning morning at Creg-ny-Varn, I had discovered nothing untoward in the vast room; no incriminating evidence to support my claim against Kinrade. It remained a cold, lifeless, shrouded space with much of the ornate antique furniture stacked and covered with dust sheets. But on the day of the ball, with caterers and florists and technicians and porters coming and going, the room was gradually beginning to wake and warm and prepare itself for another major event. Only when I saw the size of the buffet table and the vast number of wine glasses that were being polished and set out did I realise the scale of the party. Kinrade was certainly sparing no expense and by the end of the morning, with a little magic from my polish and duster as well as the dozens of professionals who scurried tirelessly to finish their work, the Grand Hall was beginning to resemble the final scene from Cinderella. I looked down at my grubby clothes and laughed.

Then came the hand on my shoulder.

'I've done a terrible thing.' Dominic appeared grey, like a ghost from the past, which quite suited the old-fashioned stately look of the room. I didn't say a word, trusting him to come out with it himself. 'If I was a Catholic, I would seek out a priest right away.'

'But?' I urged, sensing this could take a while.

'There is no one I can admit my crime to.'

I hadn't got a clue what he was talking about and guessed that, being rather fed up with the party preparations, Dominic was nudging me for a few naughty games. Beneath the doleful expression, I spotted a spark of mischief.

'If it's that bad, then you'll most likely need severe punishment.'

A little colour returned to his cheeks, accenting the several days of stubble growth that roughened his skin. For the first time I noticed how the colour of his eyes was graduated in deepening tones of brown, almost black. Surely no one could possess such intense eyes without bearing the burden of an equivalent secret? I shuddered and shook such serious thoughts from my head.

'You'd better come with me.' In case he protested and in case I changed my mind because of flashes of Connor and what might have been, I gripped Dominic by the arm – his strong, hard-working arm – and dragged him to the door of the library. The door that was always locked.

'Got a key?' I knew he would have.

'I'm not sure that –'

'I've already seen what Kinrade has done to my father's library. Is he likely to disturb us?' That feeling again, spreading through me as surely as the fingers of sunlight grip the horizon on a clear day.

'He ... he's out. He won't be back for a while.' Then the stammer again, this time accompanied by an eruption of perspiration on his top lip, which would mean nothing to me until much, much later.

'What are you waiting for then? Open the door.'

Dominic grappled with a number of keys until he found the correct one. He slowly pushed open the door to reveal the room that I had seen several days before, only this time my view was from another angle and I saw even more of Ethan Kinrade's kinky handiwork.

'Who *is* this man?' I muttered inaudibly. I stepped across the wooden floorboards, which creaked underfoot, and trailed a hand over the swathes of black and scarlet satin lining the walls. I presumed the bookshelves were still concealed behind the drapes and paraphernalia. 'I don't know what half this stuff's for. Do you?' I turned to Dominic, who didn't seem able to answer my question. I took his silence to indicate compliance and he didn't even protest when I plucked the keys from his hand and sealed us in what can only be described as a bondage parlour.

It didn't matter to me any more that I felt this way. The sizzling and searing inside me that accompanied the strange situations I had found myself in since returning to the island were beginning to feel normal. In fact, I was thoroughly enjoying the thrill of experimenting with Dominic's need for submission and Liz and Lewis's desire to share. And in a small, heart-rending way, it helped to overcome the realisation that all was lost between Connor and me. Any possibility of a life together had dissolved the day I left the island fourteen years ago. It was fate. Heavy-handed fate. I had to accept that the past could not be reclaimed, if indeed we were ever on the path of true love in the first place.

'Strip.'

Dominic hesitated, as if he expected me to say something completely different. Exactly what, I don't know. With our silent track record and our current surroundings, it was impossible to believe I would have said anything else. But that hesitation, his relieved expression...

Naked in the garishly decorated room, Dominic looked desolate. I was reminded of a winter tree alone in the hedgerow, the stiff boughs of his limbs completely leafless and the trunk of his body fixed firmly in the ground.

'On you get,' I ordered and gleefully watched Dominic's buttocks separating slightly as he folded his naked body around the hard surface of what looked like a higher than usual hall table. The difference was that tan leather straps hung from five different places on the wooden frame and these, I supposed, were for me to secure him with. 'Breathe in,' I said and tightened the first and largest band around his middle. The stiff leather nipped at the skin of his back and cut a firm line across his girth. I saw the striations of tensed muscle, developed from years of hard physical work, struggle against the restraint, and, as I shackled his wrists and thighs to the spanking frame's sturdy legs, Dominic let out pitiful whimpers. It was a perfect display of weakening strength.

'Perhaps this will teach you not to do bad things.' The truth was, I didn't care what he'd done. If he'd broken a glass, then I was happy to watch as his buttocks flushed from the sting of a tawse slapping across his unmarked flesh. I selected a suitable instrument from half a dozen that hung from a rack positioned conveniently near the spanking frame. Kinrade had designed the layout of the room very carefully, ensuring that everything was in easy reach. It gave me another insight into the workings of his mind: the mind that I would be challenging in only a few hours.

'Maybe this will help you remember exactly what it is that you've done.' I raised my arm and delivered a small, sweet whip to his skin with a black riding crop. Quite suitable, I thought, for a man of the country.

Dominic inhaled sharply but didn't make a sound.

His buttocks clenched in readiness for another swat. This time it was harder and the crop left a pale pink line on his skin.

'Am I jogging your memory?'

Dominic shook his head at which I stung him again and again with the tip of the leather crop until I could see the dark outline of his balls quivering between his legs. Unable to resist, I drew the crop up between his legs, brushed it across the soft skin of his sac and watched in delight as he strained against the strapping around his wrists and thighs. He moaned loudly and turned his head to the side.

'Is it coming back?'

'Oh yes,' he admitted. 'But I'm too ashamed to confess. Punish me as much as you will but you won't get it out of me.'

I walked around to the side of the wooden frame and knelt down. Dominic had developed a sturdy erection despite his predicament.

'I get the impression you're enjoying this and that was not the intention.' I touched the crop to the end of his penis, picking up the bead of moisture that had erupted. 'If you continue like this, I'll be very, very annoyed.'

Dominic acknowledged what I said but I don't think he took me seriously as the more I whipped his bare buttocks, the more determined his erection became. I decided to untie him and address the problem in a different way. In the middle of the room there was a tall, metal frame, again with shackling points that would allow me access to Dominic's most sensitive areas – the parts that seemed to be thwarting his attempt at absolution. I steered him to the contraption and cuffed his wrists and ankles, both stretched wide apart so that I could deal with the problem freely.

'This' – I pointed to his cock, which surely couldn't get any harder without unloading the pressure – 'is the root of your problems.'

Dominic shook his head. The man was genuinely filled with – was it? – guilt. I paused a moment and studied his narrowed eyes. Their natural darkness had deepened, and gentle but pained lines had formed at the outer corners. His mouth was curled, as if he had tasted something sour, and his head was tipped to one side as if his neck was unable to support it. I approached him and stood close, his face a few inches higher than mine.

'You really are eating yourself up, aren't you?' I didn't know I was doing it until I felt the warm, silken skin in my hand and the irregular stubble on his chin scouring my lips. I stroked his erection, pulling it to painful limits while I teased his mouth with mine. My body pressed against his flat, firm belly, touched with a light covering of hair from his navel down, and I felt him tense as the rhythm of my hand increased. His breathing became jerky and forced and a frown pinned his eyebrows together.

'Stop!' he cried and the vehemence of his demand made me back away instantly. 'If you carry on, I'll come and that's not right.'

Now I didn't know what to think. I had assumed, perhaps wrongly, that the kinky scenario was designed for pleasure and that when I had brought him to orgasm, I would demand that he do the same to me. It was only fair.

'You don't like me?' I couldn't think of anything else to say.

'Look what you've done to me. Of course I like you.' Dominic's voice was gravelled and strangely filled with regret. I didn't understand so, lacking any other ideas and unwilling to return to my cleaning duties, I knelt and took Dominic's still erect cock between my lips. It wasn't as if he could do anything to stop me, even if he was drowning in guilt from something I knew nothing about.

Because I was unsure whether Dominic would oblige and push his mouth between my legs and ease the heat that was welling there, and because I couldn't be certain that he would kiss me or touch my breasts the way I liked, or even try a flick of the crop across my own naked bottom, I slid my jeans down and worked a couple of fingers into the wetness that had virtually soaked my panties. It was as if I had completed a complicated electrical circuit – the lightly-veined cock filling my mouth and nudging my throat, and the tender touch of my own finger – and all over our bodies thousands of silent volts shocked us into a series of spasms as we climaxed.

With Dominic's slackening penis still entrusted to the warm cocoon of my mouth, it was fortunate for him that his guilt remained private. The temptation to bite would otherwise have been too great.

9

I thought Steph would have insisted on my preparing for the party with her at Connor's cottage, especially as she should have been trying to make up with me for stealing my diary, not to mention the man I could have loved. But she was obviously still mad at me for nearly kissing Connor although, strictly speaking, I should be angry at her. Strangely, though, as hard as I tried, my irritation was now limited to the inconvenience and frustration of not being able to add to my journal rather than the obvious embarrassment associated with losing it. That, coupled with her likeable cheek, made it very hard for me to loathe the girl, even though, on another, deep-rooted emotional level, I should have been clawing her eyes out. It was obvious that she had won Connor over completely.

So I bundled up my dress and at least persuaded her to give me a lift to the cliff top before darkness came so that I could boil some water for a wash.

'It takes ages,' I told her, thinking of how easy it would be to slip into Connor's bath.

'But I bet it's quite exciting, washing standing up.' That wasn't the reply I was hoping for.

'You obviously haven't tried it then.'

'Hey, I've been travelling for months and put up with some pretty grim facilities at hostels along the way. I'm no stranger to hardship.'

I glanced at her while she pulled the Land Rover onto the verge at the top of the beach track. 'Of course you're not,' I said with a full helping of sarcasm. 'Thanks for the ride.' I opened the door.

'This is for you.' Steph caught my arm and presented me with a large toiletries bag. 'You might find some of this stuff useful.'

'Thanks.' I tried to sound grateful as I stepped out into the wind that had whipped up from the north. My hair lashed around my face and I had to fight to hold onto the dress as its skirts billowed.

'See you later!' And Steph crunched the gears through a three-point turn and tooted as she drove back to the estate. Back to Connor.

Thankfully, the fire was a brilliant bed of orange with small flames still licking at a crazed and ashen log. After a quick poke and more fuel I was able to remove my coat without a deep shiver setting into my bones.

I hung up the dress, which had fortunately survived the windy walk to the beach cottage, and filled the iron cauldron with water. My father had once used it to boil shellfish and I smiled as I recalled popping the rubbery whelks and cockles into my young mouth. I had spat them out immediately. I heaved the large pan on top of the fire and tiny bubbles soon began to fizz at its bottom. While the water was heating, I took a look inside the flowery bag that Steph had given me. An attempt, I supposed, to get back on my good side, although I wondered why she was bothering.

A floral scent wafted out as I studied the contents. There was a packet of soap petals that really smelled of sweet summer roses, a bottle of body lotion and a tub of moisturiser plus more practical items such as deodorant, a razor and shampoo. I grinned.

'Thanks, Steph,' I said and then stopped short when I pulled apart the clip on another compartment of the large bag. Aside from a selection of make-up, perfume and nail polish, Steph had included some beautiful jewellery – an antique necklace with a huge jade pendant hanging beneath other coloured droplets, and a matching bracelet and several rings – but also, wrapped carefully in layers of tissue paper, an ornate tiara that looked more like a crown than a hair decoration. I stared at it. It would look stunning with my gown and tears started as I realised that my father had never seen me in such an outfit. The thought made me more determined to shame Ethan Kinrade in front of the island's entire social elite. And for that I had to look my absolute best.

I began at the bottom and worked up. Steph had thought of everything and I was able to give myself a quick pedicure and paint my toenails a shameless scarlet. I shaved and exfoliated and massaged body lotion into my skin so that, with the remains of my Spanish tan, I was smooth and glowing. Sadly, though, I knew that tonight was the one night when no one would have the chance to enjoy my pampered body. I would be too preoccupied with overthrowing Kinrade to give thought to any naughty antics. Besides, Connor would be there as my date, and if I couldn't have him...

The water began to simmer and I added a splash of cold so that when I drenched the sponge, again from Steph, and added some bubbles I was able to give myself a decent all-over wash. I lathered my hair, soaked it in an intensive conditioner and wrapped it in a towel. After drying my body, I put on the stunning red lingerie that Liz had given me and gently eased the sheer stockings up my legs. Before putting on the gown, I sat huddled in my outdoor jacket and carefully painted my fingernails the same shocking red as my toes. Already I was taking on an air of superiority which I knew was vital in my attack against Kinrade.

I couldn't think about food. My stomach swirled and churned like the blue-black sea that dumped weed and driftwood and the occasional tin can onto the shore. It was getting dark so I lit all the candles and pulled the grubby curtains across the window to block out the worsening weather. I thought about my imminent journey. It was tough enough in regular clothes, in the ball gown I didn't expect to make fast progress across the rocks.

By six o'clock I was nearly ready. I had fought with the skirts of the dress, continually stepping inside the wrong layer and terrified of tearing the vintage fabric. I was nestled within the bodice and, with the help of Liz's boned basque, my breasts rose above the low neckline in gentle and tempting hillocks. It was my hair that was proving difficult to style because it was still slightly damp so I pulled out all the pins, released the chignon and mussed my hair by the fire. Then my cheeks turned red from the flames so I cooled them with a chilled sponge, which messed my make-up so I had to redo that. At seven o'clock, I inserted the final grip into a very professional hairstyle – a tight twist rolled high on the back of my head with several seductive tendrils winding down my cheeks – and took a candle into the back room of the cottage to inspect myself in the cracked mirror that was hanging crookedly on the wall.

The yellow glow provided an eerie light, making me wonder if what I was seeing was real. The mirror was frosted with over a decade of dust and salt, which gave my reflection a timeless quality. I saw not myself but a society woman from several centuries ago. The crown twinkled in the flickering light and, when I put on the feathered mask, I knew that Ethan Kinrade would surely crumble when I revealed who I was and stated my intentions.

'Nice job!' I gathered up my skirts, gave myself a wink in the mirror for luck, put on my walking boots and warm jacket and stuffed the high-heeled shoes into my pockets.

As I left, I took one last look around the beach cottage and I'm sure I caught sight of Connor and me as kids, chasing each other around the old furniture while my father mended his nets. I heard our excited squeals as we were promised a trip on his small fishing boat and saw the delight on our faces when my mother arrived with a picnic basket hooked on her arm. The happiness, the laughter and all the potential that went with my memories would keep safe in the little cottage, fuelled by the flames that flickered in the grate.

I closed the front door and stepped out onto the shore, where my breath was taken away by the stinging north wind.

Frustrated by my slow progress, I scrunched my skirts high around my thighs so that my legs were free from the swathes of antique fabric and I was able to navigate the treacherous rocks. Also, I was terrified of ripping the dress because paying for it would have been way out of my reach. Besides, I had absolutely no need for such a gown after the evening was over.

I arrived at the cliff top panting, perspiring beneath my jacket even though the night had brought a temperature of only two or three degrees, and I had bruised my shin on a jagged rock. My hair, thankfully, had mostly resisted being torn down by the wind that was steadily increasing, although I didn't hold out much hope for its survival as I still had a long walk along the road ahead. My cheeks smarted from the cold.

'Would madam care for a lift?'

Suddenly, the barren scene was floodlit by two bright cones of car headlights and I had to shield my eyes.

'Connor, is that you?'

I felt an arm around my waist, guiding me to the source of the light. A strong arm which, when we reached the vehicle – a white limo! – removed my old jacket and replaced it with a scarlet velvet cape trimmed with snow-white fur. My escort was dressed in a similar robe and wore a velvet and gold crown, beneath which was a black mask. Only the firm lines of a nose and clean-shaven jaw remained visible along with several strands of heart-warmingly familiar bronze-coloured hair poking beneath the crown. It had to be Connor!

'My queen,' he said and held open the door of the limousine. 'We have a ball to go to.' I grinned inanely and climbed in as gracefully as I could.

Once inside the warmth of the car, which was silent apart from the gentle hum of the engine, I unfurled my hitched-up skirts and settled into the plush leather of the seats. Connor slid in beside me and tapped on the glass that separated us from the driver. I was relieved to be free of the tormenting wind whipping at my skin and the incessant crashing of the waves.

'It's a pity that it's such a quick journey by car up to Creg-ny-Varn.' I trailed my hand over the door leather and opened and closed the drinks cabinet in front of me. 'Amazing,' I said, dumbstruck, having never been in such a vehicle before.

'We have one stop to make along the way.' Connor removed his mask to reveal his intense grey eyes. They flicked over my body continuously, studying every detail. 'You look beautiful, Queen Ailey.' And he took my hand and kissed it.

I couldn't speak. None of this made sense. Perhaps it was the dress transporting me back into a fairytale time or maybe I'd fallen and hit my head on a rock and I was lying on the shore, the tide creeping over me, and I was lost in a dizzy fantasy world that could never be. Either way, I felt deliriously happy and, for once, free from the adrenalin rushes that had plagued me all day at the prospect of confronting Ethan Kinrade.

'Your majesty,' I giggled and before I knew it we were turning into the driveway of Creg-ny-Varn. 'I thought we were making a stop along the way.'

'We are.'

In a moment, we had bypassed the big house, which looked resplendent with fairy lights strung across the façade and through the winter trees. Numerous flares illuminated the driveway and already guests were starting to arrive. The limousine came to a stop at the entrance to the Glen Broath distillery.

'Follow me. There's something I want to show you.'

Connor took my hand, leaving one free to grapple with my skirts, and we walked across the damp cobbles and into the distillery. It was cold and the sickly sweet smells somehow seemed different in the dark, even more cloying than usual. I was thankful when Connor led me right through the main distillery, past the copper mashtuns and huge fermentation vats, not even stopping at his office but going deeper into the ancient building to the very heart of the whisky-making process.

'This is where we mature the whisky in oak barrels, sometimes for up to twenty-five years.' Connor guided me through the door into a pitch-black, extremely damp space and I was relieved to be still wearing my walking boots as I noticed the floor give under my feet. I was standing on wet earth. I couldn't understand why we were there.

'That's really interesting.' I already knew all this but didn't want Connor to think I didn't appreciate his impromptu tour of Glen Broath. It seemed an odd time to choose, though, as Kinrade's ball was about to begin. I fumbled in the dark for his hand, not enjoying the oppressive atmosphere and virtual blindness. His fingers entwined with mine as he led me deeper into the store.

'Some of these barrels have come from France and some from the United States. Many contained bourbon or amontillado and oloroso sherries before the whisky.' Connor pulled me on, guided by a faint light seeping under the door. Then he stopped, fished something from a shelf and lit a candle which gave off just enough of a glow for me to realise that the cold room went on forever. As far as I could see in every direction were racks and racks of ginger-coloured barrels.

'That's impressive,' I said, truly meaning it. The sleeping barrels, some undisturbed for several decades, represented the very essence of Connor's being.

'We have many blends as well as pure single malts. My father taught me well and I pride myself on creating the finest spirit I can.' He held the candle under my chin. 'I have something special for you to taste. Come.'

We walked down the avenues of barrels, the soft earth breathing a fusty sigh as our footsteps disturbed its surface. Connor set the candle on a small table that had obviously been prepared earlier. It was decorated with a white linen cloth, a single red rose in a slim vase and two tulip-shaped glasses. Two chairs were pushed neatly under the table and Connor pulled one out for me.

'What's this?' I smiled, completely bemused, but sat down anyway.

'I want you to taste a very special whisky. It began life fourteen years ago.'

'When I was twelve,' I said with a laugh. *When I left the island*, I thought silently.

'My father brought it into being at the request of Patrick Callister.'

'Dad?' I chilled and my skin erupted in a thousand goose bumps at the thought. I could almost feel him, watching, holding his breath as Connor retrieved a bottle of golden liquid from behind a nearby barrel. He removed the stopper and slowly poured two measures into the glasses. He then sat in the other chair.

'This is for you,' he said seriously. '*Really* for you.' His hand reached out across the table and gripped mine as I clenched the glass. I noticed a slight tensing in his jaw, a flicker underneath his left eye, but most of all I saw the sincerity in his eyes and for that brief moment I forgot why I had returned to the island. My mind was completely free of Ethan Kinrade.

'Tell me what you think.'

I copied Connor and swirled the whisky inside the glass. Then I dipped my nose into the vapours and inhaled, almost recoiling at the strength of the fumes. I closed my eyes to prevent them from smarting. After the initial shock, I was surprised and teased by the multitude of aromas.

When Connor sipped, so did I, drawing in the searing liquid and coating my tongue. Again, numerous tastes too foreign to define filled me and almost immediately I felt the whisky lining my throat, kissing its way through my body.

'You like?' Connor's eyes glinted in the flickering light and I guessed he would see the same effect in mine. It was a magical moment.

'Delicious,' I said, not knowing any technical language to use. But I meant what I said.

'Take a look at the bottle.' Connor passed it to me and I read the label.

Glen Broath. Ailey's Single Malt. Aged in oak for 14 years. For my Angel.

I sighed and drew a finger under my dampening eyes, laughing a little to conceal my emotion.

'He never forgot about you. When my father retired as stillman, he gave me instructions to let it mature for as long as you were away. None of it will ever be exported. Your father wanted it kept on the island. It was the only part of you he had to hold on to, I suppose.'

'He'd be so happy that I got to taste it then.' I didn't know what to say. I was overcome. 'His angel,' I added.

'You were. And he was fanatical about the humidity in here and controlling the losses from the barrels, as if he might lose you all over again.'

Connor forgot he was talking to someone who knew little about whisky distilling. I tipped my head sideways, frowned and drew another sip of my whisky. *My* whisky.

'While in the barrels, a proportion of whisky evaporates through the wood and is lost to the heavens.' Connor gestured upwards. 'It's known as the angels' share.'

I looked up at the distant rafters of the vaulted barn and suddenly it all made sense. I had been beckoned home by the angels, sent by my father. What was once a thought, my father's thought, had now become reality. I had finally come home to claim what was rightfully mine.

'Ready to party?' I asked and once again my head was swimming with possibilities. At last, I was ready to confront Ethan Kinrade.

Fifty or so guests had already arrived but even in the time we were standing in the hallway, having our invites checked and being offered a glass of champagne, a queue of headlights formed down the long drive of Creg-ny-Varn and bizarrely dressed party-goers filtered into the house.

Again, I was overcome with emotion but fought to keep my feelings contained. How my father would have loved this colourful spectacle filling his home. As instructed, everyone had arrived in fancy dress and no expense had been spared on the outlandish and imaginative costumes. From West Indian carnival outfits with orange and green headgear to belly dancers and naughty nurses and schoolgirls, the women had surpassed themselves in a display of anonymity, because every outfit included a mask of some sort. The men were more conservative, arriving as soldiers and diplomats and cowboys, and Connor was the only king I could see. I gripped his hand tightly as we were ushered through to the Grand Hall.

'Wow,' I said and twirled as much as my heavy dress would allow. 'I might hate every cell in his body but he's done a pretty damn fine job of organising this party.' At that moment, the music began and the sounds of a small orchestra filled the hall.

'Would you care to dance?' Connor didn't wait for an answer but led me to the centre of the floor.

'No one else is,' I said with a giggle, almost tripping on my dress. Fortunately, I'd remembered to remove my heavy boots and socks and replace them with the red high heels, although dancing in them was going to prove tricky.

'Then all the more reason to take to the floor.'

'That's what I've always liked about you, Connor McBryde. Your desire to be different.'

'To be alone, more like.' A flash of sadness in his eyes. 'Something I'm resigned to for now.'

Several other couples had joined us in the centre of the vast room and were choosing to gallop to the polka rather than meander slowly as we were. I pressed my body against his, immediately sensing the gentle mound beneath his trousers.

'But you've got Steph to . . .' I trailed off and turned to stone as I heard a small ripple of applause. A number of guests were laughing and thanking and introducing and all of them used the words 'Ethan' or 'Kinrade'. I reluctantly prised myself away from Connor and darted off, scanning the room in search of him.

Up until now I had doubted that he really existed, but when I caught sight of the black leather, the strapping and buckles and the tight collar around his neck, I knew that he did. I followed him through the crowds, shoving between ludicrous characters with the fast beat of the music urging me forward. For a moment I lost him even though he was taller than most of the guests. I followed the greetings that tracked his passage through the Grand Hall and, my heart exploding beneath my ribs, wished Connor was beside me.

'Ailey!' A hand caught me from the side, halting my progress, and Steph was squealing in my ear. She looked fantastic in the can-can girl costume that I helped her pick out the day before. The skirt was outrageously short at the front with black and crimson frills, and with her jet-black wig, fishnet stockings and garish jewellery I hardly recognised her. She wasn't going to let me go before she'd studied my costume.

'That dress,' she gasped. 'So perfect. Does he love it? Did the limo arrive?'

'*You knew?*' I whispered but hadn't time to question her now. I stood on tiptoe and searched the room but the chain-bound gimp was nowhere to be seen.

'Looking for someone?' Steph had to shout above the music.

'Yes, Kinrade. Seen him?' Several people bumped me and I couldn't spot him anywhere. There must have been about two hundred guests filling the hall now and thankfully, because of the mask which I refused to remove, I didn't have the painful experience of greeting the large number of locals who would undoubtedly remember me and be intrigued to hear where I'd been for the last fourteen years.

'Apparently he's going to give a welcome speech soon. What's up? You seem so agitated.' Steph came close and grinned, whispering in my ear. 'I'm off to find Connor. I have something really important to get off my chest.' She placed a hand on her breasts, easing them higher in their already precarious position.

I nodded feebly and the room fell silent. The colourful gowns of the dancing women blurred together in vibrant streaks. I felt the rush of air as the couples swooped past me, and still heard Steph's words ringing in my ears.

She was going to tell him that she loved him.

I was on a crazy merry-go-round, hanging on to a wild horse as it spun me faster and faster. Really, it was my life that was spinning out of control. As I looked over my shoulder, I saw Connor standing alone, bemused, sipping champagne, and then suddenly, almost directly in front of me, was the black, leather-clad figure of Ethan Kinrade greeting more guests. I felt split in two.

'Mr Kinrade,' I called out but my throat seemed to be filled with sand and he didn't hear me. I turned to look at Connor through the crowd and now Steph was by his side, her arms flung around his neck and her cleavage pushed up against his king's robe. She pushed her mouth to his ear – a little kiss, perhaps? – and then she withdrew, laughed and brushed his mouth with her painted lips. Connor's eyes began searching around the room, no doubt to see if I, his date, had caught him in a clinch with Steph.

Kinrade approached me, held out his hand as if I was in a line to greet him. Up close, he was larger than I'd imagined. His legs and head were covered in smooth black leather while his upper body remained naked but criss-crossed with a series of chains and straps. He wore gloves and a collar around his neck and, most frightening, a black leather mask that covered his head apart from eye- and mouth-holes. A row of pure white teeth was exposed through the tight mouth-hole so I assumed that he was smiling at me.

'Mr Kinrade.' I nodded but refused his hand. My heart banged in my chest as I stood dumbstruck in front of the man who had caused me so much anger and resentment during the last few weeks. Unable to hold his mysterious, faceless gaze, I switched my view to the naked skin of his chest and its layer of dark hair. There was a light sheen to his skin, indicating that he perhaps wasn't quite as cool as he would have everyone believe. And there was nothing I could do to prevent him taking my hand, raising it to his mouth and delivering not a kiss but a bite.

'Ouch!' I retracted my hand. 'How fitting that you've come as a gimp, Mr Kinrade.' But he was gone, annoyingly swallowed up by the crowds. I didn't have to wait long for another appearance though, as he stepped onto a small platform beside the orchestra. I began my journey through the guests, pushing and shoving to get to where he was standing in front of the crowd, ready to receive their adoration in *my* house. How dare he bite me!

I caught sight of Connor to my left, still busy with Steph, and I tried to look away but felt drawn to their private embrace. I kept tripping on my skirts so I hitched them up and then I thought I spied Dominic across the room although I could have been mistaken because, of course, he was wearing a mask. I just longed for someone familiar by my side.

'Ailey, that's never you?' I turned to see a belly dancer and Zorro. Even through their masks, I could tell it was Liz and Lewis. I could never forget Liz's sumptuous breasts, the way they oozed over the cups of her sequinned costume bra. 'You look stunning. Where did you get that dress?' she asked.

'No time to tell you. Come with me.' I grabbed Liz's arm and pulled her through the crowds towards Kinrade, who was now holding a microphone. As we drew closer, I realised that the oversized and studded black pouch at his groin was going to be at face height when I confronted him. It was all I could see as I broke through the crowd into the small clearing in front of the stage and I was convinced that I could even smell him – the raw tang of a needy man, who was now only a couple of feet away. Ethan Kinrade parted his lips, revealing a salmon-coloured tongue within the leather head gear. The microphone was buzzing and squealed before he spoke.

'Ladies and —'

I hurled myself onto the stage. I had meant to step up gracefully but tripped on the endless layers of my skirt and landed at Kinrade's feet in a heap of fabric and frills. I stood as quickly as I was able, aware that there was a scuffle near the door as two large men in dinner suits headed my way. Someone screamed. Kinrade dropped the microphone as I bumped his legs and so I grabbed it and finally managed to get upright.

'Ladies and gentlemen,' I yelled through the screeching microphone. Part of my chignon had dislodged and chunks of hair hung limply around my neck. 'This man is an impostor! He is a low-down scumbag thief and has wormed his way into my family estate to steal what clearly isn't his.' Gasps and noises came from the crowd followed by a loud ripple of surprise as I removed my feathered mask. 'My name is Ailey Callister and Creg-ny-Varn is my family ... hey ... stop ... get *off* me!'

I was suddenly on my back with my legs kicking and my arms flailing and beating the two bouncers who carried me away.

'Let *go*, you big thugs. That gimp has stolen my home.' All my struggling was useless and seconds later, as I was carried out into the entrance hall, I heard the muffled voice of Ethan Kinrade apologising for the interruption and continuing his speech of welcome to an appreciative audience. As I was dragged down the corridor, I heard applause and whistles for the man who was obviously so popular with the locals.

'You can stay in here until you calm down,' one of the thugs said, while the other unlocked the door to the library. 'Mr Kinrade doesn't want anyone disrupting his party and if you make any more noise, I'll tie you up to that rack.'

I was about to yell abuse but thought better of it. I didn't stand a chance against those two brutes and besides, I knew that I could escape through the trapdoor in the floor and hopefully get back to the Grand Hall to have my say. They couldn't stop me that easily. The two bouncers slammed the heavy oak door and I heard them turn the key.

'Right,' I said, wishing that I wasn't weighed down with the ridiculous, albeit beautiful, dress. Even taking two paces in it caused me to trip and move as if there was no gravity. 'Where's that hatch?' I stood by the door and figured out where my father's desk used to be and therefore where the door to the underground tunnels should be, but the room was so different with its lurid décor and equipment that it was hard to pinpoint the exact spot. 'Here, I think.'

I peeled back a rug but there was no trap door. Then I realised that it must be buried beneath the weighty iron bed frame straddling the middle of the room. Kinrade had obviously shifted the equipment around since I crept through the basement a few days earlier. I sighed, realising that I would struggle to move the frame on my own.

'Damn you, Kinrade,' I cursed as I put my body against the ancient bed, although it hardly looked like a bed any more as it had no mattress but wooden slats, chains and shackles at each corner. It moved about an inch and, as I pushed for all I was worth, I heard a ripping sound as I tore the hem of my dress.

'That's it,' I spat. 'It's coming off!' I pulled at the fasteners on the bodice and then fumbled with shaking hands to untie the ribbons that held the skirts together. When the last one was undone, the entire five layers of skirts dropped to my ankles and the bodice hung open, allowing me to draw a full breath. I gathered it up and placed it on a chair. I couldn't afford any more damage.

Now, wearing only the basque, panties and stockings that I had borrowed from Liz, I felt more able to move the bed. The deep red lingerie, with its overstated trim and the firm lines of bone that pushed up my breasts into a surprisingly swollen cleavage, somehow made me feel stronger and more confident and gradually the bed began to slide across the boards. I was heaving and pushing and concentrating so hard while leaning over the end of the iron frame, my legs wide apart for better grip, that the sharp sting of a hand on my bottom nearly made me faint with shock. I swung around to be confronted by the gimp. Not only had Kinrade bitten my hand, he had now slapped my ass.

'What do you think you're doing? How dare you treat me like this! Do you have any idea who I am?' I was breathless from the effort of moving the bed and now I was suffering a massive adrenalin rush, my heart ramming against my ribs at a frightening rate. None of this was going as planned.

'I'm sorry,' he said and bowed his head.

He said *sorry*.

'Why did you smack me? Why did you bite me? In fact, why did you steal my house?' My words tumbled together and Kinrade didn't seem to be able to reply. He maintained his bowed head and let out an involuntary sigh. He wasn't the tower of strength I had imagined.

Finally, he spoke. 'You're right to be upset, Miss Callister. And yes, I do know who you are.' Kinrade's voice was quiet and muffled through the restraints of his mask. I imagined that without it he would have sounded a little more forceful. As it was, I could barely make out what he was saying.

'Did you have to work very hard to con my father into changing his will?' I circled Kinrade in order to intimidate him. He might have caught me in my basque and stockings but it was perfect timing as far as I was concerned. I had never felt so powerful and now, equal in height because I had slipped back into my red high heels, all I needed was to take hold of that chain round Kinrade's neck and get him tied to the metal frame. His humiliation would be off to a flying start.

'Well?' His silence infuriated me. Recklessness swelled within me.

'I did no such thing.'

'Do you know how much this house means to me?' Ethan Kinrade was not behaving like even a quarter of the man I had imagined he would be and, while his body was a thousand times better than the portly, lazy specimen I had conjured, he simply had nothing defensive to say. He caught me looking at the pink nubs of nipple peeking from between the straps that bound his upper body.

'So you were quite content to walk away with my entire inheritance and not feel one bit of guilt?' I retrieved a riding crop, the one I had used on Dominic earlier, and flicked it against my thigh. Before he replied, Ethan Kinrade breathed in so sharply that he coughed and choked on his own surprise. 'Dressed like that,' I added, 'you're asking for punishment.'

It came naturally now, having rehearsed on Dominic, and my hands were itching to lay the crop across his ass. Several hours ago, I would never have imagined that my encounter with Kinrade would result in me threatening him with the beating he deserved, but the man evidently had a penchant for such activities, dressed as he was, and here in with the transformed library, with all the evidence it contained, I didn't feel in the least bit afraid to deliver it.

'You have every right to punish me.' Kinrade's voice was wizened and fearful. Perhaps it was all a trick and he would suddenly pounce and overcome me.

'Take off your leather pants,' I ordered, not believing for one minute that he really would. 'Perhaps you should have thought of the consequences before you decided to claim Creg-ny-Varn as your own.'

Then Ethan Kinrade, all six feet two of him with his wide, angular shoulders and strong arms and ridged stomach and anonymous face, bent down and slowly peeled off his trousers. When he stood tall again, I saw that he was wearing the leather cock harness, the box of which I had found in his bedroom, and that his entrapped penis was already beginning to strain within its limits. I couldn't take my eyes off it.

'Perhaps you'd understand if you knew –'

'You're not in any position to answer back, Mr Kinrade. If I scream, I can have the island's entire social set witness your unusual taste in underwear *and* I'll claim that you stripped me against my will. What's it to be? Obey my simple instructions or be laughed off the island by your guests?'

Kinrade opened his pink mouth and I assume was about to offer a feeble excuse but a sharp thwack of the crop across his bare buttocks soon silenced him. I smiled as his cock bulged within the leather harness.

'Follow me,' I ordered and dragged him over to the metal frame where I had previously shackled Dominic. To my surprise, Kinrade obeyed and I soon had him strapped up with his arms and legs spread wide. As the tips of my fingers burned for a touch of his erection, I was filled with a sudden sense of *déjà vu* but put it down to the rush of adrenalin and other heady feelings that raced through me.

'This isn't at all what you think, Ailey.' His voice trembled although I could sense its natural depth and the desire that it carried. Kinrade was as excited by this situation as I was, although neither of us was about to admit it.

'That's Miss Callister to you.' I surprised myself and knew that, aside from the revenge that I had craved for so long, this was simply another naughty scene from the diary I still hadn't reclaimed. Then thoughts of Connor, who was as far away as ever, drove me to take a sharp swipe at Kinrade's ass cheek. To my surprise, his pale skin was already decorated with a number of red lines.

'Taken a beating already?' I said but I don't think he heard me. Kinrade was too busy twitching and moaning as I trailed the flimsy tip of the crop over his cock. I resisted the urge to wrap my fingers around it and pull it into my mouth for several bites plus a long, deep passage down my throat before leaving him stranded, unable to bring himself to orgasm. I would have done that, if it hadn't been for the image of Connor freshly branded in my mind. I doubted that he would ever allow me to humiliate him like this and honestly, I wouldn't want to. My desire for Connor lived in a different psychological compartment in my brain. With Connor, I knew I'd feel as if I'd come home.

'Did I tell you to get an erection?' I stung his firm buttocks again, slightly puzzled by the existing grid of welts. 'Did I tell you to steal my property?' I thwacked him in time with my words and thought he might come there and then, something I wouldn't have been happy about. I tugged on the chain that was attached to the end of his cock harness, causing him to writhe and buck as much as his restraints would allow. 'If you come, I'm going to fetch a dozen of your guests to see their host strung up and helpless.'

I was beating Kinrade with such vehemence that my hair came completely loose and tumbled around my shoulders and face in an unruly mess. While I was careful to make the crop deliver only a sharp sting, I beat him incessantly, urged on in part by my captor's moans of pleasure, though what really drove me was a head full of revenge and the desire to see him overthrown. I was a mad woman and screamed and chastised him with every blow.

Kinrade shot a creamy arc and at exactly that moment my action was arrested. An arm came down around my shoulders and another around my waist and a firm but soft voice urged me to calm down.

'Ailey, Ailey, stop. Do you even know what you're doing?'

I turned to see Connor, frowning and pressed up close beside me while staring at the strung-up Kinrade.

'He deserved it,' I snapped. 'And look, he even enjoyed himself.' I trailed the crop through the milky puddle at Kinrade's feet.

'Do you know who this is?' Connor's incredulity annoyed me.

'I'm not stupid. Of course I do. Ethan Kinrade is the man who stole my inheritance and ...'

Connor nodded and peeled the gimp mask off Kinrade's head to reveal a surprised and sweating face. His hair was stuck to his scalp as if he had been swimming and he had red marks beneath his eyes and mouth.

There was a sudden tightening in my chest, as if I

had been laced roughly into a tiny corset, and the entire world lost its colour and became ghostly grey.

'Oh my God,' I whispered and felt dizzy and sick, and then there was a rushing in my ears that sounded like the ocean rising in my head. Connor tightened his grip on me and, as my body wilted and my knees gave way, the last thing I saw was Dominic's face framed within the metal rack.

10

The party continued until four a.m. We could hear the beat of the music, which had been taken over by a DJ at midnight, even through the thick slate walls of Connor's cottage. When he brought me there, I didn't speak for an entire hour until steady sips of Glen Broath had warmed my throat and loosened my tongue.

I was still in a state of shock.

'How could I have been so stupid?' I asked miserably. I was wrapped up in Connor's robe again, having been carried across the grounds of Creg-ny-Varn in my underwear. Still drowsy from disbelief, I had been vaguely aware of Connor's heavy breathing as he puffed through the freezing night heaving me and my heavy antique dress back to safety. He didn't think I should be left alone with Ethan Kinrade.

'He'd conned me all along, making me believe he was the gardener.' I let out a sob, not really crying but trying to justify my emotions. Really, I was mad as hell.

'Did you ever give him a chance to explain?' Connor looked at me fondly, almost pityingly, and I was thankful at least that he hadn't written me off as a mad woman. Actually, it seemed that he liked looking after me. He stoked the fire, tucked a tartan blanket around me, busied himself in the kitchen and brought me a snack, and kept up a steady supply of tea and whisky. Connor almost seemed pleased about my predicament.

'I don't think you really understand, do you?' In fact, I *knew* he didn't understand. To make him do so I would have to reveal how Dominic and I had indulged in several intimate moments aside from the whipping session Connor had just witnessed. This latest episode I could write off as madness and anger, a fleeting moment of insanity, and Connor was well on his way to believing me. As much as it pained me to conceal what I had been up to during my short time on the island, at least not revealing the truth wasn't exactly lying.

'So let me get this clear. You were snooping around Creg-ny-Varn when Mr Kinrade caught you.'

'No, Dominic the gardener caught me.'

Connor pushed his hands through his hair. 'And this man told you his name was Dominic?'

'Yes. He told me when we were in his gardening hut. It was quite homely in there.'

'And you saw him subsequent to this, never suspecting or thinking that he was Mr Kinrade?' Connor was shaking his head, unable to get a grasp of my story. 'Surely you saw him in the house. You were the cleaner.'

I was about to reply and tell him how I'd been led to believe that Mr Kinrade was away but we were interrupted by someone knocking at the door. I assumed it was Steph returning from the party. I was hoping to have more time alone with Connor.

'You have a visitor, Ailey.' Connor returned to the living room with Ethan Kinrade, or rather Dominic, as I was still used to knowing him. I leapt up from my cosy cocoon to confront the man I had recently flogged in pent-up frustration. 'I'll give you two a moment alone.' Connor wisely ducked out of the room.

'That is, if you think I'll be safe.' It was Kinrade's

attempt at a joke and I didn't laugh. He had changed out of his fancy dress costume and was now wearing a pair of jeans and an old grey sweater with a waxed jacket on top. He looked far more like the Dominic I knew and I wouldn't have been surprised if he'd brought along a wheelbarrow.

'You'll be safe,' I replied, sitting down. My legs had gone weak again.

'As long as I don't bend over, right?'

'Oh, stop it!' I scooped the blanket around me to prevent the shiver that was creeping up my body. 'You were asking for it anyway, dressed in that costume. And you should have thought about punishment when you stole my inheritance and –'

'If you'd shut up for a minute, maybe I can explain.' Ethan Kinrade sat down beside me and when I opened my mouth to protest – how could he possibly explain? – he silenced me by placing a finger over my lips. Then he began.

'I have never had any intention of stealing Creg-ny-Varn from you. In fact, the opposite could be said to be true.' He pushed his finger harder against my mouth as another protest tried to escape. 'I have been desperately trying to locate you since the day your father died.'

I bowed my head and just managed to speak through his finger, although it came out muffled. 'You have?'

'Investigators have been trying to track you down all over Europe. You've cost me a small fortune and then you arrive of your own free will anyway.' Kinrade snorted a resigned laugh and removed his hand from my face, hopeful that I wouldn't interrupt. 'Do you honestly believe that I wanted to take your family home from you?'

'The newspapers said you had.'

'Pfah. And you believed that?' Kinrade went and helped himself to a whisky. He turned, one hand jammed in his jeans pocket, the other holding the glass. 'I was left with no choice but to look after the estate. With your father gone and my mother too distressed to cope, I couldn't watch the place go to ruin. I was hopeful that one day I'd find you and be able to hand over the property. Creg-ny-Varn is a burden that I never chose. I'm happy pottering about the gardens but when it comes to running an entire estate, I'm not your man.' He downed his drink and then said nothing, evidently allowing me time to talk.

'I see,' was all I managed initially. 'So, in a way, you *are* the gardener.' I wanted there to be some truth in all of this.

'Correct.' Now it was Kinrade's turn to be embarrassed. He had begun the lie. 'I didn't reveal who I was immediately because I wanted to size you up first. I couldn't hand over the estate to just anyone.'

'And then?' I was trying to regain that little bit of power.

'Then things got a bit out of hand. Or should I say, *in* hand.' He laughed and sat down again. 'You did something to me, Ailey. You unleashed something –'

'And that reminds me. What exactly have you done to my father's library?'

'You mean my collection? I've been an avid enthusiast of all kinds of bondage and fetish gear for many years now. The items in your father's library only constitute about a quarter of what I own. The rest's in storage. The costume I wore tonight was a very rare Victorian outfit that I found in an auction in London. Cost me a fortune.' Kinrade spoke as if it was as normal as stamp collecting or butterfly catching. 'I didn't think it would hurt if I arranged some of my collection in the library. The house is so vast.'

'Do you even live in the house? It doesn't seem like it.'

'The truth is, I enjoy being outside so much that I mostly sleep in the gardener's hut. I have the dogs for company and, with the stove going, it's toasty warm. I suppose it's my way of trying to unleash myself from the burden of the estate.'

I was suddenly reminded of the beach cottage and understood the appeal of an uncomplicated life. 'The house has become your museum then.'

'I suppose so.' Ethan sighed and stared at me intently. 'I'm an avid collector. I have many books on the subject too.' He bowed his head and took a deep breath. 'The thing is, Ailey, you do something to me – something thrilling and dangerous, like nothing I've ever found in a woman before. You have a unique, strangely innocent power over me that I'm reluctant to lose.'

'You don't have to sweet-talk me,' I said, noticing a flutter deep in my stomach. 'And whatever you're into is fine by me.' I couldn't look back at him.

'No, really. I've never felt like this before and honestly don't know how I'm going to, well...' Kinrade trailed off, evidently uncomfortable discussing his sexual needs.

'Get what you want?' I finished for him, feeling the seed of something devious growing inside me.

'You've unlocked something in me that I can't explain. Something that I can't live without.'

'You haven't lost a diary, have you?' I asked sarcastically. Ethan looked puzzled but didn't ask what I meant.

'Managing to sort everything out?' Connor returned and crouched on the floor by the fire. I didn't feel that I had quite finished with Kinrade but nodded all the same.

'I was just leaving. I think Ailey and I have reached an understanding.' Kinrade stood and spoke directly to me. 'Your father never changed his will to accommodate my mother. You are still the sole beneficiary of the estate. I'll notify the executors in the morning and they'll be in touch with you. I'll leave the property by the end of the week.'

I was jolted by guilt. I liked Dominic. There was something earthy and raw about him, like he was an essential part of the estate.

'Where will you go?' I tried not to show how keen I was.

'Perhaps England. My mother's staying with relatives in Yorkshire. I may join her.'

'Creg-ny-Varn still needs a groundsman,' I said. I stood and walked Dominic, Ethan, whoever he was, to the cottage door. I clutched the blanket around my shoulders. 'And the position comes with a cottage too.' I stared into his dark eyes, indicating just how serious I was.

'Any other perks?'

'Let me see.' I rolled my eyes in pretend thought. 'I could see to it that you get tied up once a week and get a good hiding. Would that entice you to work for me?' I held out my hand and Kinrade gave it a firm shake. 'You'll even have somewhere to house your huge collection of kinky gear. I shall turn over the Grand Hall to displaying your artefacts and, of course, you'll be free to inspect them any time you wish.'

'I doubt if I'll ever get a better offer.' He was about

to step out into the cold north wind but stopped and turned back to me again. 'You want to know the real reason I kept up the charade so long?'

I nodded as the wind stung my cheeks and chilled my bare feet.

'Because I wouldn't have stood a chance with you if you'd known who I really was. Ailey Callister would never have bedded Ethan Kinrade.'

And as he stepped out into the night, I understood completely.

We watched the sun rise. A thin band of orange spread behind the hills as Connor cooked breakfast. We had talked, sipped more Glen Broath as if it contained all the answers, dozed in each other's arms and then woken as the light seeped through the curtains.

'So what will you do?' Connor asked. We were eating in the living room and I had my legs curled underneath me. 'About the estate.'

I blew out and put down my knife and fork. Bacon had never tasted so good. Why is it food tastes so good after sex?

'How do you feel about having me as your boss?' I'd already made up my mind the second that Connor's fingers had slipped into my hair and his lips had pressed against mine. Estate or no estate, I wasn't leaving the island.

He laughed. 'After what I saw last night, quite intimidated. Can I expect to see you at the distillery with your crop?'

'After hours, maybe.' I snuggled back into the blanket, embracing the feeling that came after making love to someone so special. I slipped a hand between my legs to feel that the wetness was still there, that I hadn't imagined it.

'You'll be staying then.' It was a statement rather than a question and I could sense the relief in his voice.

'I'll be staying home,' I reiterated and pulled back the blanket so that Connor could see what I was doing. He put down his plate and crawled across the floor to me just as he had done a few hours ago. He took my hands and clasped them in his own.

'Welcome back, Miss Callister. It's been a long time.'

'Too long,' I replied, trying not to think of the logistics that would be involved. There would be time for that later.

Connor kissed the inside of my thighs, working up my legs to the glistening space that he had recently entered as if he was the only man that ever had any right to be there. He flicked his tongue over my eager clitoris and between the still swollen folds of my sex, tasting his own seed and preparing me all over again. I leant back in the chair and eased my legs apart further, encouraging him to delve deeper with his tongue.

I sighed, feeling blissful and abandoned while Connor greedily tucked into me. There was so much catching up to do that I didn't think that we could ever be separated. I wanted to explore each bit of his mysterious body but also every part of his mind, discovering devious desires that he had never dared to admit before.

'It turned me on, seeing you punishing Kinrade.' Connor slid up my body and opened the robe to reveal my breasts. He'd already set them on fire from the attention he'd given my pussy. In fact, my whole body had been aching for him again from the minute he came deep inside me several hours before, pumping his many years of frustration back where it belonged.

We had been talking, me subdued, him coaxing and understanding. The warmth from the fire had given my cheeks a rosy glow and with the whisky that I had taken to calm me from my shock, I was relaxed and melting into the sofa. Connor sat beside me and with each breath, each encouraging sentence with which he relieved my embarrassment, he eased himself a little closer until I could feel the beat of his heart against my side.

I knew it would happen. As our breathing synchronised and our faces aligned, our profiles painted with the yellow flicker of the flames, our mouths drew together as if we had been connected by a thread for fourteen years. His lips were so soft and full, searching but gentle and quite unlike the selfish mouth of Marco that I was used to. Connor was giving while secretly exploring and he coiled his arms around my shoulders as I cradled his face in my hands with a touch light enough to hold a butterfly. The kiss probably only lasted half a minute but contained my whole life. To be kissed by Connor was to know that I was safe for ever.

It hadn't stopped with simply a kiss, although tender looks and muted sentences between the further meetings of our mouths filled the next half hour. Each of us knew that we wanted to hold and touch something more intimate while our tongues collided. Strange how something I would have once never considered possible – our kiss – had now become not enough.

Connor took the lead, tracing a meandering path with a finger along my collar bone and down the valley between my breasts. He was touching my skin, the oversized robe having fallen open conveniently, and found the way to my upturned nipple. He knew I liked it because my back arched and I sucked in a breath, my fingers increasing their hold on his neck.

Impatient for more and daring enough to admit it, Connor loosened the belt of the robe and peeled the soft, thick fabric from my shoulders. Like an artist, his large hands drew the outline of my body, tracing a sketchy image of me while his lips coloured me in. He cupped my breasts, studying them like he was in a life-drawing class, and then brought his mouth onto them, delivering a strawberry wash of watercolour to my skin.

'You are so beautiful. More than I'd imagined all these years.'

'You've thought about me?'

'Constantly.' Connor's admission drove his eyes to match the colour of the grey sea before a storm. 'You've grown up in my head. I made you into my perfect woman. In my imagination, we're already married.'

'Already?' I didn't need to say more. If I searched deep enough, it was all in my head too.

He continued with his art, painting colour all over my body until he arrived at the very core of me, where his attention to detail was equal to the masters'. Meanwhile, I fumbled with his shirt buttons beneath the frills of his silly king's outfit – *we were finally king and queen* – and exposed his warm body and a waft of his delicious musky smell. I dotted tiny kisses across his chest, the reddish-blonde fuzz that grew there tickling my nose, and inhaled the scent of his skin to burn in my memory for ever.

We were playing a game, taking turns, each more daring than the last. Connor was winning and plainly at an advantage when his fingers slipped inside my panties. His touch messed up my internal circuitry and lights and sparks twinkled through me as his fingers walked their way to my heart.

'I didn't think that you wanted me,' I admitted breathlessly. I could feel my juices welcoming his finger as he carefully slipped inside me. It wasn't an appropriate time to speak, but it was relevant to his desire for me. 'I thought you and Steph...' I trailed off. Saying another woman's name didn't seem right either.

'Steph and me?' Connor withdrew his fingers and I knew that our game was temporarily on hold. My sex pulsed from his sudden departure. He began to laugh. 'She's my cousin.'

I don't know how long I waited before replying. It seemed like hours but was probably only a few seconds. 'Oh.' I wasn't laughing. 'And?' I was trying to avoid ridicule. Again. So I acted like I already knew. 'Cousins have relationships, too.'

'Not these two cousins.' He stroked hair away from my forehead and planted his hands lightly on my shoulders. 'Steph has been trying to get us together since she knew you were on the island and realised you were the woman that I had written to her about over the years.' His eyes were transparent. I knew he was telling the truth. 'Steph's a great believer in fate and when I told her not to mess with it, she told me that she was a part of it so how couldn't she interfere. She's – how can I put it? – exuberant, forceful. She did at least keep reasonably quiet and not reveal my feelings to you.'

'Wouldn't it have been easier if she had?' My head was spinning.

'You didn't return to the island because of me. If it wasn't for Creg-ny-Varn, then you wouldn't be here. I wanted you to genuinely want me.'

'I felt the same.'

'Then it would have been stalemate without Steph. She convinced me not to give up. She insisted that you had never stopped wanting me.'

'How did she know?' Even as I was saying it, I realised that it was all in my diary.

'I never read a page, before you ask. Steph, being Steph, has read it from cover to cover and alluded to your feelings constantly. Don't be angry with her. In fact, you should be flattered. You've inspired her to kick out and go after her dreams. She's going to drama school.'

I laughed. 'She'll do well then.'

'It was her idea that we go to the party together as king and queen, after I'd told her about our childhood games. She orchestrated the limousine, too.'

'And showing me the whisky? Was that her idea?'

'All mine, actually. And it's convinced me that fate did have a hand in this. What was I to do with a hundred and fifty crates of *Ailey's Single Malt*?' He leant over me and kissed me again. 'Something brought you back here. I don't care what, as long as my angel stays this time.'

I sighed. 'I'm going to be drinking whisky forever.'

'Until we're ancient,' he replied, before working tiny kisses down my stomach, across the gentle rise of my pubic bone and into the cleft of my eager pussy. And that's where he stayed for a long time, deftly bringing me close to orgasm, knowing that when he pushed himself inside me, sliding into my body as we lay beside the fire, I would climax within the first dozen and most intimate strokes that would ever happen between us. Then he could work me up again, kneading me from the inside out – in fact, working my mind with tiny teasers and the promise of everything to come – until I clenched around him again as he jetted high inside me.

And that's where we were again, having had breakfast, talked, drifted through the drowsiness that follows first-time sex; that place where you're so tired but can't bear to sleep in case you forget.

Connor was at my breasts again, suckling noisily with his hands trapped beneath my buttocks on the sofa. Even with limited finger movement, he managed to find the tight little hole of my bottom and, using lubrication already present, slipped the tip of one finger inside me. I stiffened, unsure of the new feeling it gave me, although it was still a familiar shot of pleasure. My squirming seemed to tempt his finger deeper and with every millimetre he gained I was awarded another thrill from this secret place.

'Oh, Connor,' I whispered, driven to tugging at his hair and dragging my nails down the skin on his back. 'It's like my life has been simmering, waiting on hold until I could come back to you.'

My admission caused him to grip me tighter and press his solid cock against me. I fumbled with his clothing and freed his erection, wasting no time in turning him over and applying my mouth to the very tip. I sucked and nipped at the thin crepe skin and Connor twitched and moaned and held my head, wanting me to plunge him deep down my throat. But I held off for as long as I could, teasing every last unbearable sensation from him and lapping up the beads of salty liquid that escaped involuntarily.

'Slow down or I'll come,' he said breathlessly. I could hardly believe that it was Connor's deep, rich voice saying such a thing to me. Grinning with my mouth full was tricky but in my head I was beaming. I eased off on the tip-to-base rhythm and ran my tongue around the sensitive ridge at the head, familiarising myself with his foreign geography. But Connor couldn't wait. He got his arms around my body and moved me onto my back, gently easing me onto the floor so that I was lying on the soft blanket with the fire bathing my left side in warmth.

Then, as easily as if we had been lovers for years, Connor slipped inside me, slowly savouring the feel of new territory as I had just done with him. His chest vibrated gently with a low rumble of approval and I knew that, even after only a few strokes, he was on the brink of orgasm.

'Not yet,' I whispered, pulling him down upon me so that his tense arms and shoulders relaxed. I gripped his tight buttocks and wrapped my ankles around his thighs, giving me good leverage so that I could work while he drifted back from the inevitable release. A minute or two later and I was on the edge myself, grinding my sex against his groin, burying his cock so deep that I was convinced he was in my womb, and then I stopped, savouring the delicious feelings gripping my body.

'Are you ready? I can't wait any long ... er.' Connor took control and hauled himself back onto his hands, his face, crumpled with desire, only a foot above mine. He thrust a few more times, virtually escaping my sex each time he drew back, but then driving home with such force that I was unable to prevent the explosion of my orgasm. As the shockwaves subsided, Connor came with half a dozen terrifyingly powerful shudders, which sent me fluttering into a second climax.

I lay in his arms, watching the flames rise and fall in the stove and listening to the comforting sound of his breathing. I realised that everything I ever wanted was on this island.

Steph and I had ridden together in the taxi. She insisted that Connor should not disrupt his working day – he had a container arriving for an overseas shipment of whisky – and besides, she promised to return very soon. They kissed each other tentatively on the cheek, as cousins would.

'I expect to be bringing a new hat with me,' she said with a grin as the taxi dropped us at the sea port. The ferry loomed in the harbour, the Legs of Mann proudly displayed on her red funnel. I held my hair back as the wind lashed round the corner of the terminal building.

'And why would that be?' I grinned as my cheeks smarted from the cold.

'For the wedding, stupid. He's not going to risk losing you again.'

We went inside for coffee and warmth. Our friendship had been short and plagued with misunderstandings, but it was wearing into something solid and worthy of prolonging through the years. I wrapped my hands around my hot mug.

'I have something for you.' Steph rummaged in her pack and withdrew a packet tied up with brown paper and string. She slid it across the laminated table.

I didn't open it right then but tucked it inside my jacket, next to my heart, next to Connor and the takeaway warmth he had bestowed on me. 'And I have a gift for you.' I took out a bottle of my whisky and showed her the special label.

'That's a wonderful thing to have. I'll think of you every time I take a dram. I've learnt a lot from Connor over the last week. My father needs to be more commercial if the business is to survive. Connor's father retired gracefully but mine refuses to hand over to a woman.' Steph grinned, pointing at herself, and I couldn't tell if it was because she was upset at being sidelined or pleased that she wouldn't have the responsibility.

'Connor tells me you're going to London.'

'To seek my fortune. I want to go to theatre school.'

'You'll make it,' I said, reaching out for her gloved hand. And I knew she would. Steph was driven, her unique brand of energy inspiring and fuelling the lives of those she touched.

'What about you? Are you going to move back to Creg-ny-Varn?'

'Oh yes,' I replied without hesitation. 'I can't leave again. My heart, my memories, my future – it's all there, waiting for me.' Damn that tear that caught in the corner of my eye. 'And if you don't come and visit us, I'm going to . . .'

'What, write bad things about me in your diary?' Steph laughed out loud, making the old couple at the next table turn their heads our way. 'I'd like it if you did.' She squeezed my hand.

'My diary-writing days are over. It's got me into too much trouble.' More to the point, I knew I wouldn't have time or even the need to spend hours each day transcribing my secret thoughts. With a big estate to manage and a man in my life, I was going to be busy. And then there was Dominic to keep in check and Connor would need to be introduced to Liz and Lewis . . . A flickering smile grew on my lips as I recalled the dirty secrets Connor had already revealed to me about his latent desires. He'd made me promise that I would wear the naughty underwear that night and take to him with my riding crop. He didn't want Kinrade to be the only recipient of my kinky admonishment.

'It seems to me that your diary has got you into the perfect situation. And you shouldn't be too hard on me. It was fate that made me take it. I had a part to play in bringing you two together.'

It was too late to be angry at Steph and I had already figured out that she was the type of person that you simply couldn't get mad at. From the moment she first approached me on the inbound ferry, she had worked her cheeky charm on me and unwittingly shaped the rest of my life. How *could* I do anything but forgive her?

The departure of Steph's ferry to Heysham was announced and all remaining foot passengers were required to embark.

'Will you go straight to London?' I held her hand as we walked to the ticket collector, both of us lugging her large pack.

'I'll return to the Highlands first. Let Dad know gently that I'll be leaving.' She sighed wistfully.

'I'll invite you to my première,' she said, laughing, and handed over her ticket.

We kissed and hugged, our cheeks pressed close for a second, each sharing the other's scent, the other's dreams.

'Bye, Steph,' I called out as she disappeared down the walkway. 'And thanks.'

She didn't turn but instead raised a gloved hand in a cheery salute and then she was gone, as the deep blast of the ferry horn resounded through the building.

I didn't have much to move, and it wasn't even worth sending for my belongings in Spain. Of course my mother was upset but when she realised that there would be a wedding in the summer and that she was invited, the thrill of resurrecting old ghosts was too much to turn down. She was desperate to see Creg-ny-Varn after all these years.

'I'm so happy for you, Ailey,' she confessed. 'And Connor was always such a lovely boy.'

'He's a lovely *man*, Mum,' I corrected. 'Every mother's dream.'

And then she had babbled about Marco and the farm and the village and the dreadful party of German tourists that she'd had to endure for an entire week while they explored the mountains in the winter. I'd hung up feeling that she wasn't quite in the right place, hoping that perhaps she would return one day, too. I realised this about myself, that living so far away from the island could never be sustained. I had merely been ripening in the sun.

'That's nearly every room sorted out,' I said, spinning round in the vast space of our drawing room. 'No more dust sheets and hiding away the antiques. This place needs to be lived in and loved and filled with –'

'Kids?' Connor interrupted. He gripped me around the waist and sank his mouth into my neck.

'I was thinking more of our friends and dogs and ... well, there's no harm in trying. That's the fun bit. But I'm selfish. I want you all to myself for a while yet. There's so much I want to do to you in so many places ...'

Connor's mouth devoured my words and my naughty thoughts spun in a muddle. He lay me down on the tapestry sofa and unfastened my jeans. With his mouth still attached to me, I couldn't protest that we might be interrupted, that Ethan had promised sprays of winter foliage and holly and ivy for our festive decorations. I couldn't even let him know that I had just seen Ethan walk past the window with his wheelbarrow and our eyes had met, briefly, as Connor grappled one-handed with his belt before pushing his erection straight inside me without thought of anything else.

Ethan had hesitated, gathering enough from the hazy image through the glass to realise that he would need a punishment later when he confessed to spying on his new mistress.

There was a sharp rap on the door before it clicked open followed by a rush of cold air winding through from the hallway.

'I hope I'm not interrupting.' If Ethan had come in a moment earlier, he would have caught Connor sliding from between my legs, spent, quickly satisfied and eager to finish the domestic arrangements that I had begun.

'Not at all, Ethan,' I said, raising my eyebrows and playfully lashing my hand across his buttocks when Connor's back was turned. Connor was going to have to get used to me keeping my staff in order. Indeed, I was rather hoping he could help. 'Did you get some Christmas greenery?'

'Loads of it. I've left it in the scullery.' His words were slow and thoughtful. 'Are you moving in too?'

Connor turned, realising that he was being spoken to. 'Yes, I am. My cottage will be cleared by the end of the week.' He walked up to me and wrapped an arm around my waist in a kind of masculine semaphore that told Ethan I belonged to Connor.

Ethan addressed me. 'The cottage, Miss Callister. Is there a chance that I could rent it from the estate? As much as I enjoy the elements, the gardener's hut doesn't have a bathroom and now this house is occupied...'

Ethan Kinrade was asking me for a roof over his head. I grinned the biggest smile since I had arrived on the island. The large man stood before me, having effectively made himself two inches tall by asking that question.

'You may not be able to afford the rent,' I replied, offering him a large pout. 'A gardener's wages won't go very far.'

'I could perform extra duties, Miss.' His deep voice didn't suit the grovelling but I was enjoying it.

'That was what I was hoping you would say, Ethan.'

Connor laughed and pinched my bottom. 'You're incorrigible,' he said to me. 'But right. There are many things you can do to earn your keep. Just make sure you're never idle and the cottage is yours. Right, Ailey?'

'Right,' I agreed and Ethan had to watch while Connor landed a deep, searching kiss on me and squeezed my ass for a good few minutes. Next time, I promised myself, we would go all the way with Ethan watching and then tie him up for a good spanking because he had spied on us. Despite my recent climax with Connor, I was ready for it all over again, and Ethan certainly was, judging by the bulge in his work trousers.

'That's very kind of you both,' he said and I actually thought he was going to bow. 'I won't let you down and I'm happy to do anything you wish.'

Connor and I glanced at each other and he sent me a knowing wink. He had previously let slip some of his secret fantasies, which were similar to some of Lewis and Liz's naughty preferences. Connor, it turned out, had a desire to be watched.

'So you've never done anything like that before?' It was later that evening and we were sitting on the floor of the beach cottage, huddled by the fire and pulling spiced meat off chicken legs. I'd gone to fetch the last of my belongings and we'd decided to make an evening of it, taking a basket stuffed full of food and wine. I knew I would miss the remote simplicity of the place and although we both agreed to make full use of the cottage in summer for fishing trips and beach barbecues, I couldn't just walk away without one last goodbye. Connor poured more red wine and grinned at my question, his teeth twinkling almost as brightly as the numerous tea lights we had lit around the room.

'I've been waiting for you to teach me. That is, if you're not too busy punishing Ethan.' Connor lay back on his elbow and the glint in his pale eyes told me that he was teasing me.

'I'm Lady of the Manor now. I have certain duties to perform and if that involves –'

He smothered my talk with a kiss and I could taste the wine on his lips and the desire on his tongue. Thousands of ideas flashed through my mind and I could hardly believe that Connor was saying such things to me.

I pushed gently against his chest. 'Come here,' I said hopefully, standing up and skipping to the window like a frisky kitten. 'Please be there,' I whispered and blew dust off the binoculars. I focused on the little cliff top cottage but, although the lights were on, Liz and Lewis were nowhere to be seen. 'Pass me the torch.' Bewildered, Connor watched as I flashed the light out of the window and intermittently took a look through the binoculars.

'Bird watching?' he asked.

'Kind of. Ah, wait. Look!' I handed the binoculars to Connor and guided his view to the cottage. When he let out an excited hoot and had to adjust the growing bulge in his jeans, I knew that he had spotted Liz undressing provocatively. It was fortunate that I'd told them we would be down at the beach cottage when Lewis had telephoned earlier.

'She's incredible,' Connor said, his voice clogged and slow.

'You wait,' I giggled and unfastened his jeans, deciding to work with my mouth on his never-satisfied cock while he took in the delights of Liz's striptease.

'Is there a man there yet? That's Lewis, her husband. They performed for me the first night I stayed here. It was the start of a very special adventure.' Connor didn't speak so I buried my face again in his warm groin and nuzzled and sucked and chewed upon the delightful package that would be mine for ever.

'There's a man, naked, taking her from behind. Right in front of the window.' Connor's words were half-formed, partly from disbelief and partly because he was so close to coming in my mouth he hardly dared breathe.

Finally, so he could satisfy me, Connor pulled himself from my mouth and handed me the binoculars. 'Your turn.' He stripped off his remaining clothes while I took a look at the view.

'Hey,' I said and pulled a face at Connor. 'They've got binoculars now. They want to watch *us*.'

I noticed the swallow, the twitch on his jaw, the extra-long blink as it dawned on him that already he would be indulging in one of his fantasies.

'I can see life's never going to be dull with you about, Ailey Callister.'

And he wasted no time in peeling off my layers of

warm clothing and lifting me up so that my legs were wrapped around his buttocks as he seated me carefully on the erection that shone in the moonlight.

Later, exhausted, excited that we had struck a special kind of bond with Liz and Lewis, Connor and I lay in each other's arms by the fire. The high tide washed at the door-step rocks, gently reminding us of the power of the sea that rocked back and forth only a few feet away.

'I've a present for you.' I pulled at my jacket and retrieved the brown paper package that Steph had given me. Some of the string had come loose.

'An early Christmas gift?'

I shrugged. 'Could be. I hope you enjoy it. It's just that I don't want it any more. Far more interesting things happen to me when I'm not trapping my thoughts within its pages.'

Connor unwrapped it and flicked quickly through the tatty leaves of my pocket-book, as if he was trying to take in everything at once. He snapped it shut and held it against his chest and then pulled me even closer as we melded for warmth beneath the fur throw.

'Thanks,' he smiled and even as the word fluttered around my head, my eyelids drooped and closed.

Reclaiming my life had been a tiring business. It was only when Connor shifted to reach for his glass, perhaps an hour later, that I saw him thoughtfully turning each page of my diary, his eyes absorbing every line, every word. One side of his face was lit by the fire, the rest of his expression in shadow. I closed my eyes and went back to sleep.

Visit the Black Lace website at
www.blacklace-books.co.uk

FIND OUT THE LATEST INFORMATION AND TAKE ADVANTAGE OF OUR FANTASTIC FREE BOOK OFFER! ALSO VISIT THE SITE FOR . . .

- All Black Lace titles currently available and how to order online
- Great new offers
- Writers' guidelines
- Author interviews
- An erotica newsletter
- Features
- Cool links

BLACK LACE — THE LEADING IMPRINT OF WOMEN'S SEXY FICTION

TAKING YOUR EROTIC READING PLEASURE TO NEW HORIZONS

LOOK OUT FOR THE ALL-NEW BLACK LACE BOOKS – AVAILABLE NOW!

All books priced £7.99 in the UK. Please note publication dates apply to the UK only. For other territories, please contact your retailer.

THE DEVIL INSIDE
Portia Da Costa
ISBN 0 352 32993 9

After the usually conventional Alexa Lavelle suffers a minor head injury whilst holidaying in the Caribbean, and in order to satisfy her strange and voluptuous new appetites, she is compelled to seek the enigmatic and sophisticated doctors at an exclusive medical practice in London. Their specialist knowledge of psycho-sexual medicine takes Alexa into a world of bizarre fetishism and erotic indulgence. And one particularly attractive doctor has concocted a plan which will prove to be the ultimate test of her senses, and to unleash the devil inside.

Coming in August

IN PURSUIT OF ANNA
Natasha Rostova
ISBN 0 352 34060 6

Anna Maxwell is a pixie-like bad girl with a penchant for brawny men, determined to prove her innocence when accused of stealing from her father's company. Los Angeles-based bounty hunter Derek Rowland sets off in pursuit of his fugitive, discovering that Anna's resolve is as strong as her libido. Derek's colleague, Freddie James, is convinced that Derek is being taken for a ride – and not the good kind. Freddie, meanwhile, is engaged in her own rather delicious struggle with a new lover. The sexual stakes rise as desires and boundaries are pushed to their limits.

DANCE OF OBSESSION
Olivia Christie
ISBN 0 352 33101 1

Paris, 1935. Devastated by the sudden death of her husband, exotic dancer Georgia d'Essange wants to be left alone to grieve. However, her stepson Dominic has inherited his father's business and demands Georgia's help in running it. The business is *Fleur's* – an exclusive club where women of means can indulge their sexual whims with men of their choice and take advantage of the exotic delights Parisian nightlife has to offer. Dominic is eager to take his father's place in Georgia's bed and passions and tempers run high. Further complications arise when Georgia's first lover, Theo Sands – now a rich, successful artist – appears on the scene. In an atmosphere of increasing sexual tension, can everyone's desires be satisfied?

Coming in September

THE PRIVATE UNDOING OF A PUBLIC SERVANT
Leonie Martell
ISBN 0 352 34066 5

I love the sound of heels on a bathroom floor in the morning. It sounds like . . . Mistress.

Madame K, *femme fatale* and sexual subversive, 38, is an uncompromising deviant. She exacts her pleasures through the disciplinary art of male humiliation, where attention to aesthetic detail is lovingly realised, and punishment is not given lightly.

Simon Charlesworth, cabinet minister, 52, is undergoing a crisis. Party politics, domestic routine and thoughts of mortality have recently begun to crush his soul and he is desperately seeking something. He hungers for authentic experience and excitement – but he doesn't yet know what form this might take.

When these two very different personalities meet by chance one evening in a bar at Victoria Station, London, the wheels are set in motion for a descent into sexual excess and an exploration of the human condition at its most primal. Through a series of humiliating and extreme adventures Charlesworth achieves the divine oblivion of erotic ecstasy. But there is something in Madame K's past that is due to return. Something that could cost Charlesworth everything he owns.

THE MASTER OF SHILDEN
Lucinda Carrington
ISBN 0 352 33140 2

When successful interior designer Elise St John is offered a commission at a remote castle, she jumps at the chance to distance herself from a web of sexual and emotional entanglements. Yet, as she sets to work creating rooms in which guests will be able to realise their most erotic fantasies, she finds herself indulging in fantasies of her own, about two very different men.

Blair Devlin – overtly sexy and self-confident – is a local riding instructor. Max Lannsen – the Master of Shilden – is darkly attractive but more remote. All they seem to have in common is their hatred for one another. Then, when Elise's sensual daydreams become reality, she discovers that each man's future depends on a decision she will soon be forced to make. To which of them does she really owe her loyalty?

Black Lace Booklist

Information is correct at time of printing. To avoid disappointment, check availability before ordering. Go to www.blacklace-books.co.uk. All books are priced £6.99 unless another price is given.

BLACK LACE BOOKS WITH A CONTEMPORARY SETTING

☐ ON THE EDGE Laura Hamilton	ISBN 0 352 33534 3	£5.99
☐ THE TRANSFORMATION Natasha Rostova	ISBN 0 352 33311 1	
☐ SIN.NET Helena Ravenscroft	ISBN 0 352 33598 X	
☐ TWO WEEKS IN TANGIER Annabel Lee	ISBN 0 352 33599 8	
☐ SYMPHONY X Jasmine Stone	ISBN 0 352 33629 3	
☐ A SECRET PLACE Ella Broussard	ISBN 0 352 33307 3	
☐ GOING TOO FAR Laura Hamilton	ISBN 0 352 33657 9	
☐ RELEASE ME Suki Cunningham	ISBN 0 352 33671 4	
☐ SLAVE TO SUCCESS Kimberley Raines	ISBN 0 352 33687 0	
☐ SHADOWPLAY Portia Da Costa	ISBN 0 352 33313 8	
☐ ARIA APPASSIONATA Julie Hastings	ISBN 0 352 33056 2	
☐ A MULTITUDE OF SINS Kit Mason	ISBN 0 352 33737 0	
☐ COMING ROUND THE MOUNTAIN Tabitha Flyte	ISBN 0 352 33873 3	
☐ FEMININE WILES Karina Moore	ISBN 0 352 33235 2	
☐ MIXED SIGNALS Anna Clare	ISBN 0 352 33889 X	
☐ BLACK LIPSTICK KISSES Monica Belle	ISBN 0 352 33885 7	
☐ GOING DEEP Kimberly Dean	ISBN 0 352 33876 8	
☐ PACKING HEAT Karina Moore	ISBN 0 352 33356 1	
☐ MIXED DOUBLES Zoe le Verdier	ISBN 0 352 33312 X	
☐ UP TO NO GOOD Karen S. Smith	ISBN 0 352 33589 0	
☐ CLUB CRÈME Primula Bond	ISBN 0 352 33907 1	
☐ BONDED Fleur Reynolds	ISBN 0 352 33192 5	
☐ SWITCHING HANDS Alaine Hood	ISBN 0 352 33896 2	
☐ EDEN'S FLESH Robyn Russell	ISBN 0 352 33923 3	
☐ PEEP SHOW Mathilde Madden	ISBN 0 352 33924 1	£7.99
☐ RISKY BUSINESS Lisette Allen	ISBN 0 352 33280 8	£7.99
☐ CAMPAIGN HEAT Gabrielle Marcola	ISBN 0 352 33941 1	£7.99
☐ MS BEHAVIOUR Mini Lee	ISBN 0 352 33962 4	£7.99

☐ FIRE AND ICE Laura Hamilton	ISBN 0 352 33486 X £7.99
☐ UNNATURAL SELECTION Alaine Hood	ISBN 0 352 33963 2 £7.99
☐ SLEAZY RIDER Karen S. Smith	ISBN 0 352 33964 0 £7.99
☐ VILLAGE OF SECRETS Mercedes Kelly	ISBN 0 352 33344 8 £7.99
☐ PAGAN HEAT Monica Belle	ISBN 0 352 33974 8 £7.99
☐ THE POWER GAME Carrera Devonshire	ISBN 0 352 33990 X £7.99
☐ PASSION OF ISIS Madelynne Ellis	ISBN 0 352 33993 4 £7.99
☐ CONFESSIONAL Judith Roycroft	ISBN 0 352 33421 5 £7.99
☐ THE PRIDE Edie Bingham	ISBN 0 352 33997 7 £7.99
☐ GONE WILD Maria Eppie	ISBN 0 352 33670 6 £7.99
☐ MAKE YOU A MAN Anna Clare	ISBN 0 352 34006 1 £7.99
☐ TONGUE IN CHEEK Tabitha Flyte	ISBN 0 352 33484 3 £7.99
☐ MAD ABOUT THE BOY Mathilde Madden	ISBN 0 352 34001 0 £7.99
☐ CRUEL ENCHANTMENT Janine Ashbless	ISBN 0 352 33483 5 £7.99
☐ BOUND IN BLUE Monica Belle	ISBN 0 352 34012 6 £7.99
☐ MANHUNT Cathleen Ross	ISBN 0 352 33583 1 £7.99
☐ THE STRANGER Portia Da Costa	ISBN 0 352 33211 5 £7.99
☐ ENTERTAINING MR STONE Portia Da Costa	ISBN 0 352 34029 0 £7.99
☐ RUDE AWAKENING Pamela Kyle	ISBN 0 352 33036 8 £7.99
☐ CAT SCRATCH FEVER Sophie Mouette	ISBN 0 352 34021 5 £7.99
☐ DANGEROUS CONSEQUENCES Pamela Rochford	ISBN 0 352 33185 2 £7.99
☐ CIRCUS EXCITE Nikki Magennis	ISBN 0 352 34033 9 £7.99
☐ WILD CARD Madeline Moore	ISBN 0 352 34038 X £7.99
☐ SAUCE FOR THE GOOSE Mary Rose Maxwell	ISBN 0 352 33492 4 £7.99
☐ THE DEVIL INSIDE Portia Da Costa	ISBN 0 352 32993 9 £7.99

BLACK LACE BOOKS WITH AN HISTORICAL SETTING

☐ MINX Megan Blythe	ISBN 0 352 33638 2
☐ THE AMULET Lisette Allen	ISBN 0 352 33019 8
☐ WHITE ROSE ENSNARED Juliet Hastings	ISBN 0 352 33052 X
☐ THE HAND OF AMUN Juliet Hastings	ISBN 0 352 33144 5
☐ THE SENSES BEJEWELLED Cleo Cordell	ISBN 0 352 32904 1
☐ UNDRESSING THE DEVIL Angel Strand	ISBN 0 352 33938 1 £7.99
☐ FRENCH MANNERS Olivia Christie	ISBN 0 352 33214 X £7.99
☐ LORD WRAXALL'S FANCY Anna Lieff Saxby	ISBN 0 352 33080 5 £7.99
☐ NICOLE'S REVENGE Lisette Allen	ISBN 0 352 32984 X £7.99

☐ BARBARIAN PRIZE Deanna Ashford	ISBN 0 352 34017 7 £7.99
☐ THE BARBARIAN GEISHA Charlotte Royal	ISBN 0 352 33267 0 £7.99
☐ ELENA'S DESTINY Lisette Allen	ISBN 0 352 33218 2 £7.99

BLACK LACE ANTHOLOGIES

☐ WICKED WORDS Various	ISBN 0 352 33363 4
☐ MORE WICKED WORDS Various	ISBN 0 352 33487 8
☐ WICKED WORDS 3 Various	ISBN 0 352 33522 X
☐ WICKED WORDS 4 Various	ISBN 0 352 33603 X
☐ WICKED WORDS 5 Various	ISBN 0 352 33642 0
☐ WICKED WORDS 6 Various	ISBN 0 352 33690 0
☐ WICKED WORDS 7 Various	ISBN 0 352 33743 5
☐ WICKED WORDS 8 Various	ISBN 0 352 33787 7
☐ WICKED WORDS 9 Various	ISBN 0 352 33860 1
☐ WICKED WORDS 10 Various	ISBN 0 352 33893 8
☐ THE BEST OF BLACK LACE 2 Various	ISBN 0 352 33718 4
☐ WICKED WORDS: SEX IN THE OFFICE Various	ISBN 0 352 33944 6 £7.99
☐ WICKED WORDS: SEX AT THE SPORTS CLUB Various	ISBN 0 352 33991 8 £7.99
☐ WICKED WORDS: SEX ON HOLIDAY Various	ISBN 0 352 33961 6 £7.99
☐ WICKED WORDS: SEX IN UNIFORM Various	ISBN 0 352 34002 9 £7.99
☐ WICKED WORDS: SEX IN THE KITCHEN Various	ISBN 0 352 34018 5 £7.99
☐ WICKED WORDS: SEX ON THE MOVE Various	ISBN 0 352 34034 7 £7.99

BLACK LACE NON-FICTION

☐ THE BLACK LACE BOOK OF WOMEN'S SEXUAL FANTASIES Ed. Kerri Sharp	ISBN 0 352 33793 1
☐ THE BLACK LACE SEXY QUIZ BOOK Maddie Saxon	ISBN 0 352 33884 9

To find out the latest information about Black Lace titles, check out the website: www.blacklace-books.co.uk or send for a booklist with complete synopses by writing to:

> Black Lace Booklist, Virgin Books Ltd
> Thames Wharf Studios
> Rainville Road
> London W6 9HA

Please include an SAE of decent size. Please note only British stamps are valid.

Our privacy policy
We will not disclose information you supply us to any other parties. We will not disclose any information which identifies you personally to any person without your express consent.

From time to time we may send out information about Black Lace books and special offers. Please tick here if you do <u>not</u> wish to receive Black Lace information. ❏

Please send me the books I have ticked above.

Name ....

Address ....

....

....

....

Post Code ....

Send to: Virgin Books Cash Sales, Thames Wharf Studios, Rainville Road, London W6 9HA.

US customers: for prices and details of how to order books for delivery by mail, call 888-330-8477.

Please enclose a cheque or postal order, made payable to Virgin Books Ltd, to the value of the books you have ordered plus postage and packing costs as follows:

UK and BFPO – £1.00 for the first book, 50p for each subsequent book.

Overseas (including Republic of Ireland) – £2.00 for the first book, £1.00 for each subsequent book.

If you would prefer to pay by VISA, ACCESS/MASTERCARD, DINERS CLUB, AMEX or SWITCH, please write your card number and expiry date here:

....

Signature ....

Please allow up to 28 days for delivery.